Like One of the Family

Black Women Writers Series
Series Editor: Deborah McDowell

Like One of the Family

Conversations from a Domestic's Life

Alice Childress

INTRODUCTION BY TRUDIER HARRIS

Beacon Press   **Boston**

Beacon Press
25 Beacon Street
Boston, Massachusetts 02108

Beacon Press books are published under the auspices
of the Unitarian Universalist Association
of Congregations in North America.

Library of Congress Cataloging-in-Publication Data

Childress, Alice.
Like one of the family.

(Black women writers series) (Beacon paperback)
Originally published: Brooklyn : Independence
Publishers, [1956].
Bibliography: p.
I. Title. II. Series.
PS3505.H76L5 1986   813'.54   86-73367
ISBN 0-8070-0903-2

MY GRANDMOTHER
Eliza Whitc
who loved life

CONTENTS

CONTENTS

CONTENTS

INTRODUCTION *by Trudier Harris*

KNOXVILLE, TENNESSEE, is an unlikely place to meet black artists, unless they happen to be invited for special occasions. In December of 1978, Alice Childress and I were there participating in the conference on Black American Literature and Humanism held at the University of Tennessee. In one of the lulls, during which artists and scholars had an occasion to mingle, Childress asked me if I had read any of her work. Although she mentioned the titles of several of her books (even giving me an autographed copy of her novel, *A Hero Ain't Nothin' but a Sandwich*), I found the title of one—*Like One of the Family . . . conversations from a domestic's life*—especially intriguing. Having known many black women who worked as domestics, including several in my family, I could not wait to read Childress's depictions of their interactions with their employers.

When I returned to Williamsburg, Virginia, I searched for the book—long out of print—and for more information about this writer who had written so much but been read so little. Childress's life reflected a nurturing and support that would later evolve into the striking independence characteristic of her work. The great-granddaughter of a slave who was abandoned by her former master at Emancipation, Childress was born in South Carolina in 1920. She therefore grew up with a sense of life from the underprivileged side of the veil. Raised by her grandmother Eliza, Childress was taken at the age of five to New York, an archetypal journey from the South to the promised land of the North that generations of blacks had taken before her. Grandmother Eliza encouraged Childress to jot down certain ideas because they were worth remembering, thereby offering the support that eventually led her to become a writer. The grandmother instilled a sense of value in Childress—value of herself as a human being and of her thoughts. This priceless estimation of her own worth encouraged Childress to explore the world of literature, to seek out those voices, as Richard Wright had done with H. L. Mencken, Theodore Dreiser, Sinclair Lewis, and others in the 1920s, which could enhance her perceptions of the world and her own budding artistry. That she is primarily self-taught, not a high school graduate, is a wonder considering her accomplishments since those exploratory days of the thirties and forties.

Childress's upbringing and struggles in New York effectively influenced the kind of writer she would become. She says of herself: "I attempt to write about characters without condescension, without making them into an image which some may deem more useful, inspirational, profitable, or suitable."[1] She has also commented that she concentrates "on portraying have-nots in a *have* society, those seldom singled out by mass media, except as source material for derogatory humor and/or condescending clinical, social analysis."[2]

Before these ideals could be realized, however, Childress had to serve a long apprenticeship. As her young adult years had already revealed, the dream of better opportunity in the North was elusive. She pursued a variety of jobs, including assistant machinist, photo retoucher, saleslady, and insurance agent as she worked relentlessly to gain audiences for her work as a playwright, actress, and novelist. She also did domestic work for a few months; the day she quit she surprised her employer by throwing her keys at her head. The woman later asked her to return to work. This "only work" that Childress could find turned out to be valuable, for it provided her with firsthand experience of the job situation she would later depict in *Like One of the Family*. Her first commercial acting success came with the American Negro Theatre, where she originated the role of Blanche in their famous production of *Anna Lucasta* in 1944. She later played the same part on Broadway with the original cast, which included such stars as Canada Lee and Hilda Simms. For this she was nominated for a Tony award.

Childress began to be published in 1950 when her short play, *Florence*, appeared in the journal *Masses and Mainstream*.[3] She first directed the play in 1949 at the American Negro Theatre, where she served as actress, writer, drama coach, and director. But Childress's first major success came with the Greenwich Mews Theatre 1955 production of *Trouble in Mind*, a play in which she challenged directly the stereotyped presentations of blacks in the theater. The main character, Wiletta Mayer, an aging black actress, is once again called upon to play a role that she knows is antithetical to the feelings of a black mother for her son. In the play within the play, entitled "Chaos in Belleville," she is required to give up her son to the white men she is told will protect him when she *knows* that he will be lynched for the "crime" of voting and urging other blacks to vote. Wiletta tries to lead the cast in a walkout of the racist production. However, paltry bids for stardom win out over principle, and the cast opts to pursue a project they do not believe in and from which they know the white director will release Wiletta for challenging his authority. The price of black human dignity is too dear for them to pay, so they smile at racial insults and try to retain some vague notion of what they believe is their professionalism. But at the end Wiletta still envisions the kind of work she wants to perform.

The extent to which the play challenged prevailing images of black character is attested to in Childress's alternate endings. The more militant option, demanded by the producers to show togetherness and black and white unity, had the cast leave the theater behind a marching Wiletta. Only when the racist director agrees to call in the author for the requested changes do Wiletta and the cast agree to continue work. Childress disagreed with this version because it let the director off the hook, gave him the right to "do it for them." Childress considered it wishful thinking that the races would agree to change. The original two-act version, published in Lindsay Patterson's *Black Theater* (1971), ends after Wiletta's criticisms and with the certainty that, on the morrow, she will no longer be a part of the cast.

The black woman in *Trouble in Mind* who would not be quiet when silence negated her humanity anticipates, in her almost apologetic outspokenness, the militant Mildred of *Like One of the Family*. After reading the book, I was converted to an abiding faith in the voice of Alice Childress that was strong enough to inspire my first book-length project—on domestic workers in Afro-American literature.[4] Although I eventually treated several other writers in the study, Childress and Mildred were my motivation and inspiration. A part of that study included interviews with women who had worked as domestics, and Mildred was the source of the anecdotes I used in trying to get them to talk with me about their work. Mildred's description of being tested for honesty, especially in a conversation like "The Pocketbook Game," was one of the tangible, ongoing ties she had to many of these domestic workers. Even in 1980 and in 1981, black women were still being tested for their honesty in white women's houses, and they were still being cheated out of their rightful wages.[5]

Childress's voice in *Like One of the Family* was different from most I had heard. She dared to test assumptions about the expected in Afro-American literature. Instead of a handkerchief-headed black woman, or one bowing and scraping before her "quality white folks," Mildred stood up straight and tall. Childress's dramatization of Mildred and of her other characters was lifelike and the issues concerning them immediate. In this collection of crisp conversations of two to three pages each, I shared the adventures of a black maid, a day worker who told her friend Marge about her experiences with the white folks in the New York area. The conversations were structured as dramatic monologues so that although I never heard Marge's voice, I felt her presence and intuited her thoughts through my own reactions to the stories Mildred told. When Mildred said she had snatched a newspaper out of her white employer's hand at breakfast one morning, I wanted to say, as Marge implies: "Aw come on, girl, naw you didn't!" And, like Marge, I wanted to pat Mildred on the back for being so daring. When Mildred stands toe-to-toe with the preacher and tells him, in terms comparable to Langston Hughes's Madam Alberta K. Johnson in "Madam and the Minister," exactly why she hadn't been coming to church, I wanted to join Marge in her symbolic outcry: "Move, girl, them lightning bolts you stirred up might zap me." And when Mildred plans parties for the children in her apartment building and gives them lessons in black history, I wanted to applaud an author who could create a sassy character but who could also transcend stereotypes in that creation.

In its conversational form, *Like One of the Family* is an example of one of the patterns of interactions so characteristic of women who frequently integrated art into their life-styles.

Women who did not have the leisure to compose and who did not consider themselves artists in any traditional sense of the word made art out of conversation in the way that Paule Marshall relates the women did in the West Indian community in which she grew up in New York. And as Kathryn Morgan maintains of the storytelling process that enabled her to learn of her infamous great-grandmother Caddy and eventually to write a book about her, the stories "were usually told in the kitchen while my mother was preparing a meal or performing some other chore. She never sat to tell them and sometimes we would have to follow her from room to room to hear the end of a legend."[6] The careful words, the artistic turns, the striking images—all were relevant to making order out of chaos, to shaping an imaginative response to a world that often stifled imagination.

In the traditional places that characterize the differences between the gathering and storytelling sites of men and women, kitchens become comparable to barbershops and cooking takes the place of shooting pool. Instead of moving out of the usual realms of their environments to share experiences with others, women frequently tell their tales where they are—in the dining room or living room while they are shelling beans for dinner, ironing, or while chastising their children (indeed, the stories might be instructional in the chastisement). Tasks do not interfere with performance, and art and life are synonymous. So too with Mildred and Marge; they make no distinction between art as life and art as artifact. Creativity is not something that they put on and take off as occasion warrants.

The alternate endings to *Trouble in Mind*, which preceded the publication of the first Mildred conversations, establish a precedent for the delicate balance Childress tries to maintain in *Like*

One of the Family. Her conversations hover precariously between wish fulfillment and reality, between the desire of the person of low social status to be self-assertive and concern with the potential consequences of such behavior. In all her adventures with her white employers, Mildred the maid is a combination of lady in shining armor charging off to attack insensitive racist infidels and the black woman of flesh and blood who knows that a direct confrontation with her white employers could lead to physical violence against her as quickly as it could lead to her dismissal. Day workers were noted for quitting, not showing up, or telling off the inconsiderate. They did not rely on long-term situations.

Childress chooses to depict a day worker rather than the "old faithful" family servant, to push the limits of possibility for what a black domestic in the mid-twentieth century demanded of her employers. In the sixty-two conversations in this volume, Childress allows Mildred to discuss a range of topics that others might judge antithetical to a domestic's intellectual ken, and the character raises issues that others would perhaps have her overlook. Mildred begins with many stereotypical attitudes and concepts about blacks and consistently refutes them when they violate her humanity. She is especially iconoclastic about historical notions of where she should and should not be—both psychologically and physically.

The concept of physical space—and its attendant psychological implications—has as its basis the broad concept of place for all blacks. Place can refer to status, to physical location, or to both. Status encompasses the sense of place slaves very quickly learned was expected of them; status and physical location include the sense of place the sharecropper landlord consigned to his black tenants, as well as the sense of place the blacks on southern buses were taught was theirs. Place in any context espouses the hierarchy of masters and slaves, owners and owned, privileged and nonprivileged.[7]

By directly confronting her employers in a violation of the expected behavior of domestics, Mildred adds the psychological disturbance to the physical disturbances she effects by meeting them in their living rooms. In the initial, title conversation, "Like One of the Family," Mildred challenges that time-honored lie about domestic workers as she simultaneously violates physical space. Her white employer brags to a visiting friend about Mildred: "We just *love* her! She's *like* one of the family and she *just adores* our little Carol! We don't know *what* we'd do without her! We don't think of her as a servant!" Mildred explodes the myth by asserting that she has none of the privileges of one of the family, not even the dog, for it can sleep on the "satin spread" where Mildred cannot; the child is "likable" rather than adorable, "but she is also fresh and sassy," forcing Mildred to restrain herself from spanking her on occasions. But Mildred's tour de force comes in her description of the work apportioned to various family members, especially the black one: "After I have worked myself into a sweat cleaning the bathroom and the kitchen . . . making the beds . . . cooking the lunch . . . washing the dishes and ironing Carol's pinafores, . . . I do not feel like no weekend house guest. I feel like a servant." And Mildred uses the occasion to demand better wages and more respect.

In "Let's Face It," Mildred further rejects the concept of physical spatial limitations; she deliberately sits down in the presence of a visiting white southerner who is lecturing her on the proper place for "Nigras." He has waited restlessly for the opportunity to talk with Mildred because he has stereotyped her as the "right" sort of "Nigra." He has called her "sister" (tantamount to "Auntie") and has complimented her on the good, stable sort she seems to be in these changing times. Because of examples like her, he is not losing his faith in "Nigras." Mildred then shocks the man by sitting in a big leather chair opposite him in the living room. When he relates the tale of one of his colored friends, a black minister, the epitome of an Uncle Tom, she upsets him further by threatening to go to Alabama and whip his model "Nigra." By settling herself in the living room of the white family for whom she works, at the same eye level with the guest and in a chair similar to his, Mildred eradicates the physical symbols of inequality. In being sassy, she refuses to recognize psychological inequality. In this case and others, she is *driven* to stand up for her rights.

Mildred also redefines physical and psychological boundaries in "Interestin' and Amusin'." Given a small amount of time to do some yea-saying, she uses it to make a nay-saying speech on World War II. Serving at a buffet cocktail party for Mrs. H., Mildred is struck by the company's overuse of the words "wonderful" and "amusing." When the hostess asks Mildred's opinion, having cooed to her guests about how *wonderful* Mildred is, she opts for a response that will eliminate the hint of laughter from those who clearly find her "amusin'." When Mrs. H. tries to shush her after Mildred claims a motherly interest in all young people, not just young men going off to die, she ignores her and continues: "I do not want to see people's blood and bones spattered about the streets and I do not want to see your eyes runnin' outta your head like water. . . . When there is true peace we'll have different notions about what is *amusin'* because *mankind* will be *wonderful*."

By putting Mildred on the side of life, meaning, and substance, and by placing her in the living room, Childress succeeds in passing judgment on the people at the cocktail party who really engage in none of those things. Mildred, the assumed bottom rail culturally and intellectually, becomes the top rail morally and racially, for as a black maid Mildred represents blacks whether she wants to or not. But representative as she is, she is also decidedly individual. She has her individual triumph as the audience recognizes the truth and seriousness of what she says in contrast to the falsity and triviality of what the whites have said. One *Mildred*, a black maid whom they have considered inconsequential and utterly lacking in intelligence, turns the intellectual tables on them all.

Debunking myths and demanding change—that is the pattern of interaction throughout *Like One of the Family*. Childress allows Mildred to violate all the requirements for silence and invisibility that were historically characteristic of domestics. Mildred questions authority by confronting white women about their child-rearing habits in "Inhibitions" and gives them helpful hints on raising children in "Listen for the Music." Mildred also forces her white employers to confront specific stereotypes they have about black people. In "The Health Card," a white woman indicates her stereotyped belief that blacks are unclean and unhealthy by asking Mildred to show proof of the status of her health. She believes that her family can contract germs from Mildred because she lives in "filthy" Harlem. Unabashed, Mildred lets the woman know that she expects the same show of health cards from her and her family. Indeed, one must be careful, Mildred exclaims to the woman, "and I am glad you are so understandin', 'cause I was just worryin' and studyin' on how I was goin' to ask you for yours, and of course you'll let me see one from your husband and one for each of the three children . . . Since I have to handle laundry and make beds, you know . . ." Mildred's ploy succeeds; as the two women stand there smiling at each other, the white woman guiltily and Mildred indulgently, perhaps they construct a bond that emphasizes their mutual humanity. At least, that is the intention of the encounter.[8]

Mildred insists, further, upon polite requests and respectful actions from the children, as in "Inhibitions." She does not believe it is the maid's responsibility to allow a child to play in the hamburger that everyone has to eat for dinner. The child's temper tantrum and the white woman's frustration and plea for leniency only intensify the problem. Mildred finds herself confronting two children rather than an adult and a child. The mother can finally see the problem she has created, but only because Mildred pushes the limits of authority and politeness. A similar focus on politeness underscores "Mrs. James." The white woman in this conversation refers to herself in the third person to emphasize to Mildred the distance between them and the formal courtesy she expects. Mildred takes the occasion to let Mrs. James know that black women deserve the titles of "Mrs." or "Miss" as much as white women do.

Mildred constantly challenges the use and abuse of black domestics. In "I Hate Half-Days Off," she recognizes the need for collective representation to protect domestics from excessive labor. A white woman interviews Mildred for a job and describes work days that will begin before breakfast and end "after the supper dishes"; she describes the half-days off with a calculation typical of devious politicians: "Well, you have one half-day off every Tuesday and one half-day off every Sunday and every other Thursday you get a full day off, which makes it a five and a half day week." The woman also has a cagey plan to pay only on the first and the fifteenth day of each month so that she can get a free week's work. Of such "brilliance," Mildred sarcastically concludes: "How come all of them big-shots in Washington that can't balance the budget or make the taxes cover all our expenses, how *come* they don't send for that woman to help straighten them out?" Mildred also recognizes the need for organized representation for black domestics in "We Need a Union Too."

In "On Leaving Notes," again a white employer tries to trick Mildred into extra work. At the end of the day, just as Mildred is leaving, she finds a note pinned to three house dresses. The woman has requested that Mildred take them home, wash and iron them, and return them the next day; she has appended a dollar to the lot, considerably less than the seventy-five cents per housecoat that the nearby laundry charges. The work is outside the agreement Mildred has with the woman; therefore, she leaves the mess and complains the next day of the attempted exploitation. Mildred is consistent and generally effective in her bids to protect her labor and to bring about change in the process.

Interspersed throughout the conversations is a strong nationalistic pride as well as a simple philosophy for living. Mildred values black people, especially black children, and she is touched acutely by the prejudices that affect them. This is particularly evident in "Ain't You Mad?" but also in conversations such as "Got to Go Someplace," in which she laments the lack of public recreational spaces for black people. But Mildred also stresses interpersonal and communal sharing, evident in her recounting work experiences to Marge, attending funerals ("I Go to a Funeral"), visiting friends ("Weekend with Pearl"), and going to parties ("Dance with Me, Henry"). She expresses a poetic sensibility in "I Wish I Was a Poet," and, throughout the conversations, she generally exudes a joy at being alive.

More often than not, Mildred is able to make her points in relatively polite and certainly witty ways. Not so in "Ain't You Mad?" The racial anger underlying many of the conversations surfaces overtly in this one, and it is here that Childress comes closest to being a propagandist; the message is consciously allowed to become more important than art and direct lecturing takes the place of witty manipulation. Mr. and Mrs. B. complacently insist over their leisurely breakfast that "you people," meaning blacks, must be angry about a recent attempt to integrate a white university. When Mr. B. asks Mildred what is to be done, her reaction approaches violence. She "hollers" rather than attempting her usual ploy of moral suasion: "What the hamfat is the matter with you? *Ain't you mad?* Now you either be *mad* or *shame*, but don't you sit there with your mouth full 'tut-tuttin' at me! Now if you mad, you'd of told me what *you done* and if you shame, you oughta be hangin' your head instead of smackin' your lips over them goodies!" Further screaming and disagreement ensue, with Mildred comparing the helpless woman trying to integrate the school to Mrs. B., who would have the law and the Klan to assist her if she were threatened. The ugly encounter continues until Mrs. B. jumps up, waves a newspaper in Mildred's face, and insists that she go home. It is at this point that Mildred angrily snatches the newspaper and offers parting advice on the responsibility of all human beings to make the world a better place.

Mildred represents conscience and concern, her employers insensitivity and condescension. By noting the casual way Mr. B. finishes the "last piece of buttered, jellied toast" and the offhand way Mrs. B. swashes down her bacon "with a gulp of coffee" as they consider the wretchedness in Alabama, Mildred emphasizes the distance between black and white: between the security, stability, and complacency of the B.s' life on the one hand and the insecurity and disruption that Autherine Lucy must have been experiencing—insecurity and disruption that Mildred herself shakes at the thought of—on the other.[9] Mildred selects detail here to make the B.s seem like villains whose place in society prevents them from ever sympathizing with or even understanding what vitally concerns the black community.

"Ain't You Mad?" is the only conversation in which Mildred is sent home. Significantly, she is not fired though she radically violates every sort of spatial boundary set for the domestic; but it is also significant that only in this conversation do she and her employers fail to reach a new level of understanding. Usually, the people she enlightens as to their ignorance accept their enlightenment. They are shocked that they have been so narrow-minded concerning racial issues; they evince an eagerness to change. They and Mildred recognize their mutual humanity and Mildred works harmoniously with them for at least a few more days or weeks—a pattern which might occur once or twice in real life, especially in Mildred's New York and in the life of a maid with so vivacious a personality as Mildred's, but which surely could not be the norm. "Ain't You Mad?" is striking, therefore, in that it is the least realistic confrontation in the conversations, yet it has the most realistic, least optimistic ending.

It is significant that the conversations were initially published in Paul Robeson's newspaper *Freedom* under the title "Conversation from Life" and continued in the *Baltimore Afro-American*, as "Here's Mildred," for audience is a key factor in how the episodes are developed. In creating Mildred, a heroine of the black working class, Childress may have been influenced by Langston Hughes's Jesse B. Simple, another heroic figure conceived for audience approval and interaction. Serialized in the *Chicago Defender*, Hughes's tales featured a gregarious, beer-loving, bar-hopping Harlemite who shared his adventures in the white world and his homely philosophies with a meticulously correct black man named Boyd, who usually provided the motivating frame for Simple's reflections. Indeed, as early as 1950, Childress adapted Hughes's *Simple Speaks His Mind* for the stage in a show entitled *Just a Little Simple*. With his common-sense philosophy and his belief in dignity for all human beings, Simple shares with Mildred a recognition that human value must not be determined by one's status in a society.

It was appropriate that Childress's conversations should originally appear in *Freedom*, for they were militant in nature. Her iconoclastic portraits of a working-class woman who fought her exploitative situations in very creative ways touched close to the proletarian themes which were historically true of black characters in American history—Nat Turner, Frederick Douglass, Sojourner Truth, Harriet Tubman. Mildred's militancy, therefore, could have been viewed in the larger, worldwide political context of breaking the yoke of the bourgeoisie on the masses of workers. Childress says that she "wrote the pieces originally for Paul Robeson's newspaper *Freedom* for no compensation at all, then for five dollars per column. The *Baltimore Afro-American* ran them all (one per week) for twenty-five dollars each and then I wrote new ones for them (unpublished) for the next year or two."[10]

Mildred identifies herself as a *Negro* (as did the earlier nationalist Marcus Garvey), yet many of her actions equal or surpass those of the consciously militant blacks and Afro-Americans of the 1960s. Her nationalistic sentiments would be echoed later in the writings of Nikki Giovanni and Sonia Sanchez, and her concerns about South Africa anticipated what is a prevailing concern in the 1980s. The term that would later be assigned to complacent middle-class blacks, therefore, did not at all apply in substance to the vivacious, racially conscious Mildred as she paraded across the pages of the *Baltimore Afro-American*.

The many domestic workers who subscribed to that paper and who found themselves in situations equally or more restricting than Mildred's could applaud her victories; the conversations thereby transcended their individuality and responded to a collective consciousness. When Mildred says no, sometimes in thunder and always with humor, the domestic workers who could and could not do so had found their voice. Those who managed to protest against overwork and general physical abuse found some new stratagems to employ after reading about Mildred's exploits. And perhaps there were others who were so much a part of the families for which they worked that Mildred's feats simply seemed incredible. Whatever the gamut of responses, the column brought to light the daily problems of the little people, the invisible people, those who don't seem to matter statistically but who, like those in Douglas Turner Ward's *Day of Absence* (1966), have in reality the capacity to stop the worlds in which they work from functioning. Ward's domestics and other "menial" workers go on strike one day and cause such confusion among the whites that they riot. Childress says that in reaction to her column, "floods of beautiful mail came in from domestics (male and female) telling me of their own experiences." They gave their approval to Mildred's exploits and escapades and then told their own stories of protest.

With this audience-based sense of performance, then, Childress could incorporate her theatrical background into the showman's side of Mildred's personality, and she could co-opt this traditional medium to present her depictions of Mildred. In newspapers, therefore, Mildred is a stage personality, performing for her readers as she performs for Marge and for those of us who read of her exploits today. On stage, she creates a legend of herself, one that we can question, alter, or correct, but one that we cannot deny her in the process of creation, for that process is solely within her control. We may fuss and fume at being held outside —like the situation of the storyteller who allows us to identify with his hero, but who will not allow us to add, subtract, or correct him *while he is in the process of relating the tale*—but such is the nature of Childress's artistry at work in the newspapers and in *Like One of the Family*.

The collection of monologues was originally issued by a small Brooklyn-based publisher in 1956. The publishing history of the volume demonstrates the exploitation of women writers endemic to the publishing industry. Childress is stoic in describing her experience: "I never received a penny in advance from the book from the publisher and not a dime in royalties. He also sold the German rights and other European rights without my consent. A lawsuit would not have paid for the legal fees required. I have been compensated by pieces taken from the book and used in school books—particularly 'The Pocketbook Game' and 'The Health Card'—here and abroad." The named conversations illustrate, in their tremendous popularity, the wit and humor of a writer who refused to be undone by the foibles of individuals who would not be fair with her. And, ironically, such exploitation allowed Mildred's voice to be heard by the select few who would listen; her sass cannot be weighed in gold.

Perhaps those in a position to review the original publication chose not to do so because of Childress's former association with Robeson, or perhaps they chose to ignore it because it went against the prevailing grain of the time. Whatever the reason, *Like One of the Family*—as near as I have been able to uncover—was reviewed only once in the four years following its publication. That lone review appeared in *Masses and Mainstream* in July 1956,[11] an appropriate place considering the history of that journal and Childress's personal history. Mildred's fans from the newspaper might have been aware of the volume, but no black journal voiced a response to it, although Richard Wright's *Pagan Spain* and James Baldwin's *Giovanni's Room* were both reviewed in black magazines such as *The Crisis* in 1956. If the maids and butlers who applauded Mildred in *Freedom* and the *Baltimore Afro-American* did not know that the book had been published, then Mildred was lost to them as well. The volume apparently went underground, and only a few copies remained to document Mildred's voice, one of which I was lucky enough to acquire in 1979.

The voice that Childress found in Mildred resonates in the characters of her subsequent books: in Benjie's independence and (sometimes wrongheaded) defiance in *A Hero Ain't Nothin' but a Sandwich* (1973), in Cora James's refusal to give the slaveholders any more of her soul in *A Short Walk* (1979), and in Rainbow's decision to give up the prettiest boy on the block rather than demean herself in *Rainbow Jordan* (1981). Mildred's concern for children is echoed in the books that Childress has written for them, including *When the Rattlesnake Sounds* (1975), about Harriet Tubman, and *Let's Hear It for the Queen* (1976), which Childress wrote in celebration of her granddaughter's eighth birthday.

In most of her adolescent and adult writings, Childress presents material judged to be controversial, so much so that reactionaries have banned them from the reading public. In the 1970s, *A Hero Ain't Nothin' but a Sandwich*, which deals with the drug addiction of a thirteen-year-old, was the first book banned in a Savannah, Georgia, school library since *Catcher in the Rye* was banned in the fifties. Childress says it was also among nine books banned in the "Island Trees" court case concerning the selection and rejection of school library literature. After a Supreme Court hearing her book was returned to the shelves of the Island Trees Library along with the others. *Wedding Band*, a play about an interracial love affair written early in the 1960s, was first presented by the Mendelssohn Theatre, at the University of Michi-

gan. Joseph Papp produced *Wedding Band* in 1973 at the New
York Shakespeare Festival, and he also produced it for ABC television with Childress's screenplay. When it finally aired on prime
time television, eight of the 168 television stations in the viewing
area would not carry it, and another three showed it only after
midnight. Another sixties play, *Wine in the Wilderness*, which
depicts several young blacks coming to a true understanding of
their identity while a riot is going on, was banned from television in Alabama. Such negative public reaction to Childress's
works reflects a refusal to see blacks as human, a stance that
Childress consistently undercuts in the voice of Mildred.

The significance of Mildred's voice is obvious. Childress lets us
hear the many women in Afro-American history whose occupations have silenced them. Through Mildred, we are again aware
of numerous indignities that the majority of black women
workers in this country experienced, for, indeed, the majority of
them were domestic workers. While certainly some of the southern experiences differed from the northern ones in degree, they
did not differ in kind. The women were uniformly overworked,
expected to neglect their families for those of their white employers, and frequently expected to accept hand-me-downs and
service pans—the name for leftover food domestic workers were
given to take home to their families—instead of remuneration for
their extensive expenditure of labor. By daring to look low, to
depict another character type in Afro-American fiction, Childress gave to the literature a dimension that it had rarely had
before.

Notwithstanding the silence surrounding the publication of
the volume, Childress's creation of Mildred, a working-class black
woman who commanded the attention of a volume rather than a
part of it, was unlike anything preceding it in Afro-American
literature. The tradition of the tragic mulatto in the nineteenth

century required idealized, overly educated, overly sentimental-
ized portraits of black women. The plantation tradition to which
Charles Waddell Chesnutt and Paul Laurence Dunbar reacted
required stylized figures, familiar stereotypes such as Mammy
Jane Letlow in Chesnutt's *The Marrow of Tradition* (1901), and
only fleeting glimpses of more complex female characters. More
complex characters, such as Irene Redfield in Nella Larsen's
Passing (1929), share some of the extraterrestrial features of their
nineteenth-century sisters in accomplishments, beauty, and sepa-
ration from the masses of blacks. Only Janie Crawford in Zora
Neale Hurston's *Their Eyes Were Watching God* (1937) and
Lutie Johnson in Ann Petry's *The Street* (1946) came close to
realistic presentation of working-class characters without middle-
class embellishments, but even Janie is supported by a middle-
class husband and Lutie's vision is marred by an unwavering
adherence to the destructive preachments of the American
Dream. Nor is Mildred bogged down in the quagmire of judging
herself by a standard of physical beauty antithetical to her racial
background, as is the case with Gwendolyn Brooks's *Maud
Martha*, which appeared in 1953.

Mildred breaks the mold of casting black women as alien to
or bemoaning their own experiences in order to make them ac-
ceptable to white audiences. She was conceived to reflect as
exactly as literature ever imitates life the experiences of those who
would be reading about her. Her difficulties on the job tie her
most closely to the black masses, but her conversations about
social situations as well as her own personal circumstances are
also close to home. Readers can easily imagine the encounters
Mildred had with racists at public facilities, or her partying with
friends, or her being involved in church and community work.

By selecting her character from the lower echelons of black
society, Childress exemplified her determination to respect and

present without condescension those folks who are just folks—living, loving, working, being. Childress thus anticipates the portrayal of similar characters in works by writers in the 1970s and 1980s, for example, Gloria Naylor's Mattie Michael and Ciel Turner in *The Women of Brewster Place* (1982). The lack of embellishment in characterization also anticipates Alice Walker's portrayal of Mem and Margaret Copeland in *The Third Life of Grange Copeland* (1970), and Hannah Kemhuff and Rannie Toomer in *In Love and Trouble: Stories of Black Women* (1973); these women are what they are—commoners, farmers, church workers, women who engage our attention without being painted as some superhuman examples in the form of Frances Ellen Watkins Harper's *Iola Leroy* (1892) or Charles Chesnutt's Rena Walden in *The House Behind the Cedars* (1900).

Childress, then, though frequently unread and more frequently out of print, captured in *Like One of the Family* a vein so true to Afro-American life and culture that many post-1950s creations of black women must find their genesis in her depiction of Mildred. Not a wandering, passive Janie, or a predetermined, disillusioned Lutie Johnson, Mildred is a black woman who knows that black women, even when they have been domestic servants, have had dignity and a degree of self-determination to sustain and define themselves against frightful odds.

In this sense, Childress and Mildred represent a continuity in Afro-American literature and history that was unlike any other. What they shared touched the heart of the development of Afro-American communities in this country. During slavery, black women had worked in the big houses as servants or in the fields beside black men. During Reconstruction, when the forty acres and a mule were not forthcoming, black women could still use their skills as domestics to find jobs and try to hold their families together. Some still worked in the fields, but the majority of them were domestic servants. Forced to adopt individual strategies for interacting with their white employers, and isolated from other workers, these women sometimes found themselves in a new form of slavery. If they were worked and not paid, there was no union to which they could complain. If they were accused of stealing, their claims of Christian virtue would not alleviate the charges. If they were fired without notice, they simply had to look for other employment.

Childress and Mildred showed the problems peculiar to domestic workers, and they illustrated the center from which many attendant problems in black communities had grown for the domestic herself as well as in terms of the popular conceptions of her. The integral place of the domestic in black American experience suggests that the black woman as maid is the basic historical conception from which other images and stereotypes have grown. Dependency on service pans foreshadows the dependency of welfare, for certainly that paternalistic phenomenon influenced social expectations. Sexual exploitation of the maid by the employer's husband, which is a direct extension of slavery, may have contributed its share to the stereotyped images of the black woman as hot momma or unwed mother. And the parallels continue: the relationship between mistress and maid explains, in part, other images of black women in the popular imagination as well as in the literature.

After reading *Like One of the Family*, I began to wonder why I had not heard more of Alice Childress. The reason is that like Mildred and Childress's real-life Aunt Lorraine upon whom Mildred's character is based, Childress is a writer who "refused to exchange dignity for pay." Such refusal can be costly; the cost for Childress was that her Mildred stories were printed more frequently and more widely read in other countries than in the United States. It also implied that her refusal to blunt her barbed attacks made her nationalistic views unpopular in the assimilationist climate of the 1950s. Her outspoken Mildred had little of the God-fearing, long-suffering tolerance that would characterize Lorraine Hansberry's Mama Lena Younger a few years later in *A Raisin in the Sun*.

Childress's claim to artistic freedom paralleled Mildred's claim to physical and psychological freedom in her violations of space requirements in the homes of the whites for whom she worked. Childress's refusal to adhere to the expected portrayals of downtrodden, suffering, victimized black women in literature was just as effective as Mildred sitting in the living rooms of her employers and violating their notions of what domestics ought to do and be. Both gained a freedom and a greater sense of self by not allowing outside forces to define them.

In Mildred, Childress seldom romanticizes the domestic worker, but she does suggest that that position was not ultimately so negating that it does not warrant celebration in the literature. *Like One of the Family* celebrates the image of black women most common to their history and suggests that they are no less dignified for having spent time on their knees. Mildred scrubs and soars. In both postures lies the complexity of black women.

Notes

1. Alice Childress, "Knowing the Human Condition," in *Black American Literature and Humanism*, ed. R. Baxter Miller (Lexington: The University of Kentucky Press, 1981), p. 10.

2. Alice Childress, "A Candle in a Gale Wind," in *Black Women Writers (1950–1980): A Critical Evaluation*, ed. Mari Evans (New York: Doubleday/Anchor, 1984), p. 112.

3. "Florence," in *Masses and Mainstream* 3 (October 1950): 34–47.

4. Trudier Harris, *From Mammies to Militants: Domestics in Black American Literature* (Philadelphia: Temple University Press, 1982).

5. According to Childress, many black militant domestics, led by Mrs. Nina Evans, a domestic worker, often met in a rented studio room on 110th Street in Harlem. They were trying to form a domestic workers' union.

6. Kathryn Morgan, *Children of Strangers: The Stories of a Black Family* (Philadelphia: Temple University Press, 1980), p. 15.

7. Information in this paragraph and in sections of the comments on specific conversations in the following paragraphs is taken from *From Mammies to Militants*.

8. Childress reports that "The Health Card," "The Pocketbook Game," and "Mrs. James" all happened to her as a day worker.

9. Autherine Lucy, a black woman, attempted to integrate the University of Alabama at Tuscaloosa in 1956, several years before the University was actually integrated in the early 1960s.

10. Letter from Alice Childress to Trudier Harris, dated January 7, 1980. Remaining quotations by Childress are from this source.

11. Helen Davis, review of *Like One of the Family*, in *Masses and Mainstream* 9 (July 1956): 50–51.

SELECTED BIBLIOGRAPHY
By Trudier Harris

Works by Alice Childress

BOOKS
Like One of the Family . . . Conversations from a Domestic's Life (Brooklyn, N.Y.: Independence Publishers, 1956)

Wine in the Wilderness: A Comedy-Drama (New York: Dramatists Play Service, 1969)

Mojo and String: Two Plays (New York: Dramatists Play Service, 1971)

A Hero Ain't Nothin' but a Sandwich (New York: Coward, McCann & Geoghegan, 1973)

Wedding Band: A Love/Hate Story in Black and White (New York: French, 1973)

When the Rattlesnake Sounds (New York: Coward, McCann & Geoghegan, 1975)

Let's Hear It for the Queen (New York: Coward, McCann & Geoghegan, 1976)

A Short Walk (New York: Coward, McCann & Geoghegan, 1979)

Rainbow Jordan (New York: Coward, McCann & Geoghegan, 1981)

PLAY PRODUCTIONS
Florence, New York, American Negro Theatre, 1949

Just a Little Simple, adapted from Langston Hughes's collection *Simple Speaks His Mind*, New York, Club Baron Theatre, September 1950

Gold Through the Trees, New York, Club Baron Theatre, 1952

Trouble in Mind, New York, Greenwich Mews Theatre, 4 November 1955

Wedding Band: A Love/Hate Story in Black and White, Ann Arbor, University of Michigan, December 1966

String, adapted from Guy de Maupassant's story "A Piece of String," New York, St. Marks Playhouse, 25 March 1969

The Freedom Drum, retitled *Young Martin Luther King*, Performing Arts Repertory Theatre, on tour 1969–1972

Mojo: A Black Love Story, New York, New Heritage Theatre, November 1970

Sea Island Song, Charleston, South Carolina, Stage South, 1977

Gullah, Amherst, University of Massachusetts, 1984

SCREENPLAY

A Hero Ain't Nothin' but a Sandwich, adapted from Childress's novel of the same title, New World Pictures, 1977

TELEVISION

Wine in the Wilderness, in "On Being Black," Boston, WGBH, 4 March 1969

Wedding Band, ABC, 1973

String, for *Vision* (series), PBS, 1979

OTHER

The World on a Hill, in *Plays to Remember*, Literary Heritage Series (New York: Macmillan, 1968)

Black Scenes, edited by Childress (Garden City: Doubleday, 1971)—includes a scene from Childress's *The African Garden*, pp. 137–45

Trouble in Mind, in *Black Theatre*, edited by Lindsay Patterson (New York: New American Library, 1971), pp. 135–74

"Knowing the Human Condition," in *Black American Literature and Humanism*, edited by R. Baxter Miller (Lexington: University of Kentucky Press, 1981), pp. 8–10

PERIODICAL PUBLICATIONS:

DRAMA

Florence, A One Act Drama, in *Masses and Mainstream* 3 (October 1950): 34–47

NONFICTION

"For a Negro Theatre," *Masses and Mainstream* 4 (February 1951): 61–64

"The Negro Woman in American Literature," *Freedomways* 6 (Winter 1966): 14–19, reprinted as "A Woman Playwright Speaks Her Mind," in *Anthology of the Afro-American in the Theatre: A Critical Approach,* edited by Lindsay Patterson (Cornwells Heights, Pa.: Publishers Agency, 1978), pp. 75–79

" 'Why Talk About That?,' " *Negro Digest* 16 (April 1967): 17–21

"Black Writers' Views on Literary Lions and Values," *Negro Digest* 17 (January 1968): 36, 85–87

" 'But I Do My Thing,' " in "Can Black and White Artists Still Work Together?," *New York Times,* 2 February 1969, II: 1, 9

"The Soul Man," *Essence* (May 1971): 68–69, 94

"Tributes—to Paul Robeson," *Freedomways* 11 (First Quarter 1971): 14–15

Secondary Sources

Abramson, Doris E. *Negro Playwrights in the American Theatre, 1925–1959.* New York: Columbia University Press, 1969, pp. 188–204, 258–59.

Brown, Janet. *Feminist Drama: Definitions and Critical Analysis.* Metuchen, N.J.: Scarecrow, 1979, pp. 56–70.

Curb, Rosemary. "An Unfashionable Tragedy of American Racism: Alice Childress' *Wedding Band.*" *MELUS* 7 (Winter 1980): 57–68.

Evans, Mari. *Black Women Writers (1950–1980): A Critical Evaluation.* Garden City, N.Y.: Doubleday/Anchor, 1984, pp. 111–34.

Harris, Trudier. *From Mammies to Militants: Domestics in Black American Literature.* Philadelphia: Temple University Press, 1982.

———. " 'I wish I was a poet': The Character as Artist in Alice Childress's

Like One of the Family," *Black American Literature Forum,* 14 (Spring 1980): 24–30.

Miller, Jeanne-Marie A. "Images of Black Women in Plays by Black Playwrights." *College Language Association Journal* 20 (June 1977): 494–507.

Mitchell, Loften. *Black Drama: The Story of the American Negro in the Theatre.* New York: Hawthorn Books, 1977.

———. "Three Writers and a Dream," *Crisis* 72 (April 1965): 219–23.

LIKE ONE OF THE FAMILY

HI MARGE! I have had me one hectic day. . . . Well, I had to take out my crystal ball and give Mrs. C . . . a thorough reading. She's the woman that I took over from Naomi after Naomi got married. . . . Well, she's a pretty nice woman as they go and I have never had too much trouble with her, but from time to time she really gripes me with her ways.

When she has company, for example, she'll holler out to me from the living room to the kitchen: "Mildred dear! Be sure and eat *both* of those lamb chops for your lunch!" Now you know she wasn't doing a thing but tryin' to prove to the company how "good" and "kind" she was to the servant, because she had told me *already* to eat those chops.

Today she had a girl friend of hers over to lunch and I was real busy afterwards clearing the things away and she called me over and introduced me to the woman. . . . Oh no, Marge! I didn't object to that at all. I greeted the lady and then went back to my work. . . . And then it started! I could hear her talkin' just as loud . . . and she says to her friend, "We *just* love her! She's *like* one of the family and she *just adores* our little Carol! We don't know *what* we'd do without her! We don't think of her as a servant!" And on and on she went . . . and every time I came in to move a plate off the

I

table both of them would grin at me like chessy cats.

After I couldn't stand it any more, I went in and took the platter off the table and gave 'em both a look that would have frizzled a egg. . . . Well, you might have heard a pin drop and then they started talkin' about something else.

When the guest leaves, I go in the living room and says, "Mrs. C . . . , I want to have a talk with you."

"By all means," she says.

I drew up a chair and read her thusly: "Mrs. C . . . , you are a pretty nice person to work for, but I wish you would please stop talkin' about me like I was a *cocker spaniel* or a *poll parrot* or a *kitten*. . . . Now you just sit there and hear me out.

"In the first place, you do not *love* me; you may be fond of me, but that is all. . . . In the second place, I am *not* just like one of the family at all! The family eats in the dining room and I eat in the kitchen. Your mama borrows your lace table-cloth for her company and your son entertains his friends in your parlor, your daughter takes her afternoon nap on the living room couch and the puppy sleeps on your satin spread . . . and whenever your husband gets tired of something you are talkin' about he says, 'Oh, for Pete's sake, forget it. . . .' So you can see I am not *just* like one of the family.

"Now for another thing, I do not *just* adore your little Carol. I think she is a likable child, but she is also fresh and sassy. I know you call it 'uninhibited' and that is the way you want your child to be, but *luckily* my mother taught me some inhibitions or else I would smack little Carol once in a while when she's talkin' to you like you're a dog, but as it is I just laugh it off the way you do because she is *your* child and I am *not* like one of the family.

"Now when you say, 'We don't know *what* we'd do without her' this is a polite lie . . . because I know that if I dropped dead or had a stroke, you would get somebody to replace me.

"You think it is a compliment when you say, 'We don't think of her as a servant. . . .' but after I have worked myself into a sweat cleaning the bathroom and the kitchen . . . making the beds . . . cooking the lunch . . . washing the dishes and ironing Carol's pinafores . . . I do not feel like no weekend house guest. I feel like a servant, and in the face of that I have been meaning to ask you for a slight raise which will make me feel much better toward everyone here and make me know my work is appreciated.

"Now I hope you will stop talkin' about me in my presence and that we will get along like a good employer and employee should."

Marge! She was almost speechless but she *apologized* and said she'd talk to her husband about the raise. . . . I knew things were progressing because this evening Carol came in the kitchen and she did not say, "I want some bread and jam!" but she did say, "*Please*, Mildred, will you fix me a slice of bread and jam."

I'm going upstairs, Marge. Just look . . . you done messed up that buttonhole!

LISTEN FOR THE MUSIC

MARGE, I LOVE CHILDREN, they're wonderful and I find their company real excitin'. You know how they are always askin' a million and one questions which on first thought can sometimes seem silly but if you look into them questions a little while they make real sense.

Where I worked today, there was a little boy about five years old and he was such a bright-eyed inquirin' little fellow that it was a pure joy to be around him and it was all I could do to keep doin' my work and not stop and play with him all afternoon.

One time he asked his mother a question when she was listenin' to the radio music. "Mama," he says, "where did music come from?" And she answered him in a kinda off-hand way. "Oh, men invented different kinds of musical instruments and kept improvin' them until we got pianos and harps and all kinds of horns and drums." He shook his head and said, "I don't mean that, I mean where did the music come from *before* it came out of horns and pianos."

She looked at him kind of dumb-struck and then said, "I guess it came out of men's hearts and minds because it was somethin' they were thinkin'." Well, Frankie looked at her a minute and then shook his head again. "I mean, where did it come from before it was in men's hearts and minds?"

Marge, he really had her then because she just shrugged her shoulders and said, "Frankie, you can ask the craziest questions!" But he wasn't studyin' about lettin' her off so easy. "Mama, I want to know!" Well, she laughed a little then and said, "Ask Mildred!" And so he did.

Now, you know, Marge, I don't believe in lettin' the little ones down and whether I know somethin' or not I will always try to give them at least my own thoughts on the matter so I explained to him: "Frankie, I don't rightly know that I can give you the last-word facts about it, but I can tell you what I think if you'd like to hear that." He sat down on the hassock-cushion and his big eyes was all eager. "Yes," he says, "tell me that."

"Well," I says, "there has always been music as long as there has been a world, been out there floatin' around long before it went into man's heart and mind, no two ways about it. At first man was so busy tryin' to learn how to build a fire and find food to eat that he didn't have time to *hear* the music, but it was there just the same."

Marge, have you ever noticed how little children can hang on each and every word you say just like the greatest thing they've ever heard? Well, that's how Frankie was lookin' at me. I always pause a bit in the story in order to make it more excitin' and make them help me along with it. "Where was it?" he asked, "where was it when they didn't know about it?"

"Well," I says, "it was all around them and it just kept on goin' about its music-business until they began to notice it. One night after supper, man and his wife and child were sittin' in front of the fire feelin' nice and comfortable when they noticed a sound. They listened a bit and then they heard it again!"

"What was it!" Frankie hollered. "It was the fire cracklin' and poppin'," I said, "and after they listened a while they heard somethin' way up over their heads goin' *boom-boom-boomity-boom!* And what do you think it was?"

Marge, what do you think he said it was? "A bomb!" "No," says I, "it was thunder and after a while the lightnin' went clackity-clack! And then the rain began to fall . . . *plup, plup, plup* and when it hit man's fire, the hot wood made a sound like *cu-zizzzzz* before it went out and sometimes musicians make that sound on the brass cymbals when they hit them together real fast."

I had me a real audience by this time because Frankie's mother turned down the radio so's she could listen, too.

"Since there was no television in those days, man and his family had a lot of fun listenin' to the different sounds they would hear like the *buzzin'* of bees, the wind in the trees, the cry of animals in the night goin' *ah-wooooooo, ah-wooooooo.* In the daytime they heard the waves slappin' up against the beach and sayin' *cu-swush, cu-swush,* and they heard the birds *trillin'* in the trees and they also found that when they listened to the little babies they'd hear musical, gurglin' sounds like *ah-ga-gerrr-taaaaah.*"

"That's what baby sister says," shouted Frankie. "Yes," I said, "and one day when man was hittin' one stone against the other, it pleased him to hear the rocks makin' a ringin noise like *tooooonnnnng.* And *music* began to enter the heart of man. He listened to everything, and he found that there was music all around him. It was in his own breathin' which was all timed out nice and even; it was in his heart-beat which went *ku-dum, ku-dum* all the time; it came out of the animals'

6

hoofs as they ran across the stones *tic-toc, tic-toc, tic-toc;* it was in the brook-water, goin' *curga-la-la, rerrrr-curga-la-la;* it was everywhere; it was in man's throat."

Frankie let out a nice high note, and I said, "That's right, just like that! One day man stood down in a valley and hollered up to the tops of the mountain, *la-la-deeeeee!* and the sound came rocketin' back, *laaaa-laaaa-deeeeeeee!* and man was so happy he began to *sing!*"

Frankie then gave us a line or two of "Yankee Doodle." "But," I said, "man got weary of waitin' around for the sounds to happen because he wanted to hear them whenever he felt like it, and he also wanted to hear them in a different order. Sometimes it got on his nerves to hear the raindrops first and then the birds and then something else 'cause he had a notion that if he could arrange them in a different order, they would sound better, so he went to work to make all those sounds himself. At first he whistled them out, but he couldn't get close enough to the real sounds so he began to hit sticks against one another and blow through animal horns and hit metal pieces together and things like that. And before you knew it he had some musical instruments to play on."

"Hot dog!" Frankie says, "like drums and things!" I waited until the little fellow was all charged up with curiosity again and then I went on, "But it just so happened that every man couldn't play the music although they all liked to hear it, so some played for others and they practiced together and got to be *bands.* Some of the band people played some real pretty things but other bands couldn't because the man that made up the pretty piece couldn't come and see them to tell them how to play it. So man racked his brain until he found a way to put dots down on paper so that other bands could look at it and know how the pieces should be played. My goodness, but they had a good time then and kept real busy writin' down pieces and sendin' them back and forth to each other and playin' some of everything there was to play, because as you know, these bands were all over the world and naturally they was playin' all kinds of different ways!"

"How could they read it if everybody spoke different?" asked Frankie. "Well," I says, "they did somethin' with music that they never did with no other language, they made only one set of writin' so that every blessed musician can understand the other if he takes a little time to do it."

"Well," says Frankie, "now we only hear music when the band plays it." "No, no," I says, "it's still everywhere, and if you will listen close you can hear it right in this room." We got real quiet, and after a bit he says, "I hear the radiator goin' *ta-sisssss*, and I hear the clock goin' *pip-pip-pip-pip*." "That's right," I says, "and now if you will place both of your hands tight over your ears and lift 'em up and put 'em back real fast, you will hear the music of life real clear."

He did as I told him and then his face lit up real bright. "I hear it, I hear it!" "Of course you do," I said, "and whenever you hear the music band you must learn to listen real close and that way you will find out what's *in* the music and sometimes it won't be birds or thunder or water, but it might be just a feelin' you had about somethin' once, maybe a scary feelin' or a happy feelin'. Listen long and careful and you'll be sure to hear it."

Well, that child was so delighted and pleased. "Tell me another story about somethin'!" he says, and his mother adds, "Yes, do tell us another story."

Of course, I did, Marge, 'cause not only was I enjoyin' myself but it was a good way to get out of an afternoon's ironin'.

ON SAYING NO

HEY MARGE, come on in and live a while. The coffee pot is perkin' and I have the world's best sweet-potato pie coolin' in the window. . . . Well, how was your trip last weekend? . . . That's nice, I wish I could say that I had a good time too. . . . Yes, the company came. . . . Girl, you should have been here! . . . You know I invited Susie and her husband and a few other people? . . . Sure, they all showed up and some more in the bargain. Susie brought a couple along that was visitin' with her because she thought I'd just *love* to meet them. . . . You know me, the first mistake I made was to light up like a Christmas tree and say, "Make yourself at home!" Me and my big mouth! Those friends that she thought I'd love to meet proceeded to do just that! You should have seen those two!

They hadn't been here ten minutes before they let loose with a string of *off-color* jokes. We listened in a strained sort of polite way, and I forced out a couple of weak ha-ha's, but I can tell you that the goin' was rough. . . . I did that. Yes, I kept changin' the subject or tryin' to change it. . . . No mam, they did not take the hint, and I was so mad you could have boiled a pot of water on my head. . . . Yes, the subject finally got changed but only when it suited them to do so, and in a way I kinda wished they'd stuck to the jokes. Next thing on the program they started talkin' about people. . . . Of course, everybody talks about people sometime, but I mean they got to rippin' people's personal business apart and diggin' out all manner of ugly gossip and scandal and such. They were experts on everybody's private affairs and from the drift of the conversation I could tell that few people met with their approval. Just as I thought I couldn't take any more of it we started in on the refreshments. . . . No, dear, food did not stop their mouths. Them free-loaders sat there eatin' my frankfurters and potato salad and in between bites they informed us about the wonderful *lobster* supper they'd had at *this* doctor's home and the *turkey* and *ham* feast they'd had at *that* doctor's home, and how good a hostess *this* woman was, and what a beautiful home *that* woman had. . . . If I'm lyin' I'm flyin'! . . . All the while they were talkin' they kept eyein' my drapes and coffee table and everything, and somehow or another the room seemed sort of shabby all of a sudden. I mean I'd never noticed that the drapes were kinda flimsy and faded, the lampshade is a little bent on one side, my big ashtray has a nick in it . . . you know, things like that. After they finished off two or three helpings of my salad and franks, they wiped their hands on my crummy paper napkins and started to talk about people havin' things. . . . You heard me! . . . Seems like everyone they know has a fine car, buy their clothes at the most expensive shops, know all of the most important people, have the best jobs in the world, have traveled, got this, got that, got the other. . . . And got dog! I was tired of the whole thing, especially since by this time I felt like some old raggedy crumb with no claim to nothin' no how! . . . Yes, I had drinks but it seems that all they drank was scotch and milk. Anyway I admired the way they forced down all of what I did have and then sent me scurryin' to bring back some more of that potato salad. . . . I was real relieved when we finally got to the goodby time. When I took them to the door they asked me to visit their home out in Long Island and stood there for fifteen more minutes describin' the bar in their playroom and how they knew I'd just *love* it! . . . After everyone had cleared out I felt like I'd just escaped from jail.

The next night my telephone started ringing and I don't have to tell you who it was. . . . That's right, Mrs. Lobster-Ham-Playroom herself, wanting to know could I come out on Tuesday evening. I explained how I had to work and thanked her nicely. . . . The phone starts ringing on Wednesday night, and I have to tell Mrs. Lobster-Ham-Playroom that I have club meetin' on Friday night. . . . The phone rings on Thursday and by this time, I'm tellin' one lie after another. . . . Oh, I made up some tale about my sister feelin' so sick that I'd have to help her out on Saturday. . . . Now get this, Marge! The phone rings again about a half hour later and this time Mrs. Lobster-Ham-Playroom wants to know about me comin' for Sunday dinner. I felt like something was closin' in on me and my back was flat to the wall. I closed my eyes and said, "No, thank you." Mrs. Lobster-Ham-Playroom was quiet for a second and then she says, "Why?" . . . Marge, we go through an awful lot of suffering to avoid tellin' the truth and it suddenly struck me that these people were going to keep me lyin' for a long time to come, and I said real firm-like, "Because I don't care to come and would rather be doing something else." All she said was "Well!" and then hung up on me, and again I felt free and relieved.

Go on, Marge, pour yourself some coffee. . . . The way I figure it, she needed somebody to dog around and show off in front of and I just wasn't goin' to be it. Right here and now

I'm tellin' you that from here on in, I'm gonna have the guts to say that blunt "no" instead of torturin' myself with a weak "yes" or a lie! Sure, life is too short and time is precious! And I ain't gonna squirm out of nothin' no more 'cause what kicks some people just bugs me and vice is versa!

RIDIN' THE BUS

I SURE AM GLAD we got a seat near the window, I'm that tired.
. . . What do you mean by you thought I'd never stop walkin'? I
like to sit in the back of the bus. . . . I certainly do, for many
good reasons. . . . Well, the back is always less crowded, the
air is better, it is also nearer to the exit door. . . . Why do I
sound strange to you? . . . Marge, there is no way that you can
compare ridin' in the back because you want to with ridin' there
because you have to! . . . No indeed, I'll argue you down on
that! . . . I've ridden both ways a whole lot so I can tell you the
difference.

Well, for one thing when I walked to the back of this bus
nobody was freezin' me up with stares. Have you forgotten
what it feels like? All of them eyes that always have to follow
you to your seat lookin' at you real mockin' like. Well, nobody
pays us any mind and we didn't have to die a little on the inside
because there was nothin' to this except findin' a seat. The next
difference was the fact that when we took this seat it simply
showed which one we had picked out and not which one was
picked for us. Why don't you look around you and see who else
is sittin' back here? . . . That's right, there's plenty of white
folks too. Now, if they are from the South, it's probably the

13

first time in their lives that *they* have had the opportunity to sit where *they* want!

. . . Why sure, they *can't* sit in the back down home and it seems that a lot of 'em think that's the best place to be. . . . No, I don't think of it in that way. Good, better or best, it's only the individual that can say which they like. Another thing, I get annoyed ridin' Jim Crow because you get a little more than just *separate seatin'*. You get rudeness, meanness and less for your money in every other way. There's been many a time when I was down home when the driver wouldn't stop when I pulled the cord, that is if I was the only one who wanted to get off, or if it was any other colored for that matter. I'd be so mad when he wouldn't let me off 'til we was four or five blocks past my stop. There's been many a time I've been left standin' with my hand held up to stop the bus and the driver would go whizzin' right on past. There's been other times when them drivers would go out of the way to splash a mud puddle on you. . . . Well, you know they was bein' upheld in everything they did! But the most miserable thing of all was when the back of the bus was full and the front almost empty. Yes, you'd just stand there and get madder and madder, especially when you'd be standin' by a colored mother holdin' her baby in her arms and look toward the front and see four or five white men and women ridin' along with about twenty seats between. I can tell you that although we knew it was the law, it didn't make anybody feel good to notice how the folks sittin' in the front would just go on readin' their newspapers and never even look up or feel the least bit self-conscious about us. . . . Oh yes, there are some places down South where the passengers are supposed to fill up from the front and the back as they come in, but I never liked that too much because if there were more colored we'd have to move back when the whites came on, and of

course that was worse than bein' in the back in the first place.
. . . You are right, Marge, some people still think we want to
sit with white people when they hear us talkin' about that Jim
Crow ridin' and what they seem to forget is that there was
never nothin' *equal* about those *separate* seats even though they
were all on the same bus.

Watch where this white man sits when he gets back here.
Well now, did you see that? He sat next to a colored man. . . .
No, I don't think he especially wanted to or didn't want to.
See how he's busy readin' his magazine? It is good to note also
that the colored man never noticed him sitting beside him and
went right on lookin' for his street. That's the way things *should*
be—nice and easy like with no fuss or bother one way or the
other. Sure, and when I feel like bein' exclusive, I take a *cab!*

BUYIN' PRESENTS

GIRL, I WENT all the way downtown and spent the whole after-noon buttin' around from one store to the other tryin' to find out where best to spend five dollars on Angie and her husband. I tell you, it was downright discouragin'. . . . Sure, there was lots of things, but Angie's got three children *and* a husband, and I was tryin' to get something that would sort of cover every-body at one blow. . . . No, I wouldn't get no candy because Angie's been tryin' to lose weight and that would be a mean trick to play on her since she dearly loves candy. . . . No, I didn't want to buy something just for the children because it seems a shame that people with children never get anything for themselves. After a while I decided to let loose of *ten* dollars, but even then nothin' was happenin' except my feet began to ache.

Finally I headed for home empty-handed and when I got out of the subway I went in the super-market to buy some-thing for my supper. Marge, it is gettin' so that I hate to go shoppin' in the market because it turns my heart to see the women's faces. . . . Now, Marge, I know that I don't go in there to look at faces, but how can I help it?

Take today, for an instance, I saw a woman with two little children, and she was starin' at one of the little boxes of meat which is wrapped up in cellophane like it were a necklace or something, and her forehead was all frowned up because the tiny package of beef had a sticker on it that read one dollar and forty-seven cents and wasn't hardly enough to feed one of them children.

Well, the little ones looked at her hopefully, but she moved on and bought a piece of salt pork for fifty cents, then the poor children poked out their mouths so that the mother bought them a box of sweet biscuits. Marge, I followed her all around the store and saw her look long at the coffee and then buy a package of tea. She handled some of the fresh fruit and then bought a box of dried prunes. She stopped in front of the stringbeans and then picked out a rusty old turnip.

. . . Yes, Marge, I know we all have to do like that but it sure started me to thinkin' about Angie's present and I began to pick it out right then and there.

Well, first I bought her a big, beautiful sirloin steak because I know that hasn't happened to them in a long time; next I got a tin of the best kind of coffee, a box of mixed sweet biscuits and a carton of cigarettes. After I came out of the market I stopped in the five-and-dime and picked up three picture books full of puzzles, jokes, stories, cut-outs and pictures to color. . . . Yes, that will be for the children to go along with the biscuits. Girl, I'll bet this will be the best present Angie ever got, especially since it isn't her birthday or anything. . . . That's right, this present is just because they're always nice to me, and I want them to know that I think about them too.

I have also decided to give our superintendent a half a ham the next time I get some extra cash because I know he don't eat nothin' but neckbones and such on seventy-five dollars a month. When Mrs. Ames across the hall celebrates her baby's first birthday I am goin' to give her one dozen jars of that baby food she uses. On my sister's birthday I will give her a turkey which I shall roast myself, thus saving her a couple of days cookin'.

. . . No, I will not buy any of those glass beads and party diamonds nor will I be tricked into buyin' no sleazy, satin bedroom slippers. Since we feel we must give gifts, wouldn't it be nice if everybody's pantry shelf was full after it was all over?

. . . What? . . . Oh, that's mighty nice of you, Marge, you can just give me three pounds of coffee and five pounds of rice. . . . Yes, Marge, your friend Mildred would appreciate that no end. Thank you.

IF YOU WANT TO GET ALONG WITH ME

Marge, ain't it strange how the two of us get along so well? . . . Now you see there! Why do you have to get so sensitive? . . . No, I was not reflecting on your personality or making any kind of digs! . . . Well, if you'll give me a chance I'll try to explain what I mean. . . . I've known you for years and although you've got your ways . . . Yes, yes, I know I've got mine . . . but the important thing is that we go right on being friends . . . for example, remember the time you borrowed my best white gloves and lost them? . . . I know that I spilled punch on your blue satin blouse! . . . Now, wait a minute, girl! Are we goin' to have a big argument over how friendly we are!

I said all of that to say this. Today I worked for Mrs. M . . . and she is an awful nice lady when she wants to be, but she can get on my nerves something terrible. . . . No, I do not mean that you get on my nerves too, and if you keep pickin' up every little thing I say, I'm gonna get up and go on home. . . . Well, gettin' back to Mrs. M . . . , she can make me downright uncomfortable! . . . Yes, you know what I mean, she turns my workday into a real socializin' session, and her idea of socializin' is to ask me a million questions. . . . "What do you do after work, Mildred?" and "Do you have a lot of friends?"

and "Are you married?" and "Do you have a boyfriend?" and "Do you save your money?" and "Do you like to read?" and "Do *you people* like this or that?" . . . By *you people* she means colored people . . . and I can tell you she can wear my nerve-cells pretty near the breaking point. . . . I know you know!

Well, at first I tried to get used to it because she is so nice in other ways . . . I mean like not followin' me around and dippin' into every thing I'm doing . . . yes, I appreciate that. . . . She lets me do my work, and then if anything isn't quite pleasin' to her she will tell me afterwards but it usually turns out that she's satisfied. Also I like the fact that she is not afraid of a little work herself, and many a day we've worked side by side on jobs that was too much for me to handle all alone. Also she makes the children call me *Miss* Johnson. . . . Sure, whenever anybody has so many good ways, you hate to be pointin' out the bad ones. . . . But question, question, question . . . and it wasn't only the questions. . . . Honey, she could come out with the most gratin' remarks! . . . Honestly, she made such a point of tellin' me about how much she liked and admired Negroes, and how sorry she felt for their plight, and what a *fine, honest, smart,* and *attractive* woman was workin' for her mother and so forth and so on and so forth until it was all I could do to keep from screamin', "All right, back up there and take it easy!"

Well, the upshot of it all was that I began to pick her up a little here and there in order to put her on the right track. For example, I'd say to her, "What's so strange about that woman being *honest* and *attractive?*" Well, Marge, she'd look so stricken and hurt and confused that I'd find myself feelin' sorry for her. . . . No, I didn't stop altogether but I'd let things go along a bit and then I'd have to pick her up on something again, and over a period of five or six weeks I had to jack her up several times. . . . Girl! all of a sudden she turned coldly polite and quiet and I can tell you that it was awful uncomfortable and strained in the house.

I guess I could have stood the strain but it began to tear me up when she'd say things like "May I suggest" and "Do you mind if I say" and "If it's all right with you." . . . When I had my fill of that I came right out and asked her, "Mrs. M . . . , what is the matter, you look so grieved and talk so strange 'til I don't know what to think?" She looked at me accusingly and said, "I'm afraid to say anything to you, Mildred. It seems that every time I open my mouth something wrong comes out and you have to correct me. It makes me very nervous because the last thing I want to do is hurt your feelings. I mean well, but I guess that isn't enough. I try to do the right thing and since it keeps coming out wrong I figured I'd just keep quiet. I . . . I . . . want to get along but I don't know how."

Marge, in that minute I understood her better and it came to my mind that she was doing her best to make me comfortable and havin' a doggone hard go of it. After all, everything she's ever been taught adds up to her being better than me in every way and on her own she had to find out that this was wrong. . . . That's right, she was tryin' to treat me very special because she still felt a bit superior but wanted me to know that she admired me just the same.

"Mrs. M . . . ," I said, "you just treat me like you would anybody else that might be workin' for you in any kind of job. Don't be afraid to talk to me because if you say the wrong thing I promise to correct you, and if you want to get along you won't mind me doing so. After all, if I got into all your personal business and wanted to know everything about your life and your husband and your friends, pretty soon you would be forced to correct me even though it might make me uncomfortable." "Oh, Mildred," she says, "I didn't realize . . ." "Of course you didn't," I cut in, "but can't you see that it's unfair to push a one-sided friendship on me?" "Mildred," she says, "I wanted to be friendly." "Now of course you did," I answered, "but, for example, when you told me the other day that you're going to drop by my house and see me sometime I don't appreciate that because I never invited you, and you never had me to your house except to do a day's work." She looked down at her hands as I went on. "I don't think it's fair that you can invite yourself to my house and I can't tell you that I'll be over here for tea on Sunday afternoon."

Marge, she shook her head sadly. "You mean that there is nothing that we have in common, nothing that we can talk about?" "I didn't say that at all," I said, "but let's just relax and feel our way along and not try to prove anything, and before you know it everything will go along easy-like."

She smiled then, "You mean you don't want to be treated *special?*" "Well, I do and I don't," I answered; "because I knew a woman once who was awful rude to me and said that was the way she was with everybody, no matter what color, and she didn't want to treat me *special*. I told her that if that was her general way then I'd appreciate her treatin' me special and I'd bet that other folks would like the change too." Marge, Mrs. M . . . fell out laughin' and says "Mildred, people are the limit!" . . . And I guess she's right too. . . . No indeed, I don't take that time and bother with most folks because when I run into a mean, hateful one who comes chatterin' around me about "What do you do after work?" I just give her a short smile and say, "Oh, first one thing and then another." And by the time she's figured that out, I'm in another room busy doin' something else! . . . That's right, but, as I said, Mrs. M . . . is a nice person, so I told her.

GOT TO GO SOMEPLACE

MARGE, I AM VERY SORRY and you will have to excuse me, but I don't feel like devilin' any more eggs, neither do I feel like makin' any more potted ham sandwiches, and furthermore I ain't so hot on goin' on no picnic. . . . Yes, I know it was my idea and please don't jump so salty, because I am goin'. No, indeed I would not stand Eddie up. I only said I didn't feel like goin'.

Yes, my mind is disturbed. Now you know I have never been a fearful woman. In fact I have always prided myself on how I'll stand up to anybody, but to tell the God honest truth, I get scared thinkin' of what might happen when you go on a picnic.

It gives me the shivers when I think how they been killin' up our people left and right, and how the law is always lettin' the murderers get away with it! Do you know what happened on the picnic last year? . . . No, not the picnic you went on but the other one! Well, Stella and Mike, Pearl and Leo and me were drivin' along singin' songs and havin' a nice time when all these cars came drivin' past us. Guess what? . . . I'll tell you. They were all flyin' Confederate flags and singin' Dixie! They slowed down as they passed us and jeered and hollered a lot of ugly names! There must have been seven or

23

eight cars and every one of 'em was loaded with screechin' hoodlums. I was some scared. I was afraid that Leo and Mike was gonna get in trouble, especially when I heard Leo say, "Okay, Mike, here's where we take somebody with us, 'cause damn if I'm gonna leave this world by myself!"

Stella started cryin' but Pearl reached down in the lunchbox, got the box of black pepper and hollered back to me, "The first mother's son that sticks his or her head in this car is gonna get both eyes full of black pepper!" Well, it looked for a while like we was gonna be run off the road but Leo held that car steady and wouldn't budge a inch. Pearl yelled, "Honey, we gonna hit!" But Leo still held fast to the center of the right lane. Oh yes, they went on after a while, when it looked like it might mean they was gonna crash too!

No, that wasn't all. After we got to the picnic grounds all we could see was motorcycles roarin' back and forth with Confederate flags on the handlebars. Well, you can imagine how long it took us to get ourselves together, but as hard as it was we managed to try and enjoy ourselves. When we went to the lockerrooms I pointed up to the wall and showed the girls where somebody had written, "niggers not wanted." No, we didn't mention it to the fellas 'cause our day was spoiled enough already. Yes, we had a swim and ate our lunch even though I couldn't taste it. Afterwards when we was drivin' home, we didn't sing and just before we crossed the tollbridge a white fella rolled down his car window and asked Leo if he'd give him a match, Leo gave him a dirty look and said, "Hell no!" He looked at us real funny, but we didn't pay him one bit of mind.

Marge, do you remember those two men that was killed in Yonkers just 'cause they went in a bar to buy a drink? . . . No, nothin' at all was done about it except to let the one who did it just go right on about his business! Search your mind and tell me if you remember one time when a white person got the chair or was hanged for killin' one of our folks. Well, if it's ever happened, I've never heard of it!

Don't it give you the goose pimples when you realize that white people can kill us and get away with it? Just think of it! We are walkin' targets everywhere we go—on the subway, in the street, everywhere.

Now I am a good woman, but if I was not, the law is so fixed that I can't go around killin' folks if I want to live myself. But white folks can kill me. And that is why we got to be so cautious even on a picnic.

Of course I'm goin'! I shall take my life in my hands and go to the beach. After all we got to go somewhere . . . sometime.

"THE POCKETBOOK GAME"

MARGE . . . DAY'S WORK is an education! Well, I mean workin' in different homes you learn much more than if you was steady in one place. . . . I tell you, it really keeps your mind sharp tryin' to watch for what folks will put over on you.

What? . . . No, Marge, I do not want to help shell no beans, but I'd be more than glad to stay and have supper with you, and I'll wash the dishes after. Is that all right? . . .

Who put anything over on who? . . . Oh yes! It's like this. . . . I been working for Mrs. E . . . one day a week for several months and I notice that she has some peculiar ways. Well, there was only one thing that really bothered me and that was her pocketbook habit. . . . No, not those little novels. . . . I mean her purse—her handbag.

Marge, she's got a big old pocketbook with two long straps on it . . . and whenever I'd go there, she'd be propped up in a chair with her handbag double wrapped tight around her wrist, and from room to room she'd roam with that purse hugged to her bosom. . . . Yes, girl! This happens every time! No, there's *nobody* there but me and her. . . . Marge, I couldn't say nothin' to her! It's her purse, ain't it? She can hold onto it if she wants to!

I held my peace for months, tryin' to figure out how I'd

make my point. . . . Well, bless Bess! *Today was the day!*
. . . Please, Marge, keep shellin' the beans so we can eat! I
know you're listenin', but you listen with your ears, not your
hands. . . . Well, anyway, I was almost ready to go home when
she steps in the room hangin' onto her bag as usual and says,
"Mildred will you ask the super to come up and fix the kitchen
faucet?" "Yes, Mrs. E . . . ," I says, "as soon as I leave." "Oh,
no," she says, "he may be gone by then. Please go now." "All
right," I says, and out the door I went, still wearin' my Hoover
apron.

I just went down the hall and stood there a few minutes
. . . and then I rushed back to the door and knocked on it as
hard and frantic as I could. She flung open the door sayin',
"What's the matter? Did you see the super?" . . . "No," I says,
gaspin' hard for breath, "I was almost downstairs when I remembered . . . *I left my pocketbook!*"

With that I dashed in, grabbed my purse and then went
down to get the super! Later, when I was leavin' she says real
timid-like, "Mildred, I hope that you don't think I distrust
you because . . ." I cut her off real quick. . . . "That's all right,
Mrs. E . . . , I understand. 'Cause if I paid anybody as little as you
pay me, I'd hold my pocketbook too!"

Marge, you fool . . . lookout! . . . You gonna drop the beans
on the floor!

NEW YORK'S MY HOME

MARGE, SOMETIMES OUT OF TOWN VISITORS can be a real drag if you live in New York City. . . . Well, you remember the time my friend Mamie visited me for two weeks? . . . Of course I enjoyed her company, but she almost gave me a nervous breakdown! . . . Yes girl, she came here with a list as long as your arm and had every minute of her time planned right down to the second. . . . No, I didn't mind that at all, but what got me was the fact that my time had to go right along with it. . . . Honey! She had to see *all* the museums, the Statue of Liberty, the Empire State Building, the United Nations, Radio City, Central Park, Bronx Park, Small's Paradise, Birdland, Randolph's, the theatres, the markets, and, of course, she never got her fill of bus and boat sight-seeing trips. . . . My dear, I never did so much subway ridin' and transferrin' in my natural life. . . . I can tell you that I was some worn out. About two days before she left she decided to make the rounds of all the big department stores. . . . Marge, we hit every floor in Macy's and then run over to Gimbel's and . . .

Girl! Are you out of your mind? Of course she didn't soak me for all the bills, in fact she made an announcement the first day she got here. . . . "Mildred, I'm goin' to pay my own way everywhere I go." . . . That was great, Marge, but the fact

28

remains that I had to pay *my* way and traipse along with her, and when she left I was two steps from the poor house and a nervous breakdown.

Wait a minute, I haven't told it all. . . . Well, she also had to sample all the different foods in the different restaurants. We had Chinese dinners, French lunches, Italian suppers and so forth and so on, then to cap the climax she just *had* to ride one of those horse and buggy things through Central Park. . . . Yes, we did that the day before she left. . . . There I was leaning back in this carriage, my arms full of packages and my blood pressure hittin' close to two hundred when out she comes with this remark: "New York is all right to visit but I could *never* live here. It's too much rush and hectic going all the time. The pace is too fast, the buildings are too close together, and I like peace and quiet."

My dear, you could have cut the silence with a knife because countin' to ten was not enough and I had to go past seventy-five before I dared answer her. . . . But before I could open my mouth she adds, "How do you ever stand it?" I took ten more after that and mumbled something about, "Oh, I don't live this fast all the time." . . . Believe me when I say that the prettiest sight I ever saw in my life was that big train sittin' in the station waitin' to carry her away from here. That's a fact . . . and you know I'm fond of Mamie!

Today . . . listen close now . . . *today* I get a letter from her sister June sayin' that Mamie had such a good time while she was here that she . . . June . . . had decided to spend her vacation with me next summer. My ankles started to swell just sittin' there thinkin' about it, and I made up my mind then and there that I could not go through the business of bein' personal guide on a merry-go-round for another two-week stretch. . . . Of course, she's welcome but no more of this

jumpin' through hoops for yours truly, especially when half
of the time the visitor goes back home without the least idea
of what New York City is all about or why millions of people
stay here and also like it. . . . I know it! All these out-of-
towners think we're a bunch of good-timers!

Marge, you know it is a rare thing for me to be runnin' different places . . . and even if my health could stand it, my
pocketbook can't. . . . That's right, there's hardly a small
town in the land where you'll find people goin' less than your
friend Mildred, but whenever I go away I soon find that I'm
gettin' real homesick for this New York . . . because I like it!

When I'm here, I enjoy stayin' home with the thought that
there is a million places for me to go if I wanted to, but when
I'm away I hate stayin' home with the thought that I *have* to
because nothin's goin' on. . . . Yes, mam, that makes a real
difference.

When I'm away I miss the subway. . . . No, not the rush
and crowd, but the people. I like ridin' with folks of every
race, color and kind. . . . They make stories go round in my
head, and sometimes I go past my stop because I'm so busy
imaginin' their children and homes and what kind of lives
they live. . . . One day I was in a super-market and I saw this
East Indian with a beautiful pink turban on his head. . . . Oh,
he was busy buyin' a box of Uneeda biscuits. . . . That stayed
on my mind for a long time because the turban made me
think of pearls and palaces . . . but there he was as big as life
. . . with biscuits! . . . Yes, I miss these things when I'm away.
I miss the people walkin' along with their little radios held up
to their ear so's they can listen to the Dodgers, the big ships
standin' still and mighty in the harbor, the tough little tug boats
huffin' and puffin' up the river, the fellas pushin' carts of suits
and dresses in and out of downtown traffic, people readin' all

manner of foreign newspapers and such, all the big sounds of swishin' automobiles, planes overhead and children shoutin' until it all comes together and turns into one big "New York-sound."

. . . Talk about missin' things! . . . I miss the friendliness of total strangers when they gather on a corner and try to direct somebody who doesn't speak English. . . . Yes Marge, I bet many a soul has ended up on the west side of nowhere tryin' to follow the advice of New Yorkers who are always gettin' lost themselves, even though they have been here ever since the flood. . . . Ain't it the truth? . . . I also miss the nice way your neighbors don't bother to keep up with what time you come and go or who visits your house and how long they stayed. . . . That's true, too, them same neighbors will rally-round in case of sickness or death. . . . I miss seein' the line in front of the Apollo waitin' to see all those fine stars like Nat King Cole and Sammy Davis and Eartha Kitt and Count Basie and everything. . . . Tell it now!

Talk about things to miss! . . . I miss the way the workmen are always diggin' at the street pipes. . . . It's kind of mystifyin' because you never know what's bein' dug, but you can stop and watch a little while anyway and think about nothin' in particular and then pass on. . . . Oh honey! . . . I miss *life!*

But Marge, what I miss most is a feelin' in the air, a feelin' that hits you right in the railroad station. . . . I can't describe it in words too well, but it seeps into you and it's real excitin'. I guess maybe you'd call it a "something's-gonna-happen-and-you-don't-know-what-it-is" kind of feelin'. . . . You right . . . I get sick and tired of folks sayin' "I could never *live* here" . . . because even though I may not ever get hold of enough money to travel to far-off places, I can still say I've met some fine Puerto Ricans and Irish, and Italian, and French, and African and some of all kind of folk. . . . This City is far from perfect, but it gets you to the place where you just want to try and *make it* perfect. Oh sure, I don't mind June comin' to visit, but I'm gonna try and make her see my home the way I see it!

. . . Hold on, Marge! No, I wouldn't go that far. . . . I ain't sayin' that everything here is better than any place else and neither will I take any cracks at the South! Because home is where the heart is and everybody knows their own home the best.

All I'm sayin' is I wish people would stop tellin' us "I could *never* live here."

ALL ABOUT MY JOB

MARGE, I sure am glad that you are my friend. . . . No, I do not want to borrow anything or ask any favors and I wish you'd stop bein' suspicious everytime somebody pays you a compliment. It's a sure sign of a distrustful nature.

I'm glad that you are my friend because everybody needs a friend but I guess I need one more than most people. . . . Well, in the first place I'm colored and in the second place I do housework for a livin' and so you can see that I don't need a third place because the first two ought to be enough reason for anybody to need a friend.

You are not only a good friend but you are also a convenient friend and fill the bill in every other way. . . . Well, we are both thirty-two years old; both live in the same building; we each have a three room apartment for which we pay too devilish much, but at the same time we got better sense than to try and live together. And there are other things, too. We both come from the South and we also do the same kinda work: *housework*.

Of course, you have been married, and I have not yet taken the vows, but I guess that's the only difference unless you want to count the fact that you are heavier than I am and wear a size eighteen while I wear a sixteen. . . . Marge, you know that you are larger, that's a fact! Oh, well, let's not get upset about it! The important thing is that I'm your friend, and you're mine and I'm glad about it!

Why, I do believe I'd lose my mind if I had to come home after a day of hard work, rasslin' 'round in other folks' kitchens if I did not have a friend to talk to when I got here. . . . Girl, don't you move 'cause it would be terrible if I couldn't run down a flight of steps and come in here to chew the fat in the evenin'. But if you ever get tired of me, always remember that all you have to do is say, "Mildred, go home," and I'll be on my way! . . . I did not get mad the last time you told me that! Girl, you ought to be ashamed of yourself! . . . No, I'm not callin' you a liar but I'm sayin' you just can't remember the truth.

Anyhow, I'm glad that we're friends! I got a story to tell you about what happened today. . . . No, not where I work although it was *about* where I work.

The church bazaar was open tonight and I went down to help out on one of the booths and, oh, my nerves! you never saw so many la-de-da fancy folks in all your life! And such introducin' that was goin' on. You shoulda *heard* 'em. "Do meet Mrs. So-and-so who has just returned from *Europe*," and "Do meet Miss This-and-that who has just finished her new *book*" and "Do meet Miss This-that-and-the-other who is on the Board of Directors of everything that is worthwhile!"

Honey, it was a dog! . . . Oh, yes, it was a real snazzy affair, and the booths was all fixed up so pretty, and they had these fine photographs pinned up on the wall. The photographs showed people doin' all manner of work. Yes, the idea of the pictures was to show how we are improvin' ourselves by leaps and bounds through the kinda work that we're doin'.

Well, that was a great old deal with me except that if they was talkin' 'bout people doin' work, it seemed to me that I was the only one around there that had took a lick at a snake in years! . . . No, it wasn't a drag at all because I was really enjoyin' the thing just like you'd go for a carnival or a penny-arcade once in a while.

My booth was the "Knick-Knack" corner and my counter was full of chipped-china doo-dads and ash trays and penny banks and stuff like that, and I was really sellin' it, too. There was a little quiet lady helpin' me out and for the life of me I couldn't figure why she was so scared-like and timid lookin'.

I was enjoyin' myself no end, and there was so many big-wigs floatin' around the joint 'til I didn't know what to expect next! . . . Yes, girl, any second I thought some sultan or king or somebody like that was gonna fall in the door! Honey, I was how-do-you-doin' left and right! Well, all the excitement keeps up 'til one group of grand folks stopped at our booth and begun to chat with us and after the recitation 'bout what they all did, one lady turned to my timid friend and says, "What do *you* do?"

Marge, Miss Timid started sputterin' and stammerin' and finally she outs with, "Nothin' much." That was a new one on me 'cause I had never heard 'bout nobody who spent their time doin' "nothin' much." Then Miss Grand-lady turns to me and says, "And what do *you* do?" . . . Of course I told her! "I do housework," I said. "Oh," says she, "you are a housewife." "Oh, no," says I, "I do housework, and I do it every day because that is the way I make my livin' and if you look around at these pictures on the wall you will see that people do all kinds of work, I do housework."

Marge, they looked kinda funny for a minute but the next

thing you know we were all laughin' and talkin' 'bout everything in general and nothin' in particular. I mean all of us was chattin' except Miss Timid.

When the folks drifted away, Miss Timid turns to me and says, "I do housework too but I don't always feel like tellin'. People look down on you so."

Well, I can tell you that I moved on in after that remark and straightened her out! . . . Now, wait a minute, Marge! I know people do make nasty cracks about houseworkers. Sure, they will say things like "pot-slingers" or "the Thursday-night-off" crowd, but nobody gets away with that stuff around me, and I will sound off in a second about how I feel about my work.

Marge, people who do this kinda work got a lot of different ideas about their jobs, I mean some folks are ashamed of it and some are proud of it, but I don't feel either way. You see, on accounta many reasons I find that I got to do it and while I don't think that housework is the grandest job I ever hope to get, it makes me *mad* for any fools to come lookin' down their nose at me!

If I had a child, I would want that child to do something that paid better and had some opportunity to it, but on the other hand it would distress me no end to see that child get some arrogant attitude toward me because I do domestic work. Domestic workers have done a awful lot of good things in this country besides clean up peoples' houses. We've taken care of our brothers and fathers and husbands when the factory gates and office desks and pretty near everything else was closed to them; we've helped many a neighbor, doin' everything from helpin' to clothe their children to buryin' the dead.

. . . Yes, mam, and I'll help you to tell it! We built that

church that the bazaar was held in! And it's a rare thing for anybody to find a colored family in this land that can't trace a domestic worker somewhere in their history. . . . How 'bout that, girl! . . . Yes, there's many a doctor, many a lawyer, many a teacher, many a minister that got where they are 'cause somebody worked in the kitchen to put 'em there, and there's also a lot of 'em that worked in kitchens themselves in order to climb up a little higher!

Of course, a lot of people think it's *smart* not to talk about *slavery* anymore, but after freedom came, it was domestics that kept us from perishin' by the wayside. . . . Who you tellin'? I know it was our dollars and pennies that built many a school! . . .

Yes, I know I said I wasn't particular proud about bein' a domestic worker, but I guess I am. What I really meant to say was that I had plans to be somethin' else, but time and trouble stopped me from doin' it. So I told this little Miss Meek, "Dear, throw back your shoulders and pop your fingers at the *world* because the way I see it there's nobody with common sense that can look down on the domestic worker!"

BUBBA

MARGE, LIFE JUST BRIMS over with first one thing and then
another, and if you throw all your troubles in a bag, there's
no tellin' which one will jump out first. . . . No, I didn't have
another run-in with the rent man. It's my sister. Listen to me,
Marge, and stop crochetin' that doily. . . . Oh, is it a chair-
back? . . . No, I don't want you to teach me how to make one
'cause I got other things on my mind.

Now where was I? . . . That's right! My sister. She calls me
up today and says, "Mildred, I want you to come over and
talk to Bubba 'cause he's after gettin' himself in trouble." . . .
Bubba is her son. . . . His name is John, we just *call* him Bubba.

Well, I jumped over there on the fly 'cause I'm just crazy
about my nephew.

Marge, the long and short of it was that Bubba has been
mixin' in politics and things. You know what I mean. Shoutin'
about civil rights and sendin' off petitions and carryin' signs
in front of movin' picture theatres, and Lord only knows he
don't think nothin' of criticizin' *anybody's* government *any
time!* My sister said, "Bubba's gonna land in jail!" Yes, that's
what she was worried about!

Well, I sat Bubba down and I says: "Bubba, why don't you
behave and stop worryin' your mother?"

38

Marge, you should have seen him! He's a handsome little wiry fellow, hardly bigger than a minute and got them big flashin' brown eyes and his mouth is set just so, you just should have seen him. He started pacin' the floor and when he stopped, he gave me a look. Right there and then I saw he wasn't gonna be nobody's pushover.

"Aunt Mildred," he said, "hurtin' mama is the last thing in this world I'd want to do." I jumped in right there and started on him again: "Well, doggone! Why don't you behave, why you so hard-headed!" I felt like I was pickin' on him somethin' terrible, but I couldn't afford to let him get the upper hand. I hollered at him, "You got nothin' else to do but be a worriation to your mother and drive her to the grave!"

And then he started talkin': "Aunt Mildred, I want to be free, I want some of everything there is to have, I want decent jobs, I want to go to any school that's teachin' what I want to learn, I don't want to ride the back of these buses!"

It would have been funny if the thing wasn't so serious. Florence jumped up in his face and the way she was wavin' her arms around you would've thought she was gonna take off and fly! "Listen to him!" she says, and the way she was screamin' it was a cryin' shame. "Listen to him talkin' about ridin' in the back of the bus! Don't nobody have to ride the back of the bus up here! You're in the North! Mildred he is in the North and yet always sayin' things like that!" "Now wait a minute," I said. But Bubba comes right back at her before I can fit a word in edgewise.

"I want to go down South and ride too, also North, East and West! I got rights that I want to use, and anytime I'm old enough to be called in some army, I'm old enough to fight for my rights! I want to be free! Are we *free*, Aunt Mildred?"

Well, Florence kept lookin' to me to say somethin' so after

39

I thought for a while I said, "*No*." And then I asked her, "Are we free, Florence?" And she answered, "I don't want nothin' or nobody to hurt Bubba, that's all."

He was most distressed, Marge, and the words came pourin' out of his mouth so fast it was enough to make your head swim. "Aunt Mildred, I don't have to tell you about our troubles. You know how we're treated, I'm tired of bein' kicked around and mocked."

"Go on, son," I said. And believe me when I tell you he did. "I can't close my eyes, ears and mouth and swallow down my own manhood. I can't sing no 'Tom Song' about 'All is well.' I can't crawl around and be content to eat my crust of bread and sleep a restless sleep! Damn if I can! I can't do them things and that's the size of it! It's wrong, wrong, wrong!"

Marge, Florence began to cry. "I know all that, but there's others wiser than you, Mr. *Smarty*. Furthermore, I ain't gonna have you cursin' me! Shame on you cursin' your own mama!"

"Oh, Florence," I said, "he didn't do no cursin'."

"He said *damn*, and I *heard* him!"

Bubba kept plowin' ahead: "All them 'Toms' that's supposed to be wiser than me is a bunch of mealy-mouth liars. All they're tryin' to do is hold on to the few dollars that *Mr. Charlie* lets 'em have!"

Marge, you would have thought that lightnin' had struck my sister. "I ain't gonna have you full of hatred for white folks, it just brings on misery." Then Bubba cut her off again: "I do not hate white people, I have plenty of white friends!"

"Friends!" yells Florence, "Mildred, they are all just like Bubba, always raisin' noise and fuss about things like that, gettin' into trouble!"

"And that's how I can know that they are my *friends*," says Bubba, "I'm tellin' you the truth. All of us have to go off to these wars and I'm tellin' you that it's a poor kind of man that won't fight for his own freedom!"

"Amen," I said. Then Florence spoke up softly, "I know, I know, I just don't wanna see you hurt, Bubba."

Marge, that young man put his arms around his mother and told her, "But I am hurt, we're all hurt and you've been watchin' it all your life, so I figure you can stand just about anything." That brought the two of us down to earth and I said to Florence, "Leave him alone, let him live his life 'cause he's got good sense. Maybe the two of us didn't do all of our share when we was comin' up. Now Bubba has to finish up some of our work. It's not right that these children should have so much left on their shoulders but it's real encouragin' to see that they don't mind handlin' the situation."

Well, no, Marge, she didn't get to the place where she felt all rosy and happy, but she kinda went over to Bubba's side. I stayed on for dinner and when I left they was listenin' to the radio and laughin' and talkin' like nothin' had happened.

THE HEALTH CARD

WELL, MARGE, I started an extra job today. . . . Just wait, girl. Don't laugh yet. Just wait till I tell you. . . . The woman seems real nice. . . . Well, you know what I mean. . . . She was pretty nice, anyway. Shows me this and shows me that, but she was real cautious about loadin' on too much work the first morning. And she stopped short when she caught the light in my eye.

Comes the afternoon, I was busy waxin' woodwork when I notice her hoverin' over me kind of timid-like. She passed me once and smiled and then she turned and blushed a little. I put down the wax can and gave her an inquirin' look. The lady takes a deep breath and comes up with, "Do you live in Harlem, Mildred?"

Now you know I expected somethin' more than that after all the hesitatin'. I had already given her my address so I didn't quite get the idea behind the question. "Yes, Mrs. Jones," I answered, "that is where I live."

Well, she backed away and retired to the living room and I could hear her and the husband just a-buzzin'. A little later on I was in the kitchen washin' glasses. I looks up and there she was in the doorway, lookin' kind of strained around the gills. First she stuttered and then she stammered and after

42

beatin' all around the bush she comes out with, "Do you have a health card, Mildred?"

That let the cat out of the bag. I thought real fast. Honey, my brain was runnin' on wheels. "Yes, Mrs. Jones," I says, "I have a health card." Now Marge, this is a lie. I do not have a health card. "I'll bring it tomorrow," I add real sweet-like.

She beams like a chromium platter and all you could see above her taffeta house coat is smile. "Mildred," she said, "I don't mean any offense, but one must be careful, mustn't one?"

Well, all she got from me was solid agreement. "Sure, I said, "indeed *one* must, and I am glad you are so understandin', 'cause I was just worryin' and studyin' on how I was goin' to ask you for yours, and of course you'll let me see one from your husband and one for each of the three children."

By that time she was the same color as the housecoat, which is green, but I continue on: "Since I have to handle laundry and make beds, you know . . ." She stops me right there and after excusin' herself she scurries from the room and has another conference with hubby.

Inside fifteen minutes she was back. "Mildred, you don't have to bring a health card. I am sure it will be all right."

I looked up real casual kind-of and said, "On second thought, you folks look real clean, too, so . . ." And then she smiled and I smiled and then she smiled again. . . . Oh, stop laughin' so loud, Marge, everybody on this bus is starin'.

"YOUR SOUL . . . ANOTHER YOU"

MARGE, SOMETIMES YOU CAN BE awful contrary. . . . Yes, you!
. . . No, I don't want to start no argument, but when I got
something on my mind I just got to say it.

Well, I think we all do pretty good to jump over the daily
harassments like rent, light, gas, groceries, sickness and weari-
ment, and the Lord only knows how we're prayin' not to have
another war! Now wouldn't you think that's enough worry for
all of us? . . . Just keep calm now, I'm gettin' to the point.
Sometimes, Marge, don't you long for a little beauty in your
life . . . a little sweetness? No, I'm not talkin' about hearin' a
snatch of pretty music, nor am I speakin' about smelling
flowers or dancin' no waltz, although everybody should have
a goodly share of those things too.

Now don't laugh, Marge, because I'm dead serious. . . . Oh
yes, it is very possible for me to get serious! . . . We make folks
laugh because it's better than lookin' long-faced and we "cut
the fool" because it takes precious little in the other direction
to start the tears fallin' and that don't benefit nobody except
a handkerchief salesman, but it's a shame how folks go 'long
and take each other for granted just as though they got nothin'
to 'em but their faces! . . . That's wrong because we all got

souls. . . . Why, I'm surprised at you, Marge! Don't you know what a soul is?

Well, I'll tell you—your soul is an inner something that is another you and hardly anybody knows what it's really thinkin' *except* you. Your soul is that which you expect *friends* to reach for in order to know you better. . . . Marge, it is truly amazin' the things that the soul can do! . . . It can make you call up your friends when you don't need a favor and share all your goodness and happiness with them. . . . It can make you spend time with your family, not begrudgin' and beholden with duty but with love and admiration. . . . It can make you talk to a stranger on a bus and leave 'em all flustered and pleased with themselves. . . . Oh yes, it'll make you scribble a note to somebody telling 'em you want to know if everything's goin' along smooth. . . . It'll teach you how to *accept givin'* when somebody gives you somethin'. . . . Oh, you know what I mean, Marge! You won't holler, "Oh, you shouldn't have!" or "Why did you?" . . . *A gift*—be it a present, a kind word or a job done with care and love—*explains itself!* . . . and if receivin' it embarrasses you it's because your "thanks box" is warped.

Take you for an example, Marge—when I wash your dishes you always say, "Oh, you needn't" or "You don't have to." . . . Now *I* know I needn't and *you* know it, but I just feel like givin' you that. . . . You see what I mean?

Yes, there have been other times when you've done it, like when you asked me to write your church speech and everytime I wanted to go over it with you, you'd get saltier and saltier, and after a while it seemed like I was botherin' you to do somethin' for *me!* . . . Of course I understand and I know you're sorry. We all act that way sometimes.

Well, the soul is a funny something—there's things it *won't* let you do either . . . It won't let a man ask his wife for a dance in a voice that's as dead as ashes. . . . It won't let papas and mamas turn a deaf ear to a child's talk about school and games and children's worries. . . . It won't let you work somebody for a salary that you wouldn't take for the same job. . . . It won't let you hate people because they look different from you. . . . It won't let you preach a sermon and then uphold Jim Crow.

Oh yes, Marge, I know there are people who do these things, but their soul case is worn thin . . . and when it comes to folks hatin' and Jim Crowin', they got no soul at all . . . they are dead . . . only they are not buried yet.

Yes, your friend Mildred is really serious this evenin' and I feel like indulgin' my feelin's.

Goodnight Marge.

SIGNS OF THE TIMES

THERE IS ONE THING about not havin' a lot of education, that is you can always imagine how you might have done somethin' great if you had. I often think like that and get to imaginin' what kind of great somebody I might have been. Of course, I just might have failed at the things, but, on the other hand, I'll never really know 'cause I haven't had the chance to try anything.

Today I found out what it is that I would have been real good at. . . . No, I never pictured myself as a nurse or a teacher although I mightn't of been too bad at either one of 'em. I was ridin' along on the subway when it all of a sudden come over me that I would be just grand at writin' signs. You know, I'm talkin about all those signs that you see lined up in subway trains and buses, in particular the ones that tell about race relations bein' better and everything!

Some of those signs are right nice and you can tell that they got the best intentions in the world but you can also tell that no colored people have been writin' any of them. . . . Well, I know that I would make just about the grandest signwriter in the business and put things so that they would be clear and make lots of sense!

There I was ridin' along and lookin' at people across the

aisle from me and wonderin' what they was thinkin' about and where they lived. I saw how almost all of them that wasn't lookin' in a newspaper was lookin' up at them signs and readin' 'em over for just as far as the eye could reach, so I began readin' them too.

Well, there was one very nice sign that showed colored and white and Spanish and all manner of people standin' together in a nice friendly way, they all looked pretty, especially since this sign was in color. The writin' on it said something like this, "In our city, all the people work and play together regardless of race, creed or color." Now, as good intentioned as that sign was, it struck me as havin' somethin' wrong with it!

I got to thinkin' about where I had heard somethin' like that before, then I remembered that it was at Mrs. Warren's house! Yes, I was over there one time to help her when she gave her daughter a party. Her daughter is in the freshman year at college and the house was brimmin' over with bright-eyed, lively youngsters. Well, the bell rings and in walks this dapper little fellow that turned out to be the life of the party. He was dressed real snappy and as soon as he hits the livin' room he waves his hand in the air and hollers, "Greetin's everybody, regardless of race, creed, color or previous condition of servitude!"

Honey! The house came down! Of course, they were all colored, but that wasn't the point. They were laughin' like crazy about that 'regardless' business! Why on earth does anybody have to *disregard* what folks are in order to like them? I never *disregard* people! Why, I can tell the difference between Chinese and Irish without half-tryin' and work and play with them just as well. In fact I would be foolin' myself and other folks, too, if I said I *disregarded* that there was even a mite of difference. Of course, maybe the word *disregard* could also mean that I might notice the difference but make sure and pay it no mind.

Anyway, I knew right then and there just how to fix up that sign! I would show all those different folks standin' to-gether just like they were, but I would change the readin' under it so it would say, "In our city, *all* the people work and play together." Now what's wrong with that? Folks will have got the point without clutterin' up the thing with all them *regardlesses!*

Another thing I would not do if I was a signwriter is to tell people that their friends will *envy* them if they buy this fur coat or that car or somethin'. Oh no, I would say, "Your friends will *admire* you!" 'Cause I think it is more fun to be admired than envied! . . . That's right, all them folks who envy you might turn into enemies or at least you won't be too pop-ular with them!

Yes, I know I would be a first-class, number one signwriter! I could also write things for these people who are always runnin' in some election. Very often I see posters in this neighborhood tellin' us about some man who is "tolerant." Soon as I see that I make up my mind not to vote for him. . . . No, I don't want anybody *toleratin'* me because the word *tolerate* is tied up with so many unpleasant things. You know how you hear people say, "I'm sick of *toleratin'* your foolishness!"

I also remember how my grandma used to say, "I'm not gonna *tolerate* your sassiness much longer!" And I would know that she meant that she had been puttin' up with me although she'd been mad as the devil with me and the whole thing had been a tremendous burden as well as a test of her temper-control.

Well, if I was signwritin' for that man I would have left

his picture there just like it was, but I'd change the writin' and have it read, "The man who works for *all* the people!" I bet he'd be surprised how much better that went over than the "tolerance" stuff.

. . . Sure, I'd be good at it! And I bet they pay people a nice tidy sum for writin' those things!

AREN'T YOU HAPPY?

Good morning Marge. . . . I come to borrow a cup of sugar and a half stick 'a butter until tomorrow. . . . I got a recipe for a "no egg" cake. . . . Ain't that somethin'? What will they think of next? My cousin Ellie give me the recipe for it. I told her if she come across a recipe for some "no-meat" meat balls to be sure and give me that . . . now that's somethin' I could really use.

Oh no, Marge, Ellie ain't workin' now. She can't work with that son of hers. Bobby ain't but 12 but already he's broke one rib and a arm and his forehead is always lumped up. . . . Yeah, her husband is doin' a little better on the job . . . got a little raise . . . so she quit her place . . . Bobby was climbin' up lamp posts and fallin' off of back alley fences. Child, when she heard 'bout him playin' leap frog on the roof ledge she whupped him and then figured she'd best stay home and watch him before he ruined himself altogether.

The woman she worked for wasn't bad as folks go so Ellie decided to give her two weeks notice. Well, honey, I can't tell it like Ellie can . . . you oughta hear her! Well anyway she told this lady 'bout Bobby and explained how she had to leave and . . . bless Bess! the woman fell out. . . . You heard me, she fell out! That's just what I said! There she was

51

cryin' and moanin' and just a-carryin' on. . . . Now Ellie was speechless 'cause she had no idea the woman was that crazy 'bout her. . . . When the woman gets her breath back she starts groanin': "Oh Ellie we were so fond of you and I never thought you'd leave us. . . . Oh I never thought you'd leave us."

"Never?" Ellie asked her. "Really *never?*" and that woman was dead serious.

"Ellie," she says, "I thought of us as just one big family. . . . What's wrong? Why do you want to leave?"

Well, Ellie gets her a glass of water and some smellin' salts and sat down and explained all over again . . . slowly. She tells her 'bout Bobby and 'bout her husband real clear. When she was through the woman asked her, "What have we done to you? Has anyone hurt your feelings? Aren't you happy?"

Well the upshot of it was that there was no way that Ellie could explain anything so's she'd understand it 'cause the way Ellie told it to *me*, this woman had read "Gone with the Wind" four times and . . . and . . . well, it's just given her ideas . . . that's all. . . . Look out Marge! The coffee is boilin' over. . . . Girl, stop actin' the fool now!

NASTY COMPLIMENTS

MARGE, I CAN SEE why you say you don't like this butcher shop on the corner even if they do have the best quality of meat. . . . I know you have had words with the man that owns the place, but I guess I will really avoid goin' in there after today! . . . Sure, he is sickenin'! . . . I don't pay him too much mind although I have had to jack him up about callin' me "girlie" and "honeychile," but every once in a while I will find myself wantin' a nice piece of steak and will go in there 'cause it is the closest shop to my house.

When I went in there tonight, he tries to pick a conversation with me by sayin', "There's some *fine* colored people around here, and I can say this: I'd rather know a Negro any day than to know a Jew." All the time he's talkin' he's also grinnin' at me like a chessy-cat! I suppose he thought he was payin' me a compliment!

So, I says, "You mean that if you had to keep some unpleasant company, you would rather it would be mine." He says, "Oh, no, I mean that colored people are better to deal with than Jews. A Jew will always try to take advantage of you and a Jew will . . ."

I cut him off then. "I'm not interested," I says, "because folks that talk about Jews that way will be very quick to call me 'nigger'!" "Oh, no," he says, "I'd never say anything like that!"

Now, Marge, all this time he is busy cuttin' my round steak and gettin' ready to grind it in the machine. I answered him real snappy, "You're a liar and the truth ain't in you! I have heard you say 'spick' after some Spanish person left the store. I also heard you say 'wop' one day, and I know that if you like nasty words like that you just couldn't resist sayin' 'nigger'."

Well, he looks kind of flustered-like and says, "I'm sorry, sister, all I meant was that I like you people." "I know what you meant," I says, "and I don't wanna hear no talk out of you 'bout how you think I'm better than some folks who you consider to be nothin' 'cause if the truth is to be known, I can't imagine *anybody* bein' interested in makin' *your* acquaintance!" The next thing I did was shake my finger at him and read him some more, "You oughta be tickled pink that anybody buys your old, crummy dogmeat!"

. . . Now, Marge, I know the meat is good, but I just called it "dogmeat" in order to be mean! "Furthermore," I says, "I'm not gonna buy that round steak, and I'm gonna tell all the people I see not to come in here and buy anything you got. I'll bet if everyone was to stay away from this place for a while you'd be tickled to death whenever you finally did get a customer, any customer!"

I'm tellin' you, those kinda people make me sick! . . . Sure, I remember the time that woman told you about Puerto Ricans. Ain't that some nerve! She's gonna ask *you* what you think of so many of 'em movin' in her neighborhood! I'm glad you told her that you was plannin' on movin' over there *yourself*. I guess that held her for a while! Folks who rent apartments got a real crust to come talkin' about *their* neighborhood!

Marge, if there is one thing I can't stand it's gettin' one of them back-handed compliments! I remember a man tellin' me once that he liked me 'cause I was "different." I said, "Different from what?" Then he went into a big old wringin' and twistin' 'bout how some colored people was terrible, but I was very nice. I told him, "You can get off of that 'cause I'm just exactly like most of the colored people I know!"

. . . You are so right! I know a lot of folks swallow that old line when it gets thrown at them! . . . Don't I see 'em grinnin' and smilin' with that thank-you-so-much look on their faces! But if the fools only knew that as soon as they turned their back another name was pinned on them they'd grin out of the other side of their mouth. No, *nobody* is gonna get in my good graces by tellin' me that some other folk is so distasteful to them that I look nice by comparison! We gotta straighten these name-callers out!

OLD AS THE HILLS

GIRL, WHAT HAPPENS to people in a bargain basement when a sale is goin' on? . . . It was all I could do to get to the counters or a dress rack! . . . Yes, indeed, Crumbley's had one bang-up sale today. It was so jam-crowded and tempers was so short that I decided I'd better get out of there before I got in a fist fight!

Eddie is plannin' on takin' me to Marybelle's club dance, so I thought I'd better get me a new frock to match the occasion. It is so *rare* that he will actually pick up and go to a dance, or rather, I should say that it's so rare that he will be here in town when one is goin' on. I figured that by the time he sees me in a new dress, he will figure that the dance was a worthwhile idea.

I saw this gorgeous, green evenin' gown hangin' there on the rack, and I managed to get to it. Soon as I had it in my hand, another woman reached out for it, and said, "*I* want that dress!" So I says, "That makes *two* of us!" Oh, she was some nasty! "I was here *first*!" she says, and I went on to agree with her, "Yes, you were honey, by the looks of you, I'd say that you were here about twenty years before I was!" Oh, my, but that made her hot! She stood there sputterin' and stammerin' and blushed all red in the face. All of a sudden I had a funny feelin' that made me know I shouldn't of said that, and I put the dress back on the rack and went away.

I saw some hats on a counter just as I was leavin' the store, so I pushed my way over and picked up a nice little blue felt. A girl that was standin' over on the opposite side said, "Miss, may I have that hat, please, I was tryin' to reach it!" "No!" I says, "you may not. Don't you see me standin' here, holdin' it in my hand!" So her little girlfriend who was with her pipes up, "Oh, snatch it from her!" . . . Oh, I was ready for her, "Let all snatchers come on up here to me one at a time, and I'll take care of 'em! First come, first served!" I hollered. Then the number one little girl says to her friend, "Ignore her, she must be at least *thirty-five*. When you're that *old*, you get *desperate*."

No, Marge, I didn't buy a thing. The whole time I was ridin' along on the bus I got to thinkin' 'bout how people can ride women 'bout their age. Soon as I got in a fuss about that dress, I had to tell the woman about her age and soon's those young girls started arguin' with me, they jumped me 'bout *my* age! Why are we so quick to abuse folks about how old they are and talk about years like it's criminal to get older?

I also got to thinkin' 'bout all those sayin's about age like "old as the hills," "a old has-been," "old and doddery," "been here since the flood!" Why I have even heard folk make nasty cracks when they are askin' about a old person. They will say, "Oh, is he *still* here?" Why, Marge, why are we so mean to people and get so aggravated about 'em gettin' older? Where did we learn such meanness? Where did we get the idea of insultin' folks by pointin' out their age? That's the silliest thing you ever heard of!

Well, there I was ridin' along and thinkin' my thoughts

when a elderly man came and sat down by me. . . . No, he didn't say anything, he just went to readin' his newspaper and after a while he got off at his stop. He left the paper on the seat by me and I picked it up. It was turned to the "help wanted" section and after readin' it a while, I could see why the poor fellow had left it on the seat!

Most of those ads wanted people between the age of eighteen and thirty-five. Now most folks in their forties can get away with puttin' their age back to the thirties, but if you're fifty or more, shame on you! Why is that?

Well, I guess the boss figures that most people have been wore out by the time they are forty, wore out with eatin' the wrong kind of food, walkin' up too many flights of stairs, skimpin' and skrimpin' pennies, and in other words just plain harassed to death!

. . . Of course, other folks besides bosses act real mean about age, too. I don't know why 'cause everybody keeps gettin' older from the time they are born 'til the day they die. It seems that we think youth is some special accomplishment brought about by the individual himself!

. . . That's right! On the other hand, we make fun of folks who go to a lot of time and trouble tryin' to stay young lookin'! All you have to do is read these want-ads and you'll see that them folks that are tryin' to stay young have got more on their minds than pure *vanity!*

I'm tellin' you! People advancin' in age had better stick together if they want to eat and pay rent, and when I say *people advancin'*, that means everybody, young, old or in-between.

Them years go a lot faster than we might think and the best way for a young man to prepare for his old age is to see that older folks get a square deal before the years creep up on him and catch him in the same spot. If he does that, he will have nothin' to worry about and also will not have to work free for his children in exchange for room and board. How 'bout that?

MRS. JAMES

WELL MARGE, you haven't heard anything! You should hear
the woman I work for . . . she's really something. Calls herself
"Mrs. James!" All the time she says "Mrs. James."

The first day I was there she come into the kitchen and
says, "Mildred, Mrs. James would like you to clean the pantry."
Well I looked 'round to see if she meant her mother-in-law or
somebody and then she adds, "If anyone calls, Mrs. James is
out shopping." And with that she sashays out the door.

Now she keeps on talking that way all the time, the whole
time I'm there. That woman wouldn't say "I" or "me" for
nothing in the world. The way I look at it . . . I guess she
thought it would be too personal.

Now Marge, you know I don't work Saturdays for nobody! Well sir! Last Friday she breezed in the kitchen and
fussed around a little . . . movin' first the salt and then the
pepper, I could feel something brewin' in the air. Next thing
you know she speaks up. "Mildred," she says, "Mrs. James will
need you this Saturday." I was polishin' silver at the time but
I turned around and looked her dead in the eye and said, "Mildred does not work on Saturdays."

Well, for the rest of the day things went along kind of
quiet-like but just before time for me to go home she drifted

by the linen closet to check the ruffle on a guest towel and threw in her two cents more. "Mildred," she says, "a depression might do this country some good, then some people might work eight days a week and be glad for the chance to do it."

I didn't bat an eyelash, but about 15 minutes later when I was headin' for home, I stopped off at the living room and called to her, "That's very true, but on the other hand some folks might be doin' their own housework . . . don'tcha know." With that and a cool "goodnight" I gently went out the front door. . . .

Oh, but we get along fine now. . . . Just fine!

HANDS

THAT'S A PRETTY SHADE of nail polish, Marge. . . . Oh, don't belittle your hands, child—I think they are lovely. Yes, I know you get tired of being a house servant. . . . Yes, you should have every right to be as much as you can be. But when you come to think of it, everyone who works is a servant. Why, we couldn't live without the hands and minds of millions of people.

Now you just look at anything in the room or in this apartment and try to point out something that working people didn't have their hands in. . . . Well, you can stutter and stammer all you please, 'cause you can't name a solitary thing, be it cheap or expensive.

Take that chair you're sittin' on. . . . Can't you see the story behind it? The men in the forests sawin' down the trees . . . the log rollers . . . the lumber-mill hands cuttin' up the planks . . . people mixin' up varnishes and paints . . . the artists drawin' the designs . . . all the folks drivin' trains and trucks to carry 'em . . . the loaders liftin' them off and on . . . all the clerks writin' down how many there are and where they're goin'—and I bet that's not half of the story.

Now Marge, you can take any article and trace it back like that and you'll see the power and beauty of laboring hands.

This tablecloth began in some cotton field tended in the burning sun, cleaned and baled, spun and bleached, dyed and woven. Find the story, Marge, behind the lettuce and tomato sandwich, your pots and pans, the linoleum on the floor, your dishes, the bottle of nail polish, your stove, the electric light, books, cigarettes, boxes, the floor we're standin' on, this brick building, the concrete sidewalks, the aeroplanes overhead, automobiles, the miles of pipe running under the ground, that mirror on the wall, your clock, the canned goods on your shelf, and the shelf itself. Why, you could just go on through all the rest of time singin' the praises of hands.

So you can see we are all servants and got a lot in common . . . and that's why folks need unions. Well, for example, Marge, suppose all you had was money and you wanted to make some more money. . . . Oh hush, girl! I know you wouldn't, but let's suppose. . . . Well, you'd hire ten people without any money who knew how to make tablecloths . . . and you'd sell them for four hundred dollars and pay the folks who made them one hundred of that. . . . Marge, I didn't say you would do that. . . . I'm only pretendin'. . . . Well, never fear, honey, we would form a union and tell you we wouldn't sew any more for you until you paid us fair . . . and then you'd either do that or make nothin'!

Now, contrary to some opinion, I contend that healthy folks love to work, but "a servant is worthy of his hire" . . . and they want decent pay and clean places to work where they won't be burnt up in no fire trap building, they want a little time to rest and enough pay to buy and enjoy some of the wonderful things they have made.

Yes, indeed, girl—I do get so tired of hearin' folks say, "I'm *just an ordinary* workin' man." Why, workin' people are the grandest folks in the whole wide world. They set the steamships on the ocean and the lighthouse on the land, they give us our breakfast coffee and a roof over our heads at night. . . . That's right, Marge, when workin' folks get together it should be with the highest respect for one another because it is the work of their hands that keeps the world alive and kickin'.

Oh, Marge, what do you mean "you guess they're right nice." . . . I told you before . . . YOU HAVE BEAUTIFUL HANDS!

ALL THE THINGS WE ARE

COME ON IN, MARGE! The coffee pot's on and I'm just sittin' here relaxin' over a magazine. . . . Tell me, if I was to buy a car would you envy me? . . . No, I'm not sayin' that you have a jealous nature, but this ad here says to buy this shiny car and be the envy of all my friends. . . . No, I don't usually buy such dicty readin' matter but this headline on the outside of it caught my eye. . . . Yes, it says: "Make Yourself Over." No, I'm not tryin' to run away from myself but you know, sometimes we do let ourselves go and it crossed my mind that I oughta take that fifty dollars out of my savin' account and spend it on yours truly. . . . Sure, life is short and there ain't nothin' wrong with Mildred doin' for Mildred sometimes.

Well, I bought the book in order to help me make up my mind just where and how to spend the money. . . . No, I haven't decided yet 'cause the more I read, the more disheartened I get. . . . Well, for an instance, I should get a good perfume like this one here. . . . No, I will not move my hand from over the price mark. I want you to guess how much it costs. It's called "Wild Enthusiasm" and it costs forty-five dollars a ounce. . . . Well, there you are! I'd be smellin' real nice but lookin' just the same with only five dollars left for makin' me over. It is mighty expensive but just look what it does: "Will make him lose his mind and reason at first meeting. . . . The magic of bottled moonbeams drawn from the everlasting fountain of youth . . . maddening . . . ravishing . . . wicked . . . tantalizing . . ." and so on. But I guess I won't get any of it. If it does all of that, I guess it would be dangerous to walk the street. Be like takin' your life in your hands, so to speak. . . . Yes, girl, makin' myself over ain't too easy. . . . See here, I need all these hormones in my cold cream and of course that jacks the price way up 'cause you can't buy none of that in the five-and-dime store, and since I'm a wee bit flat-chested, I'm supposed to buy "falsies." See, these are called "Just Between Us Two" and costs twelve dollars and ninety-five cents. No, I won't buy it . . . I guess I couldn't carry it off quite, and there I'd be with twelve wasted dollars on my conscience, or should I say off my chest! . . . I guess I may's well leave the fifty where it is for the time bein'. . . . Now dig this! In order to remake me, I have to have a manicure, a pedicure, my hair styled, a new girdle, foundation cream, night cream, day cream, bath lotion, bath salts, fingernail cream, toenail cream, toilet water, sachet, soap, bath oil, rouge, powder, hair remover, hair grower, curlers, straighteners, eyebrow pencil and . . . Oh honey, don't talk about the clothes! . . . I'll have to have a hostess gown, a playsuit, a evening dress, a dress suit, town dresses, country dresses, city dresses, a sport suit, a bathing suit, a bathrobe, nightgowns, slips, blouses, skirts and . . . No, I haven't forgotten my mind at all, but give me a chance. I'll have to join a book club, a record club, a picture club. Yes, and then I'll have to see the latest plays, movies, lectures, and . . . You see there! . . . I'm forgettin' the most important thing of all. . . . Yes, time! I should have one hour a day just to loll aroun' in my scented tub while I think pretty thoughts. I need time to shop carefully and make sure that

I'm buyin' only the things that suit my very own personality. I need time to plan well-balanced meals, I need time to go to the drug store and buy vitamins and all them toiletries. I need time to purchase newspapers and more magazines. I need time to do some volunteer work for churches and clubs, and I need time to answer all mail promptly and keep up with invitations and entertain lightly after the theatre and make myself into the ideal American woman and . . . What? . . . Girl, I had no idea it was gettin' so late! And here I have to make early time in the morning and be over on the East Side at eight o'clock sharp! . . . Pour the coffee, Marge! I guess I'll have to put up with bein' myself for a long while to come. But I can't help wonderin' about the women who go through that routine all the time . . . I mean . . . when it's all over, what have you got? . . . You're right. Like the song says: "Another day older and deeper in debt!"

I LIKED WORKIN' AT THAT PLACE . . .

I'LL HAVE TO ADMIT that I'm not wild about housework, but on the other hand I must also say that I'm good at it. You know what I mean, Marge. I don't short-change anybody and I don't expect them to be short-changin' me. I'm a pretty good cook, too, and I do take pride in fixin' a dish so that it looks as fine as it tastes. And when I clean up, you can tell that the place has been done, but I can get awful evil with folks that try to put me at a disadvantage. Oh, I've had lots of tricks pulled on me like people settin' back the clock in the middle of the afternoon in order to get a free half-hour on me.

Workin' for Mrs. L . . . was really kind of all right, but it took me a long time to catch on to her ways. I remember one afternoon last summer I was just gettin' ready to leave and it was hot as blazes. Mrs. L . . . strolls into the kitchen holdin' out a black organdy dress on a hanger. "Don't you think I should wear this instead of my white suit?" she asked. "No mam," I said real fast, "I think your white suit is just the right thing." "I don't know," she says, "it seems to me that the suit would be too warm." "No, no," I says, "it might turn cool later on and the first thing you know you'll catch a cold." She shook her head then. "I'll swelter in this suit. I'd better wear the organdy. After all, I can carry a stole to throw around my shoulders." "Well, I guess you know best," I told her, "but if it was me, I'd stick to that suit."

Now, Marge, the whole time we was talkin' I had one eye on the ironin' board which was still warm from me pressin' that suit and the one thought uppermost in my mind was how I could keep from ironin' that old long, ruffly organdy dress. The next thing she asked was, "Does the dress look crushed?" "Oh no," I says real quick, "it seems fresh to me." Now I must admit, Marge, that it did need the touch of a iron here and there, but time was passin', the temperature was risin' and I was a mite on the tired side. "Well," she says, "I think it needs to be ironed." And with that she plugs the iron in the wall again, so I reached over to take the dress from her, but she holds on to it real tight and says, "I will iron it." "That's all right, Miss L . . . ," I said, "it's awful hot today, I'll do it."

Marge, she looked at me kind of funny and then said somethin' real nice. "I don't feel the heat any more than you do, and if it's hot for me, it's hot for you too." And then she went on and ironed that dress.

Another time I remember was one mornin' when I just couldn't make it to her house at nine o'clock because there was a big winter coat sale down at Crumbley's Department Store, and I just had to get down and find me one. I called her up and told her that my sister had took quite sick, and I wouldn't be able to get to her until noon. Well, honey, when I got out to her place she was nice as could be, but she didn't say anything about my sister or ask me any questions.

That evenin' when I was leavin' she says real nice-like, "Mildred, if you ever have anything to do and would like to change your hours around a bit, I won't mind because you can always make up the time like you did this evenin'." And after that I never made up any stories about illness or death and one time when Eddie came in town unexpected-like, I told her about it and took the day off. Well, the followin' week I worked for her three days instead of two, and I must say that she was always nice about things like that and I really felt free and easy around her.

Mrs. L . . . was by no means what you'd call a wealthy woman, but I always enjoyed her Christmas gifts better than any others that I got from the people I worked for. I was with her two Christmases, and she never gave me the kind of things that I got from other folks like new uniforms, tough lookin', old, black pocketbooks or heavy ugly-colored stockings.

Well, the first Christmas she gave me a lovely, beaded evenin' bag with a five dollar bill in it. The second Christmas she gave me a bottle of *her* favorite toilet water and a ten dollar bill. Several times I had told her how pleasant that toilet water was and so I guess she thought I'd like to have some, too. Honey, I'm tellin' you, there's some folks that don't want you to have *anything* that's like somethin' they got.

I enjoyed talkin' with her, too, because she never nosed in my business or tried to poke fun at me on the sly. You know how some people do things like that! They will ask you, "How's your boyfriend?" and although there's nothin' wrong with the question they will be smilin' and sort of half-laughin' like it's funny as all get-out that you should have a boyfriend and also kinda meanin' that he must be a riot too!

She would tell me about the books she had been readin' and the plays she saw and about all manner of new things she would see or hear about. And I would tell her about my club meetin's and how my niece was studyin' to be in the theatre, and I also told her a lot of South Carolina folk stories and such.

I really liked the way I always knew where I stood with her because she treated me the same way all the time and never acted like a stranger when she had company call on her. You know, some folks will crowd in real friendly on you but when company calls they get kind of distant and cold-like with you. No, she didn't do that! She stayed on a nice even keel all the time and I would find myself tellin' her things about myself simply because she wasn't eaten up with curiosity about me like I was somethin' peculiar.

It didn't happen all of a sudden but one day it suddenly came to me that I thought a awful lot of Mrs. L . . . and that if she ever came to my door I'd be glad to invite her in without feelin' a strain. I found myself doin' little extras now and then and when she had a party or somethin' like that I really put myself out to make it a nice affair because I was *interested*.

No, it wasn't always smooth sailin'. There was times when she got on my nerves about somethin', but I was always free to tell her about it and get things straightened out. Yes, and once in a while I'd skim over somethin' I'd promised to do, but when she told me about it I never felt like she didn't like me or was all tied up in knots about it. 'Cause she'd just speak her mind like, "I wish you'd get to the pantry shelves on Thursday because it's inconvenient when you leave it until Monday." And I'd say, "All right." Other times I might say, "I can't do it on Thursday if you have company comin' in the evenin'." And then we'd change things around so that the schedule would fit.

There was times when the work was piled up a little like at spring-cleanin' time and then she'd pitch in, and we'd work together and get everything in ship-shape order. We'd eat lunch together and talk about what to do next, and there was no feelin' of boltin' your food down. But by and large I believe I did more work for that woman than for anybody that I've ever worked for.

She went off to California 'cause her husband was out there on a temporary job that turned permanent. Do you know what I did, Marge? I went down to the station to see her off! Yes, indeed, that's a new one for me! Just before she waved good-bye, she said, "I'm really goin' to miss you!" And I hollered out to her, "You will *never* have any trouble findin' people to work for *you* and if you want I'll send you *references* to show to the next party you employ!"

When she got out in California she sent me a note and told me that she had found a fine woman to take care of her home. That was several months ago.

This mornin' I open the mailbox and here is this card from Mrs. L . . . , wishin' me a happy birthday and promisin' to call me when she visits New York next winter. Yes, Marge, I'm sorry she moved because I really liked workin' at that place.

GOOD REASON FOR A GOOD TIME

COME ON IN, Marge, and take a load off your feet. Fix yourself some coffee and scramble some eggs, and while you're at it, you can fix me some, too. . . . Girl, I had me one fine weekend. . . . I told you I was goin' to spend a couple of days with Jim and Mabel, and believe me when I tell you I had one fine time! They know everyone under the sun, and they all came by Saturday night. And did we ball! Mabel's backyard is about as big as a postage stamp, but we all got out there and made barbecue on the grill. . . . What old lanterns? We was workin' strictly by moonlight . . . big fat full moon, too, girl!

We had cans of beer buried in a tub of ice, home-made potato salad, good old spareribs smothered in Jim's special barbecue sauce, and frankfurter weenies. And don't ask about the hot yeast rolls and cornbread!

Marge, the weather was tantalizin', real warm, and every once in a while a cool breeze would brush its hand across your face and throw its arm around your shoulder, and then you'd hear the trees whisperin' to each other . . . and between the smell of the rose bushes and the barbecue you'd get a

73

whiff of hot rolls driftin' out of the kitchen door. HONEY THEY LIVE!

And Jim can just keep you laughin' with those tall tales of his, and Mabel sings sweet enough to break your heart . . . she almost did, but we stopped her in time. . . . Well, we stayed out there and sang and laughed until the night air got a little crisp, then we gathered everything up and went downstairs to the basement. Jim has built a little bar to one side, and Mabel has made red and white checked curtains and covers for the four card tables. And, Marge, you should have seen how she had candles stuck in bottles. Yes indeed, from moonlight to candlelight! . . . Then we danced a while . . . and who wasn't no wallflower was *me* . . . but then, on the other hand, nobody was.

After a time we all sat back sippin' tall cool drinks while Mabel and Jim talked to us about makin' up a club. . . . Not so fast, Marge, I'm not usually a joiner, but this is a different kind of club. We are gonna give teas and parties and cocktail sips and bus rides and dinners and beach parties and birthday celebrations. . . . That's right, and whenever we get the notion, we'll have somebody speak to us about what's goin' on in the world. The first speaker is goin' to tell us all about African and West Indian people.

I tell you, we got so excited over what we'd do 'til there was no stoppin' us. I got up and told them that instead of givin' any free formal dances with our treasury money, we oughta put out some books by colored writers, and if we had enough, we could give money to organizations that was tryin' to make things better for everybody.

You should have heard Nellie layin' out the plans! That girl has a million ideas for makin' money and havin' a good time too. The first thing she wants to do is have a tea leaf readin' at her house. . . . Marge, you know Nellie don't do nothin' but tell a pack of lies when she reads them leaves, so we was kinda quiet about that until she went on and explained how there'd be a genuine West Indian dinner served along with the readin'. . . . Would make your mouth water: peas and rice, and souse, and garlic chicken, and cocoanut bread and ginger beer! You know I'll be there! . . . When it comes around to Al and Geraldine, they're goin' to give a box-lunch hike out to the country and play baseball.

To tell the truth, I felt kind of guilty-like. . . . You know, havin' such a whee of a good time. . . .It just didn't seem possible that we could be helpin' anybody when you enjoyin' yourself as much as that. . . . Of course, I can get you in, Marge. . . . I particularly want you to join and, of course, whenever we give affairs anybody can come if they'll let us soak them five dollars. . . . Yes, your boyfriend can join too! Girl, it makes me feel good all over to know that from now on in, my good times will count for somethin' that'll help people and make the world a better place to live in.

I'm tellin' you, it's beyond me how the people I work for are always complainin' about bein' bored when there's so many wonderful things to do!

I GO TO A FUNERAL

IF YOU'LL FIX the coffee, I'll just sit down and rest myself a bit because I'm some wore out! . . . I know you told me not to go to the funeral, but you know how people can get so insulted at a time like that! Them things leave me weak and upset, and it ain't because I'm afraid to die. I just can't seem to put my finger on what bothers me, but I guess it's a little bit of everything.

I only go to whatever funerals I have to, but even at that I've gone to quite a few. You know, I had to show up at Mitchell's service today because I'm such good friends with his sister. Well, I can't even go to a stranger's funeral without cryin' and sometimes I get to wonderin' why I have so little control of myself. And I come to the notion that it's because they *want* it like that. . . . No, I'm not kiddin'!

I got to the chapel a little early and it was all gloomy-lit with candles flickerin' shadows on the wall and a organ that I couldn't see was givin' out some real weird sad-like tones. . . . No, I said *tones* and I don't mean *tune!* It wasn't no hymn that you'd ever heard before, it was just a sort of sweetish kind of whinin' and groanin'.

Yes, indeed, the place was banked with flowers, all kinds of fancy pillows made out of roses and wreaths built up on big long stands. There was one floral piece that was made out of carnations and it was a clock with the hands pointin' to the hour that Mitchell had died!

You just shoulda seen the flowers! There was sheaves of wheat and sprays of gladiolas and everything was tied with a ribbon-bow made out of net with satin stripes on it. His casket was gray plush and it was lined inside with white satin all crushed-up in little bunches like those Christmas boxes that necklaces come in.

I had to sit down real quick because I started to cry and get weak in the knees. I was hurt and mad all over because I know Mitchell wouldn't of liked all that down-in-the-mouth kinda fixin's! Not the way he used to laugh and make jokes all the time. Why, he was one of the most happy-actin' people I ever knew. But I think what really got me was the little silver-paper words that was written across the net ribbons like "Rest in Peace," "The Dear Departed" and "We Mourn." It was a good thing that I had taken two or three handkerchiefs with me because I was a wreck!

Well, the organ kept goin' on as the people came in and last of all the family came walkin' down the aisle. I was surprised that there was so many of them because Mitchell always struck me as bein' kinda lonely-like. Of course, I knew he had his sister, Emma, and his father, but here come about thirty-five people marchin' together. . . . Oh, I suppose they were family in a cousin and aunt kinda way.

They was all dressed in black, and the women wore black veils over their hats and the men had on white shirts with black ties, plus black bands around their coatsleeves. The undertakers filed in behind them and went and sat over to one side near the front. There was a little light somethin' like a readin' lamp attached to the casket and shinin' right in Mitchell's face. The undertaker went over and put it out and then closed the lid, and the organ started goin' on louder than before!

After the family was seated the service started and the minister read his obituary. It was very nice, I guess, but it didn't sound very much like Mitchell. I mean, when the minister said, "The dearly beloved son of . . ." I got to thinkin' how his father wasn't speakin' to him most of the time because Mitchell wanted to open a shoe-repair shop and his father wanted him to be a doctor.

. . . No, I don't remember all of the obituary just little snatches like ". . . walked the straight and narrow path . . . was an inspiration in his every day life . . . lived a life of self-denial . . . humble and meek . . ." . . . No, honey, that wasn't Mitchell at all and if he *did* go through any *denial*, it wasn't *self* because he wanted some of everything there was to have and tried to get it. He just failed, that's all!

. . . Oh, yes, they had singin'! One lady sang and she had a very nice voice, but she made it tremble too much. I guess she did that so it would sound real sad-like. It sure was sad 'cause she had the whole family sobbin' and sniffin' something terrible. She sang something about "Take Me Home" and it was all about wishin' to go to Heaven.

The minister talked about him goin' to his "just reward" and that really made people cry *real* hard. It beats me why his "just reward" would strike folks as bein' so particular sad because I do think he was a good man as far as I know.

But the worst part was when the undertaker opened the casket again, and they asked every one to file up and look at him *one more time*. I smiled to myself a little because I distinctly remember that one of Mitchell's favorite records was Count Basie's "April in Paris," and he used to holler out the part where the Count says, *"one more time!"* . . . And the whole time that I stood on line waitin' my chance to look at him I could kinda hear him hummin' "April in Paris."

Yes, I guess you could say he looked all right, although I don't know why people always ask, "How did he look?" . . . No, I don't mean you in particular, I mean anybody. Marge, do you know what they had done to Mitchell? They had dressed him in a full-dress suit with a white carnation in the buttonhole and he was wearin' white gloves! . . . Sure, they had bought it special because anyone that knew him could tell you that he liked clothes that were easy-like and was especially fond of tan and gray and green and colors like that!

When the last lookin' was over, the service came to the end and the next part was goin' out to the cemetery. I rode in one of the cars that was for his friends, and there was two fellas and a girl ridin' with me. I felt a lot better as I heard them talkin' about him because they were rememberin' nice things he had said and done and talkin' about him easy and free.

My, but there was a long train of black shiny cars lined up near his grave site in the cemetery and when they started unloadin' his flowers, there was hardly enough space to put them. It suddenly struck me that this burial cost a heap of money!

Everyone stood there and cried as they lowered him in the ground, but they weren't cryin' as hard as they did in the chapel. Everyone threw a flower in the grave. I was plannin' to keep a rose to bring home and press in my Bible, but a lady snatched it out of my hand and threw it away. She said, "It's dead-bad-luck to bring flowers from the graveyard." I asked her why and she said, "It means that there will be a death in *your* family!" Girl, it looks like nobody wants to go to their "just reward"!

When we got back in the cars, we headed over to Emma's house for refreshments. . . . Oh, yes, she had all manner of goodies to eat and plenty to drink and everybody seemed a little relieved that the whole funeral business was over. People kept talkin' about how Mitchell had been "put away beautifully," "the family has certainly done handsomely," "this is the way he would have wanted it," "he would have been proud" and things like that.

I saw a lot of people that neither me nor Mitchell had seen in years, but I guess they were all wishin' just like I was that we could have just *one more time* to be better friends to him. But the past is the past.

. . . How did he die? . . . No, he wasn't sick long, he just went like that, real sudden. You know he had been tryin' to get a nice shop location for a long time, but people wouldn't rent it to him because he was colored. . . . Sure, Marge, they do like that with stores just the same as with houses! . . . Yes, indeed, they will bar your way when it comes to tryin' to buy money-makin' property. Why do you think most colored businesses are all crowded into colored neighborhoods?

Sure, we want to sell things everywhere, too! After all, there's plenty of white shopkeepers in Harlem! Anyway, Mitchell couldn't find a good place so he just miseried along in first one little out-of-the-way side street and then another. One time he tried to get some white people to rent a place for him, but that got all bolexed up in legal procedure, and his father wouldn't help him get the money although he had it to lend. So last week Mitchell dropped dead. They said it was a heart attack, but I do believe he died of discouragement.

The reason I feel so bad about the whole thing is that I know he could have had a right smart little shop for what that funeral cost.

So, Marge, if there's anything you're plannin' to do, and

ten or fifteen dollars from me would help you, let me know *now* because I do not intend to ever buy you or anybody else any of those carnation clocks or pillows! . . . I'm not sayin' you will go first! If it makes you feel better, we can pretend that I'm goin' first, and you can advance me some dollars on my next summer's vacation. And I want to thank you, too!

WEEKEND WITH PEARL

MARGE, I SPENT THE WEEKEND with Pearl and her husband. They have their place fixed up very nice. . . . Oh, yes, they have their own home now, but Pearl says that what with taxes and mortgages and painting and patching fences, walls, plumbing, windows, basement, roof and 'bout ninety-'leven other things it keeps them busy and also broke.

Anyway, we watched a lot of political speeches on their television because Leo is always highly interested in such things. It was just wonderful! . . . No, not the speakers, I mean her television set. It has a mahogany cabinet, a seventeen inch screen and very good reception. The speakers themselves were very interestin', what with the Southerners callin' all the shots and tellin' the North off every other minute.

Well, what got me Marge was somethin' one of the news commentators said. He announced that everybody on the political scene was avoidin' the use of words like anti-lynch, F. E. P. C., and other words which would not be pleasin' to the South. Ain't that somethin'! I was some hot, I tell you!

It came to me all of a sudden that he was dead right! Have you ever heard any of these politician speakers say "Jim Crow"? No, they will say the race *situation* or the *problem* of minorities or race *tensions* or somethin' like that. You may think as hard as you might, but you'll find nobody comes down to the nitty-gritty when it calls for namin' things for what they are. . . . You right, we always some "problem" and people takin' pot-shots at us is always called "tension" and why you and me who have been citizens for generations should be called "minorities" is more than I can see.

We went on after that and had quite a pleasant weekend. Leo has built a brick oven in his backyard, and he fixed some nice hickory-wood barbecue and we ate it outside under their tree. They begged me to stay and spend a week so that we could go out to the beach, but as much as I wanted to I just couldn't because I had to work for Mrs. J. this Monday.

All the way back to the hot city I kept thinkin' of those words which were "displeasin'" to the South. Well, to make a long story short, when I report to work this mornin', the first thing Mrs. J. does is give me a weak smile and waggle her finger at me, sayin', "Mildred, you did not water my geraniums last Friday, how many times have I told you that geraniums need sun and air and water!"

I don't know why I got so distressed, but I raised my voice at her, "Don't you waggle your finger at me! Besides which I'm not workin' for you this week because I need some sun and water and air myself and I won't be back here until next week, and furthermore if you don't like that you can get your-self somebody else!" And there I stood just so mad I could have snatched her. Well, she was shocked out of two years growth.

Yes, I am a little sorry that I hollered so loud at Mrs. J., although I would never tell her so. I know it isn't right to take out on one person what you feel about what someone else has done, but that is how I am sometimes. So, I'll see you next week, Marge. But wasn't that some nerve of them South-erners not likin' words like anti-lynch?

MORE BLESSED TO GIVE . . .

MARGE, I DID THE SUPER and his wife a favor this afternoon. I took their little girl to the settlement party that they give every year for "underprivileged" children. She is only five years old, so somebody had to take her. . . . Yes, it was a very nice kind of affair, but little Barbara acted up somethin' terrible!

You know, the grown-ups couldn't join in with the kids, so I was sittin' over to one side of the hall with the mothers and aunts and fathers. It was a little bit depressin' 'cause some of them had such a hangdog expression on their faces. The men, in particular, looked like they'd rather be someplace else other than where they were!

I enjoyed lookin' at the paintin's the children had done, and there was also some nice carpenter work the little boys had done for their parents to see. The teachers and instructors were also nice and friendly-like, but I never saw such a resentful bunch of children before in my whole life!

They was all washed-up and bright-lookin' as far as I could see, but they all had such sullen-sorry looks except for those few that was runnin' around and touchin' things and gettin' into all manner of mischief.

There was any number of important folks there, and they

seemed mighty proud of what the children had done. A few of them made speeches to the children whilst the little ones squirmed around kind of impatient-like. Girl, it seemed to me that they was talkin' all over the heads of those kids and really aimin' the remarks at the parents who was all over in the corner!

One woman got up to speak and every once in a while she would say somethin' about "the low-socio-economic group," and after a while I caught on to the fact that this was the high-flung name for poor people! Then a man got up, and he called off a group of hoity-toity folks that the children should be grateful to 'cause they was givin' money and time to help the settlement keep goin'! After that, a teacher explained to them how they owed so much to the ones who came in and worked without bein' paid. And on and on it went. Why, it seemed that there must have been at least a hundred folks that these little ones owed a debt of gratitude to!

. . . Well, I suppose they did 'cause they were givin' out time and money that they could of kept for themselves. The kids got up and sang little songs, and everybody seemed real proud about that and they did look real cute. One or two of them recited things, and then one little fellow got up and read off a paper. He told us how thankful the children was for the camp fund, the play center, the toys, the teachers and things like that.

After that, the party began. One lady was dressed up so lovely, she had a pretty straw hat with a feather on it and a fine fur scarf. . . . Yes, she was pretty, too, and she was givin' out boxes of candy to the children. They lined up nicely and went up and got a box one at a time and said thank you.

Yes, everything was goin' on pretty smooth until it got

to Barbara's turn. Well, when that little girl got to stand in front of the woman to get her candy she decided to just stand there! . . . I mean that she held both of her hands behind her back and wouldn't take the box.

Oh, the lady was real nice about it, she stooped down and took one of Barbara's hands and placed the candy in it, then Barbara ran back to her seat without sayin' thank you or anything else for that matter. I guessed that she must of felt a little bit shy, so I didn't think too much of it. But when it was time for ice cream and cake, that child wouldn't go and stand on line to get hers! . . . No, she sat there in her seat and when they tried to make her go up, she held on to the seat with both hands and a derrick couldn't of moved her!

Every once in a while she'd look over at me, and I'd look someplace else real fast, so's she wouldn't know that I was watchin' her. But I kept a close eye on what she was doin'.

After the kids started playin' little games and things got kinda calmed down with the visitors, Barbara took her box of candy and went over to one of the pretty lady visitors and offered it to her with a nice little smile. I tell you, that woman was some touched! Why, she almost cried! But she refused the candy and said, "No, bless your heart, it's for *you*, it's *your* candy, and you must keep it!"

Well, that child just turned around and went back to her seat. I couldn't stay out of the thing any more, so I got up and took Barbara's box from her and *I* went over to the woman and says, "She wants you to have it, she's givin' *you* a gift and it would make her feel awful good if you'd take it." The lady got so confused and upset lookin'. "Oh, I couldn't," she says, "I couldn't take anything from that child, I wouldn't feel right about it!"

"She's takin' a lot of things from you," I says, "like your

money and time and all such as that." "Oh," she says, "that's different." "Not a mite," I says. "Givin' is givin'! Now you take it so that little girl will feel as good as you do."

Yes, Marge, she kept it and then went over to Barbara and thanked her. You should have seen that baby's face light up, she looked as proud as anything!

When the party was over, I helped my little girl put on her coat and I says to her, "Barbara, do you remember the time you came up to my house and helped me to string the beans and dry dishes?" "Yes, Miss Mildred," she says. "Well," I said, "I been meanin' to pay you some money for that 'cause you are always doin' those nice things, and sometimes I like you doin' it for free and other times I like to pay, so will you take this fifty cents?" . . . Yes, she took it and we left out of there and started walkin' for home.

Soon as we got to the five-and-dime store down the street, I says, "Honey, I'm so thirsty, I'd like to have me a soft drink, but I am all run out of change so we can't get none." She smiles at me and says, "*I'll* buy you a soft drink 'cause I got money!" So we went in and had orange drinks and lot of fun chit-chattin'. Barbara had the most fun when she hands the waitress her fifty cents. The waitress starts to put the change in front of me on the counter, but I said, "No, it's *her* money." So she handed the thirty cents to Barbara.

We didn't come right home 'cause we had to look all over the five-and-dime store. We found a bag of marbles for her brother, a chocolate bar for her father and some sweet biscuits for her mother and the rest of the kids. Marge, that little girl was some happy! I guess it never struck her mind that she didn't have nothin' bought for herself. But I knew that what she needed more than anything else was to go on one good old spendin' spree from the *givin'* end!

All the things that happened today set me to thinkin' 'bout

what it says in the Bible about it bein' more blessed to *give* than to receive. All I can say to that is: And how! It is not only more *blessed*, but it *feels* better and everybody oughta get the chance to do it once in a while 'cause there's nothin' more distressin' than to always be on the receivin' end, especially when folks keep addin' up the list and askin' you to carry a load of gratitude that gets a bit too heavy sometimes!

If it's the last thing I do, I'm gonna find a few minutes to go over to that settlement and tell the teachers to have them children make up little calendars and pictures and things like that. . . . Sure, so's they'll have something to give the visitors when they line up to get that candy and ice cream! After all, let *everybody* get in on that good feelin'.

SOMETIMES I FEEL SO SORRY

You oughta hear Mrs. B . . . moanin' and groanin' about her troubles. I tell you, if you listen long enough, you just might break down and cry your heart out. That woman don't have nothin' but one problem on top of the other! If it ain't her, it's her husband or her brother or her friends or some everlastin' sorrow tryin' her soul. She's got sixty-'leven jars of face cream and lotions and stuff, but she's gettin' a big frown creased 'cross the front of her forehead just the same.

Girl, you oughta see all the stuff she's got! A handsome mink coat, a big old apartment overlookin' the river, me and a cook and a nurse for the children, a summer cottage in the country and a little speedboat that she can chug up and down the river in any time she might take the notion. . . . Hello! And what did you say! . . . Yes, indeed, that just should be me!

Today she was almost out of her mind about her brother. Her brother's name is Carl, and he is a caution! Seems like he doesn't know whether to paint pictures or write books, and it just keeps his mind in torment and turmoil. Whenever the problem gets too much for him, he drinks up a case of whiskey and goes into the shakes.

Whenever this happens, they get him into a private home that costs about three hundred dollars a week. He will hang around there while the doctors study his mind for about seven or eight weeks, and then he'll come out again to go through the same merry-go-round all over again.

. . . You ain't heard nothin' yet! She also had a very close friend who was a awful successful actress, but she got to be a dope addict, and Mrs. B . . . told me that she got that way 'cause she had so much work and personal appearances 'til it drove her to the drugs. I told her that she could turn down some of that work and do just enough to take it kinda easy-like, but all Mrs. B . . . said about that was, "Oh, the poor thing, I feel so sorry for her."

Another time her mother's arm broke out in a little rash and that thing developed into the biggest long drawn out to-do! The doctors had to analyze that woman's mind for almost a year and even then they couldn't tell whether she had a rash because of her dog's fur or on account of her husband's personality. No, I don't know if the thing is straightened out yet.

This mornin' Mrs. B . . . was all tore up because Carl wants to get married. Marge, she is in a pacin'-up-and-down fit! She thinks the girl will aggravate Carl's condition because she can paint pretty pictures, and it will hurt Carl because he can't. Honey, she worries my soul-case out with all them troubles. I have listened to more tales of woe comin' out of that woman. . . . No, she won't want no advice 'cause she never listens to a word you say. I do believe it would break her heart half-in-two if anybody told her somethin' that would end all the misery 'cause she's so used to it by now she wouldn't know what to do without it!

That woman has a pure-artful knack of turnin' the simplest things into a burnin' hellfire *problem!* When she gives a dinner party, she worries herself to death about whether she's invited the *wrong* people and left out the *right* ones! If her daughter ain't laughin' and talkin' every single minute of every single day, she turns herself inside-out worryin' if somethin' is the matter with her. If her husband sneezes she annoys him to death until he goes to the doctor for a complete check-up. She will eat too much lobster salad and then swear she's got a heart ailment when one of them gas pains hit her in the chest. . . .

Whenever things go kinda smooth-like, she takes time out to worry about the stockmarket and who's gonna be our next president! That poor woman has harried herself into the shadow of a wreck!

Marge, sometimes I think that all she would need to cure her is one good-sized real trouble. You know, like lookin' in your icebox and seein' nothin' but your own reflection! I guess she'd know what trial and trouble really was if she had a child with a toothache, no money, and a dispossess all at the same time! . . . That's what happened to Gloria last spring! . . . Sure, I guess Gloria cried a little but she took that child to the clinic, and then they moved with her brother for a while, and her brother only had four rooms for his wife and their four children!

. . . Sure, I remember the time you lost your uncle and he didn't have any insurance! And what about the time I had to send all my little savin's down home so that my niece could stay in college? You know everybody's so busy talkin' 'bout us gettin' into these schools 'til it never crosses their mind what a hard time we have stayin' there. It costs money!

I bet Mrs. B . . . would think twice about what trouble is if she had one dollar in the house and had to fix dinner for a bunch of kids like Mrs. Johnson who lives downstairs. She'd also think twice if *her* husband had lost his job 'cause the boss had to cut down and decided to let the colored go first.

. . . Marge, you may be right, perhaps their troubles are as real to them as ours are to us. I don't know about that though. I don't think I'd be goin' through the same miseries if I was in her shoes.

I've seen some trouble in my life, and I know that if I was to call up my aunt and tell her that I'd been too quiet all day or had a hang-over or didn't know whether to paint or write or something like that, she'd say, "Girl, are you out of your mind! Don't be botherin' me with no foolishness!"

I GO TO CHURCH

WELL, MARGE, I WENT to church last Sunday. . . . No, the doors did not cave in on me! And if you're going to think up jokes, I wish you'd think of new ones. It's true that I don't go very often but you know most folks go 'round Christmas and Easter time, so I thought I would surprise my pastor by goin' a week early this time. . . . Oh, the sermon was so-so, and I saw a lot of friends that I hadn't seen in a long while, but wait until I tell you what happened just as I was leavin'!

The pastor caught up with me at the door and spoke out real loud, "My, it certainly has been a long time since we've seen you! What happened to you?" Now, in the past when he's done this I always told him some lie about bein' busy or sickly or some such tale as that, but all of a sudden I decided that I was goin' to let him in on the truth. I spoke out real plain: "I haven't been comin' to church because you ain't been sayin' anything whenever I do get here." . . . Marge, he was some upset, and asked me to step into his study and explain what I meant. . . . Of course I did just that!

"Not meanin' any disrespect," I said, "but every time you give a sermon, I find that you reach way back in the book and pick out a text about people bearin' up under a whole lot of misery that the *Lord* has visited upon them. For example, the last time

I was here you told me all about Job's sores and boils, how all his children was killed off and a million and one other miseries, the whole object bein' how nicely he bore up under these things." . . . Marge, he shook his head and said, "That's in the Bible, I'm sorry you didn't like the text."

"Well, reverend," I told him, "it's true that you are the one who gets to select the sermon, but I notice that it's almost always something about people bein' destroyed or cursed or something from Lamentations. And when I leave, it's always with the feelin' that I'm lucky to be breathin' and had better be thankful that I ain't any more miserable than I am." . . . No, Marge, he wasn't offended, especially when I told him what I would like to hear.

"Reverend," I said, "the Bible also tells us that Jesus did not act *meek* and *mild* and enjoy the fact that some folks were walkin' all over others. He raised his voice and spoke to crowds, told them that the rulers were puttin' heavy burdens on people's shoulders, devourin' widows' houses. He called Herod a fox and told the people they were livin' amongst a generation of vipers. He advised people to feed the hungry, take in the stranger, visit the prisoner. He told them there was no justice in the court, he accused the rich of misleadin' the people and seekin' high places for themselves. He taught the people to break bread in common brotherhood. He taught them 'The kingdom on Earth as it is in Heaven.' And it was for teachin' and preachin' these things that he was hauled into court and charged with overthrowin' the Lord, the prophets, the religion of the land and settin' himself up as King. It was for these things that he was nailed to the cross. Today his message has become lost in stained-glass windows and mournful songs. The message of love, hope and forgiveness has been drowned out by false prophets screamin' about hell-fire and damnation and destruction."

My pastor smiled a little and said, "I asked and you told me. You've said a great deal and I'll have to think about it a while."

"Yes, reverend," I said, "and if you could find it in your heart to preach a sermon like that it would make Sunday a day of real meaning and inspiration."

And it would, wouldn't it, Marge?

I HATE HALF-DAYS OFF

GIRL, PEOPLE HAVE GOT some crust! Some folks' notion of what's *fair is* all out of whack, and it takes your friend Mildred to tell it! You know, Marge, I told you how I was sick and tired of runnin' from hither to yon in order to make a bare livin'? . . . That's right, days work can carry you all over town, workin' first for this one and then the other. There's some mornin's that it takes me a good five minutes to remember just where I'm goin' to work. So I decided to try steady time once more and look me up a permanent place to work. . . . Yes, I got it out the newspaper and telephoned the lady before the print was dry.

Honey, you never heard such a interview as she put me through. You shoulda heard her! "Now, Mildred, why do you want this job?" Don't laugh, I know you want to but try and listen. Did you ever hear such a simple question? I could of told her the truth and make mention of that nasty word *money*, but I knew that would make her sad, so I said very prettily, "Because I'd like a nice steady job with a good family."

Hot dog! I struck pay-dirt, her smile was the sunshine of a May afternoon. Sure she asked me some more things. I had to give her references, the name of my minister and my doctor, how long I worked in my last three places and how come this and why not that until we was both fair worn out with talk and more talk. Finally she seems all satisfied and made the summin' up, "I think you'll do just fine, and I hope we can make some satisfactory arrangement that'll make us both happy." Marge, before I can get in a word about what'll make me happy she takes a sheet of paper out of her desk and starts readin' off how things will go. "Mildred," she says, "on Monday you will report at eight o'clock in the mornin' and after the breakfast dishes you will do the washin'. Of course we have a machine." "Naturally," I says, then she starts runnin' her finger down this devilish list: "After the washin' you will take care of the children's lunch, prepare dinner, clean the baby's room *thoroughly* and leave after the supper dishes, that's Monday." "So much for Monday," I says, "and how about Tuesday?" "Well," she says, "you don't come in until noon on Tuesday, then you fix the children's lunch, iron, give the kitchen a thorough cleaning, prepare dinner and leave after the supper dishes." "Well," I says ,"here we are at Wednesday already." "Yes," she says, "on Wednesday you come in at eight in the mornin' and do all the floors, fix the children's lunch, do the mendin', give the foyer and the baths a thorough cleanin', prepare the dinner . . ." ". . . and leave after the supper dishes," I says. "That's right," she says, "and the schedule remains pretty much the same for the rest of the week; on Thursday you thoroughly clean the bedrooms, on Friday the livin' room, on Saturday the pantry shelves, silver, and clothes closets and on Sunday you fix early dinner and leave after one-thirty."

Marge, I must have looked pure bewildered because she adds, "Do you have any comment?" "A little," I says, "when is my off-time?" "Oh that," she says. "Yes mam," I says, and then she begins to run her finger down the list again. "Well, you have one half-day off every Tuesday and one half-day off every Sunday and every other Thursday you get a full day off, which makes it a five and a half day week."

How 'bout that Marge! I was never too good at arithmetic, but I really had to tip my hat to her. Even somebody as smart as Einstein couldn't have figured nothin' as neat as that. Before I could get a word in on what I considered the deal of the year, she played her trump card, "I will pay you two weeks pay on the first and fifteenth of each month." "But that way," I says, "I lose a week's pay every time the month has five weeks." Well, she repeats herself, "I pay on the first and fifteenth."

No, Marge, you know I wasn't comin' on that! In the first place I could see me workin' myself into such a lather that there wouldn't be nothin' to do but crawl into the doctor's office on the first and fifteenth and give every blessed nickel I had in order that he could try and straighten me out in time to meet the second and the sixteenth. In the second place . . . oh, well, what's the use? You get the picture! I backed out of there so fast 'til I bet she's not sure that I was ever there.

But it set me to thinkin'. How come all of them big-shots in Washington that can't balance the budget or make the taxes cover all our expenses, how *come* they don't send for that woman to help straighten them out? Why, in two or three weeks she'd not only get everything on a payin' basis, but she'd have enough money left over to buy every citizen a free ice cream cone for the Fourth of July, not countin' all the loot we'd have left over to bury at Fort Knox! Genius like that just pure takes your breath away. It's almost beautiful in a disgustin' sort of way, ain't it?

WHAT DOES AFRICA WANT? . . . FREEDOM!

MARGE, YOU CAN'T UNDERSTAND anything if you don't get up and go in order to keep in the know. . . . Now, you take all this talk about Africa—what do you know about Africa? . . . That's right—nothin'! Or even worse than nothin' because we don't know anything but a pack of fancy lies.

All our education about Africa comes from bad moving pictures. You know how they show us bunches of "wild folk" goin' crazy and bein' et up by lions, tigers and snakes. We see pictures about Africans dancin' all day and drummin' all night . . . and ain't it funny, Marge, how the animal always eats the African and not the white man?

Yes, girl, I went to an African meetin' tonight. No, it wasn't given by African people, but it was all about Africa. . . . Well, the evenin' started out with speakers tellin' things about Africa and how Africans are different groups of people and not all one single thing. . . . Well, like in Europe—you know there's English, French, Italians and Germans but yet you can plainly hear how they are different even though these people are all Europeans. . . . That's right, there are even more groups of Africans than there are different Europeans.

Then someone explained all about African art and sculpture, and they showed us beautiful photographs of the things.

. . . No, Marge, we didn't get to see any of the real stuff. How could we when it's all in the British Museum?

Another speaker told us about history and slavery and all such as that, finally ending up with today and what's going on *now*. And believe me when I say THINGS ARE POPPIN'! . . .

Wait, Marge, don't get excited. Save that for later. It seems that the South Africans are breakin' the Jim Crow laws! . . . Just like if you was to walk in a Mississippi waitin' room, tear down the "white" sign and sit yourself down! HOW 'BOUT THAT AFRICA! . . . Oh, honey, thousands of 'em are doin' that in trains, in the parks and everywhere.

But what bugged me was the "discussion" they had at the meetin'. Marge, you should have been there to hear the people arguin' back and forth about "WHAT THE AFRICAN WANTS" and "WHAT THE AFRICANS DON'T WANT." . . . Yes, that took up all the discussion time, and it kept battin' around from one person to the other: "The African wants this and not that" . . . and on and on it went. . . .

All of a sudden I jumped straight up and hollered, *"There ain't no mystery about that! Africans want to be free!* . . . How in the devil can you sit and hear how they're starved, whipped, kept out of schools, jailed and shot down and then ask WHAT the African wants?" . . . I went right on. . . . "You folks been talkin' so uppity 'bout 'Are Africans fit to govern themselves?' . . . 'are they educated enough?' and all such trash. . . . Let me tell you one thing," I says: "If *educated* folk can't do anything but jail, whip, starve and abuse, what in the devil makes you think *they* are anything but *unfit* to rule!"

Yes, I did! . . . I squared right off: "There's two schools of thought over there: One says *privileges for white folk alone*, while the other says FREEDOM FOR ALL." I shook my fist at them, Marge. *"Shame, shame, shame!"* I cried.

And I tell you, they got quiet when I laid down the law. . . . "Stop all this pussyfootin' pretense about 'you can't understand'. . . . Right is right and wrong is wrong. FREE AFRICA! Then I turned and asked, "Now who don't understand that?"

. . . Well, maybe I did make a scene, Marge, but I'm sick and tired of folks pretendin' they don't know the score just so they can duck the issue, 'cause we all got to go when the wagon comes and it behooves each and every one of us to "put up or shut up" as the gambler said. . . . Sure, Marge, the truth is just pure beautiful!

I WISH I WAS A POET

MARGE, I WISH I was a poet. . . . Now that's no cause for you to stop stringing the beans and lookin' at me like you was struck by lightnin'. . . . No, I don't wish it on account of I want to be famous, but I do wish it because sometimes there are poetry things that I see and I'd like to tell people about them in a poetry way; only I don't know how, and when I tell it, it's just a plain flat story.

Well, for an instance, you know my cousin Thelma stopped in town for a few days, and she stayed at a downtown hotel. . . . Yes, I dropped by to see her last night. . . . Now, Marge, when I walked up to the desk to get her room number, all of a sudden the folks in the lobby cleared a path on both sides of me and I was about to get real salty about their attitude when I chanced to look behind me and saw two old people walkin' up to the desk. . . .

No, they were white, and you've never seen such a couple in your life—a man and his wife, and they must have been in their seventies. They were raggedy and kinda beat. The old lady wore men's shoes and trousers and an old battered raincoat and on her head a man's hat. From under the hat her white hair hung in curly wisps—and she was pretty. . . .

Yes, mam, she was pretty and still she was seventy and bent and dragged her feet along instead of liftin' them. The man was dressed just as sorry as her and in his hand he carried a paper bag. . . . Marge, he was lookin' at her like every woman on earth dreams of bein' looked at, and her eyes were doin' the same thing back at him.

Honey, everyone was standin', just starin'. There was a giggle from some kid and one well-dressed woman looked like she was goin' to faint, but the old man walked up to the clerk with the old lady follerin' behind him and he said in a quavery voice, "We'd like a room for the night."

Well, you could cut the silence with a knife. The clerk hemmed and hawed while they stood there lookin' back at him real innocent and peaceful, and finally he said, "You'll have to pay in advance." "How much is the cheapest room?" the old man asked. The clerk breathed a little easier and said: "Three-fifty." The old man went in his coat pocket and brought out four crumpled up dollar bills and put them on the desk.

The clerk turned red in the face and said real loud, "You can't have a room without carryin' baggage—where's your baggage?" You could hear a pin drop when the old man placed the paper bag on the desk, opened it and pulled out two rough dry shirts. . . . Well, with that the clerk took the money, gave him a key and fifty cents change and said, "Top floor rear!"

The couple smiled in such a dignified way, and it seemed like they hadn't noticed a thing. They started over toward the elevator and then the old lady turned away from the man and made her way over to the receptionist's desk. Everyone kept their eyes dead on her, and the receptionist, who was awfully young and pretty, was almost scared out of her wits. The old lady kept makin' straight for her, and I could see that the young lady was gonna scream any second. . . .

When the old woman reached the desk, she leaned over a bowl of red roses that was there and, ever so gently, breathed in the sweet smell, and then she turned away and quickly joined her husband at the elevator, and nobody moved until the doors closed and they were gone from sight. . . .

That's all, Marge. Of course, there was buzzin' and hummin' after that, but I got to wonderin' about who they were and where they came from . . . and did they have children . . . and how much work they both done in their lifetime . . . and what it must feel like to be old and draggin' around in the cold.

That's all there is to the story and it sure don't sound like much the way I tell it, but if I was a poet, I would sing a song of praise for the love in their eyes and I would make you see the sight of a lifetime when that ragged lady bent over those roses, and I would tell how awful it is to be old and broke in the midst of plenty. . . . And that's what I mean when I say—sometimes I wish I was a poet.

ECONOMY CORNER

MARGE, as sure as my name is Mildred, I'm tellin' you that we should improve ourselves. . . . No, we are not all right as we are. We're in a rut. Here we sit watchin' the television and idlin' along with no thought of betterment. . . . Of course, it's all right to watch T.V., but we ought to be more particular about what we look at. Now instead of watchin' "Gory Story," we should find something here in the paper that will be beneficial. . . . Now, here's a show, "Economy Corner." That's a cookin' program. You know, it's all about stretchin' leftovers and fixin' up new dishes to tempt your appetite and makin' the food look more pleasin' and things like that.

. . . All right, here it is. My, isn't that a pretty kitchen with the oven in the wall and everything? We better watch sharp so's not to miss trick. . . . How to fix leftover stringbeans. That oughta be a nice recipe because we got some leftover beans. . . . Get a pencil, Marge. . . . You know, the only thing I do with the beans is warm them up again and eat 'em. . . . First thing she says is take one pint of heavy cream. . . . Marge, don't be that way! No, she didn't say where to take it from. Just take it! . . . No, she is not suggestin' that you be dishonest and lift it from the store. . . . Now take this down: one half cup of butter. . . . I don't know. . . . Maybe you could use margarine. Now you need one half pound of sliced mushrooms and one-fourth of a cup of sherry wine and . . . and four chicken breasts. . . . Girl! Leftovers can get you into some debt! Leave the dial alone! Don't turn it off. I want to see how she fixes this recipe. Oh oh, one more thing: one cup of chopped parsley. . . . No, Marge, she didn't forget the stringbeans. They're over there in that little bowl. See, now she fries the chicken in the butter. . . . Girl, don't be silly, you do not have to buy four chickens in order to get four chicken breasts. You can buy it in parts in one of those poultry stores that sell choice pieces. . . . I know it's expensive! Who you tellin'! . . . Wait, don't touch that dial! Now she's addin' the mushrooms. Now the wine and cream is mixed together for the sauce and she pours that right over the bird breasts. There now! Don't it look pretty all turned out on the platter? That's the parsley that she's bunchin' up at each end. . . . No, Marge, I'm sure she hasn't forgot the beans 'cause after all that's what it's all about. . . . Well, I'll be dog. . . . ! She's layin' them stringbeans across the top of the whole mess! Ain't that cute how they look just like little flowers? So that's how you use leftover beans! . . . Aw shucks! I know we can't afford to make that! . . . Go ahead. I don't care if you turn it off. No, girl, I just can't take any more "Gory Story" tonight. . . . I'm agreein' with you. . . . Let's just heat up our stringbeans and talk chit-chat. . . . Ain't it the truth! I guess we'd learn more by lookin' out the window than by watchin' all this nonsense. . . . You know one thing, I'll predict you this much, one of these days somebody with a little sense is gonna make a big success on T.V. by puttin' on somethin' that's good. . . . I wonder why nobody has thought of it?

IN THE LAUNDRY ROOM

MARGE . . . Sometimes it seems like the devil and all his imps arc tryin' to wear your soul case out. . . . Sit down, Marge, and act like you got nothin' to do. . . . No, don't make no coffee, just sit. . . .

Today was laundry day and I took Mrs. M . . .'s clothes down to the basement to put them in the automatic machine. In a little while another houseworker comes down—a white woman. She dumps her clothes on the bench and since my bundle is already in the washer I go over to sit down on the bench and happen to brush against her dirty clothes. . . . Well sir! She gives me a kinda sickly grin and snatched her clothes away quick. . . .

Now, you know, Marge, that it was nothin' but the devil in her makin' her snatch that bundle away 'cause she thought I might give her folks gallopin' pellagra or somethin'. Well, honey, you know what the devil in me wanted to do! . . . You are right! . . . My hand was just itchin' to pop her in the mouth, but I remembered how my niece Jean has been tellin' me that *poppin'* people is not the way to solve problems. . . . So I calmed myself and said, "Sister, why did you snatch those things and look so flustered?" She turned red and says, "I was just makin' room for you." Still keepin' calm, I says, "You are a liar." . . . And then she hung her head.

"Sister," I said, "you are a houseworker and I am a house-worker—now will you favor me by answering some questions?" She nodded her head. . . . The first thing I asked her was how much she made for a week's work and, believe it or not, Marge, she earns less than I do and *that ain't easy.* . . . Then I asked her, "Does the woman you work for ask you in a *friendly* way to do extra things that ain't in the bargain and then later on get *demandin'* about it?" . . . She nods, yes. . . . "Tell me, young woman," I went on, "does she cram eight hours of work into five and call it *part time*?" . . . She nods yes again. . . .

Then, Marge, I added, "I am not your enemy, so don't get mad with me just because you ain't free! . . . Then she speaks up fast, "I am free!" . . . All right," I said. "How about me goin' over to your house tonight for supper?" . . . "Oh," she says, "I room with people and I don't think they . . ." I cut her off. . . . "If you're free," I said, "you can pick your own friends without fear."

Wait a minute, Marge, let me tell it now. . . . "How come, I asked her, "the folks I work for are willin' to have me put my hands all over their chopped meat patties and yet ask me to hang my coat in the kitchen closet instead of in the hall with theirs?" . . . By this time, Marge, she looked pure be-wildered. . . . "Oh," she said, "it's all so mixed up I don't understand!"

"Well, it'll all get clearer as we go along," I said. . . . "Now when you got to plunge your hands in all them dirty clothes in order to put them in the machine . . . how come you can't see that it's a whole lot safer and makes more sense to put your hand in mine and be friends?" Well, Marge, she took my hand and said, "I want to be friends!"

I was so glad I hadn't popped her, Marge. The good Lord only knows how hard it is to do things the right way and make peace. . . . All right now, let's have the coffee, Marge.

I COULD RUN A SCHOOL TOO

I TELL YOU, this is a wonderful age to live in! No, dear, I'm not talkin' about washin' machines and such although I must say I'm glad somebody sat down and thought that up, too. What I am talkin' about is everybody up and at bein' something like Myrtle's daughter. . . . Well, Marge, she is goin' to actin' school. . . . That's right, she's gonna be a actress. Ain't that nice?

I was over to Myrtle's house this afternoon, and it was somethin' to see Doris goin' on before the mirror and readin' out loud and studyin' and practicin' her lessons! She's got books on top of books, and she can give you some right smart answers to anything you might ask her about plays and theatres and such. . . . Yes indeed, I'm that proud of her, and I'm glad to see her really gettin' down to her lessons, especially since it's costin' Myrtle a pretty penny. . . . Of course, she's hopin' to make some money at it and why not? Well, I had Doris about to die laughin'. . . . Marge, I told her that I believed I could run a actin' school myself because I know just how everything is supposed to go. . . . What makes me think so? Well, I've seen so many movin' picture shows until by now I could say that I've really got the hang and swing of how things are supposed to happen. That's a natural fact!

No, you cannot go by how things happen in life because they never hardly happen in that way at all. Take for example the young lady who plays the lead part. Well, she most always has a boyfriend that has got himself in trouble by tryin' to solve a murder or somethin'. . . . That's right, although I must say that I've never yet had the pleasure of meetin' anybody that had the time to do that kind of thing day in and out like they do in the movies. But be that as it may, the young lady in the story always follows her boyfriend around and gets mixed up in the thing too until finally the bad man and her boyfriend get into a big fistfight near the end of the story.

Now it is most important that when they have this fight that she remembers to retire to a corner of the room and tremble in fear. . . . No, she is not allowed to holler. She must put her hand over her mouth so as not to let the holler escape and just roll her eyes around lookin' pitiful and scared. Then the bad man will drop his gun, her boyfriend will wallow all over the floor tryin' to beat the evil man to that gun! . . . No Marge! She must *never* pick it up and give it to him or kick it out of the way. She must run to the other side of the room thus givin' them more room to roll and tumble!

You must be out of your mind, Marge! . . . Of course she can't hit the other man with a bat or do anything like that! . . . Well, it might be life but that ain't got a thing to do with actin'! Well, things keep goin' along like that, with her goin' from one end of the room to the other until her boyfriend finally gives the villain one big whoppin' right to the jaw which right will knock him out cold. After he knocks him out, he will stand there lookin' kind of groggy and beat while a little stream of blood trickles down the corner of his mouth. . . . Marge, it must come down the corner of his mouth because if it was comin' from his eye, you would expect him to have a black eye, wouldn't you? . . . And who ever heard of a hero with a black eye? . . . I don't care how many bare-knuckle licks he took, he must not have no black eyes or puffed up mouth or bashed in nose or nothin' like that! . . . Well, of course you can know he was in a fight. He can wear a little plaster patch on one cheek, he can perspire and also have his hair ruffled up. And that's how you would know!

Well now, after he knocks out the murderer, *she faints.* . . . That's right, all actresses must hit the floor at this very moment, but she mustn't fall down *bam* the way Martha did when she heard about her father passin' away. She is just supposed to whirl aroun' kinda half like and fall quietly, then her boyfriend must pick her up and put her down on the couch. . . . Now, that's a foolish question! There's *got* to be a couch! . . . No, they do not faint in rooms that don't have couches! Next thing, he pours her a glass of water from the water jug that is always full and ready and waitin' on the desk. He holds the glass to her lips, and she comes out of it gently sippin' the water and never chokes on it the way Martha did. After this, the actress begins to cry and maybe holler a little while he comforts her and keeps sayin' her name over and over. Then he kisses her and she runs her hands through his hair and tells him, "Hold me, hold me." . . . Marge, I know that is what he's doin', but she has to tell him anyway!

. . . Now you see there! That's where you're wrong! Of course *you* would help him beat up the murderer and of course you would yell your lungs out while scratchin' out his eyes, but that's not the way it's supposed to be done!

Oh yes, I'm an expert! The hero must always win the fight, he must not get mussed up lookin' except in a pretty kinda way, the bad man is always caught, the couple always lives happily ever after, nobody ever has to worry about goin' to work, everybody's got a nice place to live and nobody but *nobody* ever has to worry about how they are goin' to pay the rent or gas and light bill. And that's why I could run a actin' school and you couldn't. I know all the answers, and they're just the *opposite* of what you or anybody else would naturally think!

I VISIT YESTERDAY

MARGE, YOUR TABLE sure is fixed up pretty—flowers and everything! Stanley sure will be most impressed! I don't know what you'd do if you had money 'cause as it is you really know how to put-on-the-dog! . . . Oh, yes, me and Eddie will be here, have no fear about that! I'm goin' upstairs to get dressed right now. I would've been ready exceptin' that I had a little stop to make on my way home from work.

You know, sometimes a *duty* visit can be one of the nicest kind of things. Well, there's certain folks that I visit once or twice a year 'cause I *oughta*. Miss Jeanie is one of 'em. She was a dear friend of my Grandma. Miss Jeanie is in her nineties now and most of her old friends have passed on. So it gets kinda lonely-like for her. I put off visitin' her for a terrible long time, and then one day I just pick up and go before I get a chance to change my mind. I take her a little token and sit and chat with her for a while. I should go more often 'cause she makes fine company.

She lives with one of her grandchildren, and it is all they can do to make her sit quiet and take some ease. . . . Oh, her mind is still sharp, she can hear well and her health is not too bad but of course her strength gets taxed awful easy. . . . Yes, she loves visitors.

Miss Jeanie's mama was a slave, and she told her a lot of stories about slave-times and Miss Jeanie can go back quite a way herself and tell you things that's just pure amazin'! When I visit her I feel like I'm 'bout ten years old 'cause she will look at me and say, "Well, I declare, if it ain't little Mildred, it's really somethin' how time passes! These little *babies* are all grown up!" She says that every time we meet, and it's not long before she gets 'round to all them stories. I kinda lead her into them sort of. . . . Well, I will say, "I guess you've seen a lot of things, Miss Jeanie, and I'll bet today looks a lot different from times gone by."

Then she says, "I'm so glad for these young people comin' along now. I love 'em, and it's good to see that they goin' on and on. If my mama was to come back here now and take a look 'round, that poor soul couldn't believe her eyes! I thank God, yes, thank God, I lived these years to see it. Mildred, the good God has been good to me! Ain't many people been gifted to sight the wonders and changes that these old eyes seen!"

Today I asked her, "Can you remember any of the stories 'bout the 'old days,' Miss Jeanie?" And she says, "My recollection is long and ain't none of them stories left my mind. Don't you give no listenin' to any folks talkin' 'bout 'good ole days' 'cause wasn't no such thing, wasn't nothin' but a long tired yesterday!"

Marge, she settled back in the big arm chair and smoothed her dress apron. . . . Yes, she always wears a pretty apron even though the relatives try to keep her from doin' things in the house. Her greatgranddaughter Thelma told me, "Great-grand just insists on unpackin' the groceries when they come. She feels all the packages and looks at the labels and then lines them up nice and neat on the shelves, loves to put away groceries."

Miss Jeanie nodded her head, "'Course I like to do that! If you children seen as much old weevily meat and meal as me, you'd like to put away groceries too. I reckon my mama never seen a boxfull of groceries in all her days, never had no boxfull of nothin' but trouble! Back in them bad days folks seen nothin' but heap of work and most misery. Thing that's most hurtful to me is how my mama didn't get to look at some good days 'fore she closed her eyes.

"If I could tell you in the same words like she spoke, you'd know what I mean, but all I can do is give you a little-bitty notion 'bout them trials and things. Poor soul didn't know what a *bed* look like, never had nothin' but straw on the floor for her to sleep. Mama told me how in the evenin' the slave-folk was all bone-weary, but they'd gather together in a clearin' and build them a big old campfire. They'd sit 'round in a circle and pray and sing. After a little bit one of the overseers come walkin' over and touch some little gal on the shoulder and say, 'Master want to see you.'

"Poor little child would start to cryin' but get up and go on off with overseer so's the master could use her for his pleasure. Why you think all us colored folks is mixed up? When these children tell me 'bout what's goin' on in the papers 'bout not wantin' races mixin' in the schools, I just suck my teeth and say, 'Hmmmph! Don't want to mix by day but *do* want to mix in the dark of the night!'

". . . No, they couldn't do nothin' to stop them kind of goin's on 'cause wouldn't nothin' happen 'cept poor slaves get beat or killed! My mama told me that there was big talk 'round the campfire 'bout a black man by the name of Nat Turner. Somebody told her one time that he was gonna set everybody free. Lord have mercy, she used to pray for old Nat to hurry up and come on. . . . No, it was years later 'fore she found out that Nat had been dead long time 'fore they even heard 'bout him. He wasn't no Carolina man nohow, he was a Virginia man."

Marge, she went on like that, tellin' us one story after another. The one I liked best was how her mother married again. Miss Jeanie said, "Soon's my mama was free, she left her slave husband and got married legal to some other man. No, I never could fault her for that, 'cause who wants to have some slavemaster pickin' out somebody for you to live with, everybody know it wasn't right. Folks ought to pick and choose they own husband or wife. How's somebody gonna tell you somethin' like that? The Lord don't hold with that kinda doin' and he's gonna set his hand 'gainst folks who go 'round stampin' on others!"

Thelma fixed tea for us and we talked some more, then Miss Jeanie took me in the kitchen to see how she fixed up the pantry shelves real pretty with paper edgin' all around. "Little Mildred," she says, "see how all this foodstuff is put up so nice. Got to have all kind of food to make good dinners, got to have all kind of people to make a good world. You young folk got a great day comin'. I hear all 'bout white and black folk sittin' down and breakin' bread together. Thelma here, she knows some of 'em. This old world is gettin' more good folk in it every day. Lord, one of these mornin's you children gonna wake up and find no more hate and no more meanness. When that happens, you remember that Miss Jeanie told you that."

When I was leavin' she took my hand and said, "You just keep goin' on up and lookin' to do better 'cause everything's gonna be all right. I want you children to have a lot of en-joyment so's it'll make up for what my mama missed, and when I get to Glory, I'm gonna sit down with little Mildred's grandma and I'm gonna tell her, 'Eliza, them children are doin' just fine so don't you worry none but let's you and me sit back in the easy-chair and take a little rest.' "

Marge, it did me a lot of good to go and see that old lady, and I think I'm gonna enjoy this dinner tonight a whole lot better than if I hadn't gone.

STORY TELLIN' TIME

MARGE, THE FOLKS I work for can get some worried about me. Like for example when I went in to the job this mornin' and put my newspaper on the hall table. In no time flat Mrs. B. picked up my paper and began to go through it. "Oh," says she, "it's so seldom that I see a colored paper, do you mind if I read it, Mildred?" "No," I says, "just you go on and help yourself." I went on and changed my clothes and after a while she got up and came in the bedroom where I was makin' up her bed. "Mildred," she says, "I see here where Paul Robeson is giving a concert somewhere. You wouldn't go to anything like that, would you?"

What did I say? . . . Almost nothin'. I just finished smoothin' the spread and started for the kitchen to do the dishes. Oh, yes, I did say, "Have you ever seen such a lovely bright sunshiny day?" In a little while she drifts into the kitchen and starts nibblin' on the subject again. "I know you wouldn't go to a concert like that." . . . No, Marge, I didn't bite on the bait. All I said was, "Where did you get these gorgeous orange juice glasses?" Honey, she wasn't thinkin' of lettin' up, and she keeps pursuin' the subject. "Mildred, Paul Robeson is the kind of man who gets his people in trouble. You don't want to get in trouble, do you?" Then I said, "No, indeed, I do not want to get in trouble." Now that would have been enough for anybody but you know who. "Mildred," she says, "the only reason I ask you these things is because I feel a concern for you and I'd also like you to *know* all about the kind of people that will make trouble. I'm sure that you've heard a lot about . . ." I cut her off then. "Mrs. B.," I says, "do you mind if I tell you a story?" Her face lit up like a flashlight. "I'd be simply delighted!" Then I dried my hands and told her this story.

Once upon a time there was an old slavemaster and he owned a slave named Jim, and hardly a day went by that old Master didn't say, "Jim, you got to have a whippin'," and he'd have Jim tied down and then he'd lay on the lashes hard and fast. Old Master never gave Jim enough to eat, just weevily meal and rancid salt meat and garbage scraps. And although Jim worked fourteen and fifteen hours a day, he didn't own a pair of shoes and the only thing he had to wear was cast off rags; in fact the only thing he got regular and on time was whippin's . . . and I say that to say this: Master was mean!

Fast as Jim and his wife had children, old Master sold them so's he could send his only son, little Master, to a big fancy college to get cultured and refined. And he sold Jim's wife so that he could give his only daughter, little Mistress, harp lessons and piano lessons and embroidery lessons so's she could grow up and be a cultured, genteel and refined Miss Lady.

When the Civil War broke out and was fought and won, it worried old Master to death that he had to turn his slaves out in a cold, unfriendly world, and he stood on the big veranda that Jim had built and wept as he waved goodbye: "Who's gonna take care of you now?"

After old Master got over his cryin' spell, he formed the

Ku Klux and went out shootin' down some of Jim's relatives just to let Jim know that old Master wasn't dead yet, or even dyin' for that matter. And then he put Jim to work on his land on a share plan. . . . Jim sharin' all the work and Master's share bein' all the profit.

And Master used some of his profits to build special things for Jim's relatives like special schools, railroad waitin' rooms and county jails. He also spent some of his profits to pass laws makin' it illegal for Jim to eat in certain restaurants or go in theatres or even to marry whom he pleased or walk the streets after eleven o'clock at night. Master also told the hospitals not to admit Jim or his relatives and many of them died right at the hospital door.

In fact, old Master went so far as to pass laws against Jim's people socializin' with white folks who didn't agree with Master's plans. Old Master warned Jim that white folks who would live in the same buildin' with colored folks and laugh and talk with colored . . . well, folks like that were rabble-rousin', common, low-flung trash that were out to create trouble between Jim and old Master.

And old Master lynched thousands of Jim's kinfolks, and of course as time went by it was worth Jim's life to try and get to the polls to vote. And such misery old Master brought about . . . 'til World War I.

And then old Master calls Jim and says, "Jim, boy, we all got our faults, you got yours and I got mine. Let's shake hands and go off and fight for Democracy so's we can live in peace." And Jim tried him one time and went, but when he got back old Master started the same old burnin' and killin'.

Time went by and one day old Master called Jim and he says, "Jim, you got your faults and I got mine, but let's shake hands and go off and fight one more war for Democracy, and this time I swear on the foundations of my plantation that this is it!"

I don't know whether Jim believed him or not, but he went on and said, "All right, we'll try it one more time."

Soon as Jim got back old Master was awful annoyed because Jim was walkin' around with a uniform full of medals and raisin' merry Ned about votin'. And old Master had veterans' eyes gouged out and the killin's started all over again.

Jim fought old Master all the way down the line until one day old Master called him again and said, "I'm not goin' to ask you to go to war any more, Jim, but I got a little 'police action' I'd like you to go and see about." Yes, Jim tried one more time and when he got back he went straight on up to the Supreme Court in order to get his children in the schools. Old Master got mad as the devil and said "I'll fight you with my last breath, blood will run in the streets and I'll spend my remainin' days seein' that your children don't get into the schools!"

Then, Marge, I looked full at Mrs. B. and said, "That is all to the story but the object of this tale is simply this: *I know who makes trouble for me!*"

. . . Yes, she said something after that. I'll bet you can't guess what it was. She said, "Yes, it sure is a nice sunshiny day, and I hope it doesn't rain."

ABOUT THOSE COLORED MOVIES

YOU KNOW ONE THING, Marge, I get really salty sometimes when I listen to some of my people yammerin' away 'bout, "What's wrong with the Negro?", "The trouble with us is we *don't* do this or that," or, "Oh, Lord, when will we learn?" . . . and a whole gang of other remarks like that!

Honestly, Marge, it just bugs me to death! Now it is very true that everyone can stand some correction sometimes, but it gets awful wearisome when it begins to look like we're to blame for everything that happens to us.

For an example, I go to see a lot of movies about colored people, in fact almost all that they put out. I also have seen quite a few of them where they show colored maids and handymen and such. I'm beginnin' to get a little warm under the collar 'bout what they say!

How 'bout them pictures where people are always passin' for white? You know, they are always about some colored person bringin' misery down on themselves by passin' for white. Only the person actin' out the part *is* always white! The one who is tryin' to pass, and I say tryin' 'cause look like they never get away with it in spite of us knowin' that a heap of folks do, well, that person is supposed to make everybody break down and have a good cry 'cause they look white but ain't! I guess the folk who make the movies think that Jim Crow is all right for darker people but is awful unjust if it happens to somebody who is light-complected. It strikes me as awful strange how they wrap everything up so neat and tidy at the end. . . . Well, white people will come to the rescue and point out to the "passer" that it is more honorable to *be what you are* and improve yourself in spite of the fact. Everyone feels real happy in the end 'cause the whites can go away feelin' no fear of bein' married to, bein' the son of, the mother of, or the wife, sister, aunt or cousin of a Negro who lacked the *honor* to inform them of his race. Girl, you know that we know better than that!

Well, the whole situation is sorry enough without them askin' us to believe that them white actors are passin' when we know that they don't *need* to be passin' for white if they *are* white!

I remember seein' another picture that had a colored soldier in it. . . . Oh, no, Marge, he wasn't *passin'* for white, but he was real touchous 'bout bein' *colored*. He got so that he would have spells and things and finally it bugged him so much that he couldn't walk 'til a nice white doctor called him a nasty name, then he got up and walked! . . . No, Marge, he didn't pop him in the mouth, he just walked. That's psychology.

. . . Yes, I saw that picture 'bout Africa. Wasn't that the one that showed how good white folk can't help no colored folk 'cause they will kill good white people instead of thankin' them? . . . Yes, and didn't it also show how we just won't do right, and it ended up with a nice white man givin' another one some money to help little African boys? . . . Sure, Canada Lee was in that. . . . Yes, he's dead now. He sure was a good actor, but what I liked best was the time I saw him on the stage in a play that was about Haiti. . . . Yes, that was a show where colored folk was doin' right.

No, those kinda movies don't make me as mad as some 'cause at least you do get a chance to see colored playin' all the way through a picture instead of comin' and goin' so quick 'til you could hardly tell they was in it at all. Sometimes when I think on all those little-bitsy parts, it's more than I can understand how they all are so much alike and keep sayin' the same words all the time.

As soon as I see a colored maid that's workin' for somebody, I know that she will have a coniption-fit 'cause the lady she works for won't eat her dinner and before long the maid will say, "You eatin' just like a bird!" Or, "Somethin's worryin' you, chile, and I won't rest 'til I find out what it is!" I know that maids don't be carryin' on like that over the people they work for, at least none of 'em that I've ever met!

I will also bet that we'd never be able to figure out how much brass railin' we have polished up in movin' pictures and how many dishes we've washed and all such as that. Yes, pictures and plays will pretty much show the same kind of thing. It seems that the maid can never be married, or if she is, her husband always has to be no good, but contrary to real life, she likes him 'cause he's that way and will say somethin' like, "I don't know why I *likes* that man. I guess it's 'cause he keeps me laughin' all the time! He won't come home, and I hate to tell it, but I don't think he's none too crazy 'bout workin', but Lord! when that man hears music, he just can' keep still, he ain't much good, but I guess he's all I got, and no matter how he does, I just can' do without him!" Ain't that disgustin'?

What gets me is how the audience seems to go for that stuff

and will be blowin' their noses and wipin' their eyes 'cause they're so *touched*. . . . Yes, anybody that believes all that mess is *touched*, all right, touched in the head!

. . . No, Marge, they're not pinnin' as many bandana handkerchiefs on our heads these days, but they get the same result in other ways. Sometimes they will dress up the maid in a frumpy, old black dress and a black straw hat sittin' up on top of her head, and she will walk right nice and dignified-like, but when you boil everything down to the nitty-gritty she'll be talkin' the same old line!

Yes, I bet a whole lot of folks is real disappointed 'cause the maids they hire ain't like that at all! If the truth was to be known, they'd be searchin' a devilish long time before they found one, too!

Why, it gets so that every time I see colored comin' on in a picture, I kind of hold my breath 'cause I don't know if I can stand how they gonna have him actin'! Ain't that a shame? Who writes all that mess anyway? . . . I know it can't be the actors 'cause they sure would like to look better than that! It's a sin and shame the way they show colored people!

. . . No, I don't mean just us either! I can't see why a white man always got to play the part of a American Indian. I'm that tired of lookin' at blue-eyed Indian chiefs! Seems awful mean that they can't have a Indian play the Indian *sometimes*. And you never get to see no Chinese unless they're comical or lurkin' 'round in the shadows, waitin' to jump somebody or somethin' like that.

. . . How 'bout that! Sure, they show these pictures and plays all over the world! Marge, can you imagine some of these things bein' shown in countries where they have never had the chance to meet any colored? I bet they think that we act just the way the pictures and the plays show! . . . That's right and if they ever meet *me*, they gonna get on the wrong side of my list almost as soon as they open their mouth!

They're gonna come walkin' up to me expectin' me to laugh and grin, sing 'em a song, do a little jig for 'em, act simple and foolish, be lovable and childish, be bowin' and scrapin' and keep 'em laughin' at every word I say. I can tell you now that if that was to happen, I would most likely forget that they got them notions from some play or book, I would be too mad to be calm and cool and explain to them just what kind of person I am! I would probably cuss 'em out before I could do anything else. "What's the matter with you?" I would say. "Don't come walkin' up to me and actin' like I'm some puppy-dog or pet bird or somethin'! Are you out of your mind?" And then they would back up from me and say to their friends, "They're not like we thought they was at all. Here we was thinkin' that they laugh and play all the time and the truth is, they are *mean*!"

Yes, that would be a shame, Marge. But it's not my fault that they got all the wrong notions 'bout me, and before I could feel sorry for what they don't know, we would have had a big fuss and busted up friendship before we even got to be friends!

... Yes, that's true, too! We have seen some nice plays in the churches and halls here in Harlem. But hardly anybody ever gets to see 'em but us!

... Oh, girl, stop talkin' 'bout the Federal Theatre or people will find out our right age! ... Sure, I recall some of the plays they did. Remember one called "Turpentine"? ... That's right they did have one called "Noah" and another named "Sweet Land" and how 'bout when they did "Macbeth"! ... You sure are good at rememberin' names. Yes, there was Lionel Monagus, Mercedes Gilbert, Georgette Harvey,

Thomas Mosely, Frank Wilson, Bebe Townsend, Hayes Pryor, A. B. DeComathier, Laura Bowman, Alberta Perkins and Jacqueline Andre. . . . Oh, no, Marge, all of them wasn't on the Federal Theatre. You must have seen some of 'em someplace else! . . . Do you remember Monty Hawley? . . . Yes, a lot of 'em were *great* actors. . . . When I get to thinkin' 'bout how some folks never got to see them at all, it just tears me up. Didn't they miss somethin'!

Marge, a number of those actors are dead now. . . . I only wish that all the oldtimers that are livin' and these new actors that are comin' up now will make some pictures and plays sometimes that we could be real proud about. . . . Yes, I know that *they* don't pick out the stories, but, after all, *somebody* does.

WHY SHOULD I GET UPSET?

WELL, IT SURE IS NICE to know that you had a real good time, and I must say that I would have had a much better time if I'd gone to the picture show with you instead of over to Brooklyn. . . . Oh, no, the people were real nice, and we had a pleasant evenin' playin' cards and talkin' . . . I mean, if I had gone with you, I wouldn't have got in this big old fuss with Berniece as we was comin' home!

You know how touchous Berniece can be! Well, just the same I'd rather not be arguin' with her 'cause she is a very nice friend in lots of ways. She was real helpful when my sister was sick and if the least thing goes wrong, you can count on her to come runnin' and do whatever she can. But Berniece can act so grand and is so filled up with herself sometimes 'til she grates on my very nerves!

There we was ridin' along on the subway when in walks this drunken man. He was a Negro. This drunk has a wine bottle stickin' out of his back pocket and his clothes looked like he had spent the day rollin' around on the ground. The first thing he does is take the bottle out of his pocket and wave it around to everybody and then start takin' swigs off of it.

In the next few seconds he begun to grin at all the white folks and start dancin' a little jig. Oh, he was disgustin' all right!

Guess what that Berniece did! . . . She turns to me and says real loud, "Mildred, let's move to another car, I find this too humiliatin'!" I says to her, "He's not gonna bother us!" And she says, "I'm not afraid of that, but I do hate these people who act up like this, it's a reflection on all of us. I want to show the people in this car that we do not approve of his actions!" "Oh, you do!" I says, "I don't know what in the hamfat should make them think that we approve, and I don't notice any of them runnin' to different cars! And in fact," I says, "when we went over to Brooklyn, there was a white drunk fallin' all over his seat and I never noticed you jumpin' up to change cars!"

"You don't seem to understand," she says, "this is one of the reasons why we can't get any further than we do! Who would want somebody like that ridin' the trains with them or eatin' in the same restaurants? We'll never get our rights until we improve ourselves more! Someone like that holds us back fifty years! When we *prove* ourselves . . ."

You know, I wasn't thinkin' 'bout lettin' her run on with that foolishness! "Honey," I says, "this man ain't no reflection on *me* whatsoever. You're talkin' like a first-rate fool! Where did you get all that crazy talk 'bout provin' yourself? Why, if only the races that had no drunks in them was allowed to have rights, why, nobody in the country could vote, that's a fact! And if we had to wait 'til all the colored folks was perfect in order to be treated as citizens should be treated, we wouldn't make it. No, we'd never make it 'cause that perfection stuff falls just outside of human nature!"

She was goin' to argue me down anyhow: "Well, it makes me ashamed to see something like that happenin' when we're tryin' to get someplace!" "And that's just too bad!" I says, "I don't see why you have to fall for that old line 'bout provin' yourself. When you open the newspaper, you see all sorts of crimes and stuff that white people have done and they ain't thinkin' of givin' up their rights because of it. I hope you don't believe that all these jails are built special for us!" "No," she says, "but we have to prove . . ." I stopped her before she could say another word. "If you say 'prove' one more time, you'll force me to lose my temper. If everybody is so eager and all-fired anxious for us to *prove* ourselves, why would they fight us so when we try to get in the schools and libraries?"

Marge, she set her mouth all prim-like and got a look in her eyes that meant, "I'm not gonna say another word to you." So I went on talkin'. "Are we citizens?" I asked her. She goes right on lookin' at me like the subject is closed. "Are we citizens?" This time I said it so loud 'til she says, "Yes! Shhhhh, everybody is watchin' you." "Well," I says, "in that case, we're entitled to all our rights."

By this time the drunk had flopped down in a seat and was hummin' a tune to himself. No, we didn't move 'cause I wasn't thinkin' 'bout takin' the burden of some poor soul's weakness on my shoulders!

INHIBITIONS

MARGE, AIN'T THERE A LOT of talk goin' on about *inhibitions?*
The woman I worked for today says she does not want her
son to be inhibited. . . . This means that he can climb up the
drapes, smash up the dishes, be rude to tradespeople, sass his
parents, eat what he wants and in general act like the cock o'
the walk. When he starts in to cryin', he can write his own
ticket and get the moon with star-sauce on it. . . . You're
right, girl, he can also get in my hair and on my blasted nerves.
. . . As far as his parents are concerned they think the whole
business is "cute." I'm tellin' you, one of these days he's gonna
marry some woman and make her miserable!

Well, the point I want to make is this: I usually just gear
myself to ignorin' whatever goes on in order to get my work
done, so I've gotten used to him rulin' the house. Today was
rush day for me, and I was in a hurry and tryin' to get finished so I could make it on home. He come runnin' in the
kitchen and wanted to stick his fingers in the chopped meat
patties, and when I wouldn't let him, he started screamin'
bloody murder. His mother came rushin' in to find out what
happened, and I told her, "I won't let him play in the hamburger." She kept explainin' to him, "Mildred loves you! Mildred loves you! But she's busy." He kept kickin' up his heels
and screamin', "She does not! She does not!"

At this point his mother turned to me and said, "Tell him, Mildred, tell him you love him and explain why he can't play in the hamburger." Then I says to him, "Because I *said* not, that's why!" Well, his mama was some shocked and after she was finished givin' her son cookies, candies, kisses, and also let him go out to play, she asked if she could have a few words with me. The few words were: "Mildred, you can't deal with children abruptly, you always have to let them know the reason why things take place or else they will feel unwanted and inhibited."

"And that's bad?" I asked her. "Definitely!" she said. "Well," I says, "don't you think that should hold true for everybody? Why should *I* be inhibited? I can't tell that child why he can't do things and make any sense out of the tellin' 'cause I'm in such a inhibited state myself. I got to walk around here bein' considerate of you, and the only way I could explain to him why he shouldn't do things would throw *you* smack-dab in the middle of the explanation." Then she says, "I don't see how that can be."

So I told her, "You have spoiled that boy so rotten 'til you've made it impossible for anybody to have any dealin's with him at all. If I was to tell him why he couldn't play in the dinner, I would *have* to talk about you some. If I did that, it would put you and me in a awful strain, so I just go along and tell him don't do it 'cause I *said* so."

"Well," she says, "I'd rather you speak up and tell me just what's on your mind." "Since that's what you'd rather," I said, "here it is: the reason he can't do any and everything that strikes him is 'cause somebody has given him some wrong ideas about his *rights!* In spite of what you tell him, it is not his *right* to walk over everybody, to be rude and sassy, to hold me up from doin' my work, to make everybody sick 'cause he feels like playin' in their food. No, it is not his right to do these things or to get rewarded for *not* ruinin' the supper. He needs to be told that there are things that everybody ought to do whether they feel like it or not, and the sooner they get used to the idea, the better they will get along in the world."

Oh, Marge, she started a whole lot of goin' on 'bout how I don't understand the modern methods of teachin' children and by the time she said "you don't know" and "you don't understand" about fifty-'leven times, she began to make me mad! "Look here," I says, "I know that half the time you're givin' in to that boy because you don't want to be bothered with him!"

Marge, she looked so dumbstruck that I thought she'd faint. "Mildred!" she says, "Are you tryin' to tell me that I don't love my son?" "No, I'm not *tryin'* to tell you anything," I says. "I'm *tellin'* you that you get sick of him a whole lot of times and then he does somethin' naughty to make you give him things and try to prove that you love him! That's why you come in here hollerin', 'Mildred loves you! Mildred loves you!'"

"Well, I *never!*" she says, and I went right on talkin', "You never! That's right, you never take time out to talk to him like he's a person. You never feel like lookin' at his drawin's and talkin' about his games and things. You never tell him what's on your mind, but you will always be on hand just in time to shove a piece of candy in his mouth and start talkin' about love!"

Then she started pacin' up and down, "I never dreamed that I was such a terrible mother." "You're not so terrible," I says, "you got a whole set of inhibitions of your own. For one thing, you're always feelin' awful about how you're feelin' inside and workin' yourself to death tryin' to make the outside look just the other way. You will spring unexpected dinner guests on me and then go 'round here complainin' 'bout havin' a headache. When you do that you're tryin' to make me feel *sorry* for you so that I won't get mad about the extra work."

"Why," she says, "I would never plan to do such an underhanded kind of thing!" "No, you wouldn't plan it," I says, "'cause you've done it so much 'til it's become second nature. I notice that every time you have a few cross words with your husband, you jump in the bed and play sick 'til he buys you a ring or a watch or somethin', and you also give me a little present every time you speak cross to me or act unreasonable."

"Oh, my!" she says in a real airish way, "I wonder how my husband can stand me!" "No need to wonder," I says, "'cause I notice that whenever he goes out of town for two or three days he sure is extra-special nice to you when he gets back here, and no matter how cranky you might act, he's as humble as a little lamb for two or three days. I guess that's his way of givin' you a piece of candy, just like you do with that child."

Marge, I was sorry the minute after I said it 'cause I hate to bring a hurt look to people's eyes and you know I mightn't have said it at all if I wasn't so mad. She looked at me long and hard, "All right, I guess I deserved every bit of that." I shook my head, "Let's don't worry 'bout our just desserts 'cause if we got what we deserved all of us would be mighty happy. All we can do is go 'long and do our best without tryin' to fool anybody, ourselves in particular."

"Well," she says, "it's a deep subject, and we could talk all night long and not come up with the right answers." And I told her, "It wouldn't take nearly as long as you might imagine."

By the time the little boy came back in the house, I was ready to leave. That little devil decided that he wanted to pour the sugar bowl out on the table. . . . Who me? . . . No,

I didn't open my mouth although he kept watchin' me out of the corner of his eye.

His mother took it away. . . . No, she didn't tell him why. You know that smart little fella really knew why he shouldn't do those things. . . . Sure, he hollered, but before I left, he was quiet as a mouse and he and his mama was busy readin' a story together.

No, indeed, I don't need anybody to tell me about inhibitions, not after all the hard days I've seen and lived through!

WHAT IS IT ALL ABOUT?

MARGE, DO YOU EVER ASK yourself, "What is it all about?" I mean livin' and dyin' and the long stretch of struggle that comes in between.

I was over to my cousin Nellie's house and she had just come through a great store of trouble and it looked like a fresh supply was due any minute. Well, honey, she threw up her hands and said, "Why? Why? Why? What is it all about? I go out to work every day on a hard, low-payin' job, I live in this broke-down, high-rent apartment and I just barely manage to buy enough food so's I can keep my strength up to go back to that low-payin' job, and things go 'round like that year in and year out. For what? Why!"

You should have heard her, Marge. "Folks goin' off to war," she says, "killin' other folks, hatred scattered everywhere near and far, everybody actin' like dog eat dog and the devil take the hindmost! Every Sunday we get together and sing 'Nearer My God to Thee' and then go back to the same old scuffle come Monday mornin'."

And she's right, Marge! Ain't it awful? Just think—a man is headed for the grave. . . . Excuse me, Marge. I meant no disrespect, let's say he's headed for Heaven, but before he goes, he's got a mission to accomplish, so he says, "Before I go to Heaven, I'm gonna own all the old shanty buildings in my town and charge the poor folks so much rent that I'll be able to buy me a car and a big house with a swimming pool.

"And before I go to Heaven, I'm goin' to see that all the schools stay Jim Crow so's that different races can keep hatin' each other. I'm goin' to keep black people off of juries, also— before I go to Heaven, I'm going to drop bombs on people and also raise the food prices. Furthermore, before I go to Heaven, I'm goin' to vote against free hospitals for children. I'm goin' to build houses of prostitution and more jails to put the prostitutes in. Before I go to Heaven, I am also going to build me an atom bomb shelter, so that I will not go to Heaven too soon.

"Before I go to Heaven, I'm goin' to join the Klan and burn crosses on folks doorsteps . . . and burn folks if necessary. And last but not least, before I go to Heaven, I'm goin' to give away fifty Christmas baskets every year to the poor, regardless of their race, creed or color!"

Can you imagine that, Marge? . . . You're absolutely right, girl! Life should be more than grabbing and getting. Like I told Nellie, "Ain't it plain to see the mission is loving and working to glorify the earth and all that's in it? It's to heal the blind, not only with operations and glasses but with knowledge and learning; to cure the sick, not only in hospitals but the folks who are sick at heart; to feed the hungry! Divide the loaves and fishes among all the children in the world and see the great amount we'll still have left over. It's to find delight in one another and bring about the true brotherhood of all mankind."

Well, Marge, Nellie smiles at me and says, "Mildred, the last man that taught those things got crucified, and if he was back here today, he'd get it again!"

"Don't I know it!" I said. "But what did he say? 'Lo, I am with you always!'"

"Look around, Nellie," I said. "Every age has somebody teachin' those things, but the golden age of peace and joy will come when we stop the crucifixion!" Well, leastways, Marge, that's how I think—or else, as Nellie says, "What is it all about?"

WE NEED A UNION TOO

MARGE, WHO LIKES housework? . . . I guess there's a few people who do, but when a family starts makin' money what is the first thing that happens? . . . You are right! They will get themselves a maid to do the housework. I've never heard of no rich folk who just want to go on doin' it our of pure love and affection! Oh, they might mix up a cake once in a while or straighten a doily, but for the most part they're gettin' a kick out of doin' that simply 'cause they don't have to do it. Honey, I mean to tell you that we got a job that almost nobody wants!

That is why we need a union! Why shouldn't we have set hours and set pay just like busdrivers and other folks, why shouldn't we have vacation pay and things like that? . . . Well, I guess it would be awful hard to get houseworkers together on account of them all workin' off separate-like in different homes, but it would sure be a big help and also keep you out of a lot of nasty arguments!

For example, I'd walk in to work and the woman would say to me, "Mildred, you will wax the floors with paste wax, please." Then I say, "No, that is very heavy work and is against the union regulations." She will say, "If you don't do it, I will have to get me somebody else!" Then I say, "The somebody

else will be union, too, so they will not be able to do it, either."
"Oh," she will say, "if it's too heavy for you and too heavy
for the somebody else then it must be also too heavy for me!
How will I get my floors done?" "Easy," I say, "the union
will send a *man* over to do things like paste wax, window
washin', scrubbin' walls, takin' down venetian blinds and all
such."

She will pat her foot then and say, "Well! *That* will cost me
extra!" . . . "Exactly," I will say, "'cause it is extra wear and
tear on a man's energy, and wear and tear on energy costs
money!"

. . . Oh, Marge, you would have to put a problem in the
thing! All right, suppose she says, "Never mind, I don't want
you or anybody else from that union, I will search around
and find me somebody who does not belong to it!" Well, then
the union calls out all the folks who work in that buildin', and
we'll march up and down in front of that apartment house
carryin' signs which will read, "Miss So-and-so of Apartment
5B is unfair to organized houseworkers!" . . . The other
folks in the buildin' will not like it, and they will also be
annoyed 'cause their maids are out there walkin' instead of
upstairs doin' the work. Can't you see all the neighbors bangin'
on Apartment 5B!

PRETTY SIGHTS AND GOOD FEELIN'S

I SERVED A LUNCHEON PARTY today. . . . Yes, it was a very nice affair. It seems like it was given to benefit some orphanage, and the ladies had a very nice time chit-chattin' and playin' cards and I was mighty glad that somebody was gonna reap some benefit out of the fun 'cause wasn't nothin' else happenin'.

. . . I mean they seemed kinda bored and weary and put-upon and also acted like they'd just as soon be somewhere else. By me bein' the one who was doin' the servin' I got to hear a lot of what they was talkin' about. My, but they have done a heap of travelin'! I tell you, when we take off every few years and go down home for a week, you can bet your last dollar that we've been nowhere! Why, those folks don't think nothin' of jumpin' up and flyin' off in all directions at one time, and it would be pretty hard to name a place where most of 'em haven't been.

One sorry-faced woman told all about how she had gone to India and France and Egypt and all manner of far-off places. I couldn't for the life of me see why she looked so sad-eyed because I know that just one of those places would've set my eyes dancin' for years and years. But there she sat, blowin' smoke rings and yawnin' every once in a while. The

others took their turns and went to describin' all corners of
the world and how the food in France stood up to the food in
Spain and also how tea was made one place and how the
coffee was brewed in another. . . . Yes, it was strange how
they kept talkin' about *food,* and I did get the general idea
that of all the places they had gone nobody had looked at
very much except their dinnerplate! Why, you'd think they
had never had nothin' to eat!

Honey, they was busy rememberin' the pastry from here,
the fish from there and the wines from some place else! And
all the time sittin' right in front of them was every manner of
goody that you've ever heard of! I'm tellin' you, they had a
spread! But everybody just picked at the stuff and mumbled
about their diet. Seems like they couldn't eat unless they went
off some place far!

They raised a right-smart piece of money for the orphans
and after the affair was over I had to hang around puttin'
things in order. After the last guest was gone, I got to chattin'
with Mrs. G . . . and I asked her about the trips she had taken.
She told me about Italy and a few other places, then she says,
"The next time I make a trip, I think I'll go to South America,
I do think I'd see more and enjoy the atmosphere of a new . . ."

"Well," I says, "I always see a *lot* when I go on a trip and
although I haven't been to many places, I figure that I really
get my money's worth of sights and feelin's."

"Oh," she says, "have you traveled?" "A bit," I said, "I've
been back down to South Carolina two or three times, out
to St. Louis once and I make little short trips to Long Island
and New Jersey all year round."

"And you've enjoyed them?" she asked. "Oh, yes," I says,
"when I go travelin' I see a heap, and it's my greatest pleasure to recollect things for a long time and in that way it seems

to me I get all the good out of where I've been time and time again."

"I've been to South Carolina," she says, "and I do recall that they have a lovely Battery, the Cooper River Bridge and . . ." "Well," I says, "I remember other things more. For example, I've never had a more wonderful feelin' than lookin' out of the train window in the first early hours of the mornin'. There's a deep misty haze hangin' just a few feet above the ground, the sky is streaked with red and gold against gray, everything is quiet and still-like and it seems as though there's not a livin' soul in the world.

"The brown-wood lean-to houses look like livin' things standin' along the side of the track and watchin' the train whizz by. If you can get to the diner and have a cup of coffee at that exact time, well, you'll find that coffee tastes better at that minute than any other time. You feel cozy and close to your own thoughts, yet lookin' out the window makes you think of how big and strange the world is and how small you are."

"Yes," she said, "I do recall that feelin' slightly although I never paid too much attention at the time." "But," I says, "that's not all. You have to look sharp if you want to get the *good* out of a trip. Be sure and watch for early twilight-time and you'll really be in luck if there's a little rain happenin' at the same time. You'll see the tall cornstalks noddin' and wavin' in the fields, you'll see a horse shakin' his head and strollin' in little circles. I've always wondered why the horse pays the train no mind. And right about then the train engineer blows his whistle 'too-whoo-whoo-whooooo,' and all of a sudden I smile to myself . . . not about a joke or even anything I can describe. No, I can't name the feelin', but I smile or laugh a little to myself and it feels good to get up and rock and sway down the aisle and drink a cup of icewater out of one of those paper cups."

Then the woman says to me, "But that's on the train, what about the places you've visited?" "Oh, I enjoy the places, too," I says. "But more than the monuments and the parks and streets and such sights, I enjoy the little unexpected moments that jump up in front of you and are gone before you know it. Like when we all went on a picnic out on Edisto Island, off the coast of Charleston. The picnic was nice and there was lots of good things to eat and games to play and laughin' and talkin' and singin'. But when the picnic was over and we gathered up our things and started back to the wagon, one of those moments jumped up right in front of my eyes for almost a whole minute.

"You see, we had picnicked up on a grassy mound under a big tree, and I was one of the last ones to leave. As the people trailed down the path, some of them were carryin' the sleepin' children and their heads were bobbin' on their shoulders, the old folks were pickin' their way real slow-like so's not to stumble or fall; one little girl was runnin' to keep up with her papa and her feet was slippin' and slidin' and kickin' up the dust and everything was covered with a big silence.

"Then Reverend Carter, who was pullin' up the rear with his arms full of little campchairs for the children, started to sing 'When the Saints Go Marchin' In' and he was singin' all by himself. Somewhere off in the distance a big old lonely boat whistle hollered out—'Loooord!' And then the people joined in with the minister, 'I Want To Be In That Number!' As I stood up on that little mound watchin', I felt big and strong and able to do anything in the world. It seemed as though I was miles away and didn't know them and that they was the whole world passin' before my eyes!

"Then my friend Pete Jones came up to me and said, 'You gonna stand here all night, sister? Come on 'fore we get left!' Then the moment was gone and soon I was back with them and we was all talkin' and makin' jokes about what all we had done that day."

Mrs. G . . . looked at me and nodded her head. "You should get to travel more since you get so much out of it." "Yes," I says, "and I hope to someday but meantime I just look at everything that I can see right here at home because I know there are a lot of people savin' up their money to come here to New York and if it's worth that much to them, I oughta make it worth somethin' to me.

"If you want to see somethin' now, you get out of here on the first day of school openin' in the fall. Don't tell me these children don't like school! You never saw so much starch and hair ribbons in your life and new pencil-boxes and plastic book-bags, and sass and candy apples! Another thing you oughta catch is the children out in the street on Christmas-eve night, the hot chestnut man with that little weak whistle on his cart, folks draggin' trees through the snow . . ."

Then she says real solemn-like, "I wonder what Paris, the West Indies or Italy would mean to you?" And I told her, "Honey, I would have me a natural ball!" And I would, wouldn't you, Marge?

DOPE AND THINGS LIKE THAT

I BET YOU can't guess what happened over at the public school yesterday! . . . Miss Richardson told me that they found out that some of the school children was dope addicts. . . . No, I'm not talkin' about the high school, I'm speakin' of the elementary school! . . . That's right! Most of them children ain't over thirteen or fourteen years old! It sure *is* a cryin' shame. . . . Yes, they say they caught some young man who had been sellin' it to them! They say that he was on the stuff too!

Girl, you can't pick up a paper or a magazine without seein' somethin' about people caught takin' dope. I wonder why they do it, too. Most times you'll read somethin' about it givin' them some kind of kick or thrill or somethin' like that, but I don't believe that could be altogether true!

I worked for a woman once, and they found out that her daughter was takin' some kind of dope. The daughter was a nice enough kinda person, but she didn't never seem too thrilled about nothin', if you ask me! . . . No, she used to hang around the house lookin' real quiet-like and still all the time. There would be days when she got sort of nervous and jittery and more than once I noticed that she had awful dark circles under her eyes to be as young as she was! But for the most

147

part she was dull as dishwater and didn't seem to take too much interest in nothin'. . . .

Yes, they sent her away some place to a private sanitarium. It's a mess whenever rich people get into that kind of fix so you can imagine what it must be to have trouble like that in a poor family! When that stuff gets hold of you, it seems like it will make you steal or do anything else to get enough money to keep right on buyin' it. But the worst part of all is how it tears up your system.

. . . Sure, somethin' oughta be done about it! But what? I'm not a violent woman, but I believe I'd feel mighty close to murder if I caught up with somebody who had helped do that to a child of mine or anybody else's children for that matter.

It strikes me as doggone funny that they never catch any-body except some folk who are sellin' a few packages of it to people! I mean, it must be comin' from somewhere, and nobody is givin' it away free in order to win friends or in-fluence people! . . . No, some big people are makin' a big mint of money out of that stuff, and some folks must have got powerful rich off of strewin' it all 'round the country. How come nobody ever seems to catch up with some of them?

You should of heard Mrs. T . . . who lives down the street! . . . Yes, her son got mixed up in that foolishness and when it came time that he wanted to cure himself of it, he went into these terrible spasms and shivers and sweats. She told me, "Mildred, I come home and found my boy on the floor just retchin' and groanin' and sweatin' somethin' terrible with his eyes sunk in his head like death itself! He was crawlin' on the floor tryin' to get over to the telephone and call somebody to help him."

Girl, the tears was pourin' down her cheeks and that poor

woman had her heart brimfull of trouble and misery. Well, it got to the point that she couldn't leave the rent money in the house 'cause he would find it and use it to buy more of that poison. She said he would be 'shamed about it afterwards but it looked like when he needed that stuff, he'd get so desperate that nothin' or nobody mattered except gettin' hold of it. . . . Yes, they sent him down to Kentucky to take a cure, but when he got out, she never saw him no more 'cause he didn't come home. Every once in a while, she'd get a postcard from him with no return address on it, but after a while he stopped sendin' them, and she never heard any more from him.

. . . Well, I wouldn't say that nothin' but weak people would get themselves into such a state. No, I wouldn't say that at all unless we wanna figure that there's just millions and millions of weak folks.

. . . No, I didn't say that there are *millions* of addicts. I can't say 'cause I don't know just how many there are, but I'm talkin' about another thing I read about that has some bearin' on the matter.

I read where there is a new kinda drug that is supposed to relax folks and ease up the strain on them without havin' any ill effects afterward. Do you know that people are buyin' up them pills so fast 'til the drugstores are just plum run out of it *all the time!* Yes, mam, and bigshot people are tellin' all about how it helps them to keep goin' from day to day! There is a big rush on and almost *everybody* seems to be makin' a bee-line for them pills!

What in the world is the matter? Folks are takin' these things because they are weary and scared and tired and nervous and upset! Well, I'm glad this new stuff is harmless, too, but it clearly shows that folks would be buyin' that harmful dope if they wasn't afraid of payin' them heavy dues by ruinin' their health. Looks like people are sayin' "We're all unhappy and need some pill or somethin' to ease our minds and give us a moment's peace."

Girl, pills and needles ain't gonna change this world one little speck. Somehow folks will have to take some of the pressure off of people. They oughta get some of these great minds that's hangin' around and put 'em to work figurin' out ways and means to do it.

Don't you think there is enough of them big people to take a little bit of effort and remove that monkey that's ridin' on the backs of American people? . . .

MERRY CHRISTMAS, MARGE!

MERRY CHRISTMAS, MARGE! Girl, I just want to sit down and catch my breath for a minute. . . . I had a half a day off and went Christmas shopping. Them department stores is just like a madhouse. They had a record playin' real loud all over Crumbleys. . . . "Peace On Earth." Well sir! I looked 'round at all them scufflin' folks and I begun to wonder. . . . What is peace?

You know Marge, I hear so much talk about peace. I see it written on walls and I hear about it on the radio, and at Christmas time you can't cut 'round the corner without hearin' it blarin' out of every store front. . . . Peace . . . Peace . . . Peace.

Marge, what is peace? . . . Well, you're partly right, it do mean not havin' any wars . . . but I been doin' some deep thinkin' since I left Crumbleys and I been askin' myself. . . . How would things have to be in order for *me* to be at peace with the world? . . . Why thank you, dear. . . . I will take an egg nog. Nobody can make it like you do. . . . That's some good. I tell you.

And it begun to come to my mind. . . . If I had no cause to hate "white folks" that would be good and if I could like most of 'em . . . *that* would be peace. . . . Don't laugh, Marge, 'cause I'm talkin' some deep stuff now!

If I could stand in the street and walk in any direction that my toes was pointin' and go in one of them pretty apartment houses and say, "Give me an apartment please?" and the man would turn and say, "Why, it would be a pleasure, mam. We'll notify you 'bout the first vacancy." . . . That would be peace.

Do you hear me? If I could stride up to any employment agency without havin' the folk at the desk stutterin' and stammerin' . . . *That*, my friend, would be peace also. If I could ride a subway or a bus and not see any signs pleadin' with folks to be "tolerant" . . . "regardless" of what I am . . . I know that would be peace 'cause then there would be no need for them signs.

If you and me could have a cool glass of lemonade or a hot cup of coffee anywhere . . . and I mean *anywhere* . . . wouldn't that be peace? If all these little children 'round here had their mamas takin' care of them instead of other folks' children . . . that would be peace, too. . . . Hold on, Marge! Go easy on that egg nog . . . it goes to my head so fast. . . .

Oh yes, if nobody wanted to kill nobody else and I could pick up a newspaper and not read 'bout my folks gettin' the short end of every stick . . . that would mean more peace.

If all mamas and daddies was sittin' back safe and secure in the knowledge that they'd have toys and goodies for their children . . . that would bring on a little more peace. If eggs and butter would stop flirtin' 'round the dollar line, I would also consider that a peaceful sign. . . . Oh, darlin' let's don't talk 'bout the meat!

Yes girl! You are perfectly right. . . . If our menfolk would *make* over us a little more, THAT would be peaceful too.

When all them things are fixed up the way I want 'em I'm gonna spend one peaceful Christmas . . . and do you know what I'd do? . . . Look Marge . . . I told you now, don't give me too much of that egg nog. . . . My dear, I'd catch me a plane for Alageorgia somewhere and visit all my old friends and we'd go 'round from door to door hollerin' "Christmas Gift!" Then we'd go down to Main Street and ride front, middle and rear on the street-car and the "whitefolk" would wave and cry out, "Merry Christmas, neighbors!" . . . Oh hush now! . . . They would do this because they'd understand *peace*.

And we'd all go in the same church and afterwards we'd all go in the same movie and see Lena Horne actin' and singin' all the way through a picture. . . . I'd have to visit a school so that I could see a black teacher teachin' white kids . . . an' when I see this . . . I'll sing out . . . Peace it's *truly* wonderful!

Then I'd go and watch the black Governor and the white Mayor unveiling a bronze statue of Frederick Douglass and John Brown shakin' hands. . . .

When I was ready to leave, I'd catch me a pullman back to New York. . . . Now that's what you'd call "sleepin' in heavenly peace." When I got home the bells and the horns would be ringin' and tootin' "Happy New Year!" . . . and there wouldn't be no mothers mournin' for their soldier sons . . . Children would be prancin' 'round and ridin' Christmas sleds through the sparklin' snow . . . and the words "lynch," "murder" and "kill" would be crossed out of every dictionary . . . and nobody would write peace on no walls . . . 'cause it would *be* peace . . . and our hearts would be free!

What? . . . No, I ain't crazy, either! All that is gonna happen . . . just as sure as God made little apples! I promise you that! . . . and do you know who's gonna be here to see it? *Me* girl . . . yes, your friend Mildred! Let's you and me have another egg nog on that. . . . Here's to it. MERRY XMAS Marge! PEACE!

ON LEAVIN' NOTES!

GOOD EVENIN', MARGE. I just stopped by to say "Hey" . . .
No thank you darlin', I do not care for any turkey hash, and
I don't like turkey soup or creamed turkey either. Child, there's
nothin' as sickenin' as a "hangin' around" turkey.

Well girl, I done come up with my New Year's resolution.
. . . That's right, I made just one, and that is this: NOBODY THAT
I DO DAYSWORK FOR SHALL LEAVE ME ANY NOTES . . . You know
what I mean. Whenever these women are going to be out
when you come to work, they will leave you a note tellin' you
about a few extra things to do. They ask you things in them
notes that they wouldn't dast ask you to your face.

When I opened the door this morning I found a note from
Mrs. R . . . It was neatly pinned to three cotton housecoats.
"Dear Mildred," it read, "please take these home, wash and
iron them, and bring them in tomorrow. Here is an extra
dollar for you. . . ." And at the bottom of the note a dollar
was pinned.

Now Marge, there is a laundry right up on her corner and
they charges seventy-five cents for housecoats. . . . Wait a minute, honey, just let me tell it now. . . . I hung around until
she got home . . . Oh, but I did! And she was most surprised

to see the housecoats and me still there. "Mildred," says she, "did you see my note?"

"Yes," I replied, "and I cannot do those housecoats for no dollar."

"Why," she says, "how much do you want?"

I give her a sparing smile and says, "Seventy-five cents apiece, the same as the laundry."

"Oh," she says, "well it looks as though I can't use you. . . ."

"Indeed you can't," I say, " 'cause furthermore I am not going to let you."

"Let's not get upset," she adds. "I only meant I won't need you for the laundry."

"I am not upset, Mrs. R . . . ," I says, "but in the future, please don't leave me any notes making requests outside of our agreement. . . ." And you know, THAT was THAT. . . . No, Marge . . . I did not pop my fingers at her when I said it. There's no need to overdo the thing!

THE 'MANY OTHERS' IN HISTORY

GOOD EVENIN', MARGE. I am sorry I woke you up. . . . Yes, I know it's 12 o'clock. . . . Well, I got to work tomorrow too but I just have to tell you about your friend Mildred. . . .

Honey, I went to a Negro History meetin' tonight. It was held on account of this is either Negro History week or somethin'. . . . Why, of course it should be a year-round thing, but a week or a month is better than a "no time," ain't it?

Marge, I really "fell in" at that meeting! Let's admit it—I look good, don't I?

Well, they had several speakers. There was one pretty young colored girl who was a little nervous but she came through fine and gave a nice talk about Harriet Tubman, Sojourner Truth and *many others* . . . and a distinguish lookin' man who was kinda grey at the temples spoke about Frederick Douglass, Nat Turner and *many others*. . . . Then a middle age white woman delivered a rousin' speech about John Brown, Frances Harper and *many others*.

I noticed that everybody would name a couple of folk and then add "and many others." Well, when the talkin' was over they asked the people to speak up and express themselves. . . . Why of course I did! I got up and said, "This has been a delightful evenin' and I'm glad to be here but you folks kept talkin' about 'many others.' . . . But you didn't tell much about them.

"Now I can't think about the *many others* without thinkin'

of my grandmother because that's who you are talkin' about.
. . . My grandpapa worked in a phosphate mill in South Carolina. He was a foreman and made eight dollars a week. He and
grandma had seven children and paid eight dollars a month
rent. It cost ten cent a week for each child to go to school,
ten cent apiece for the nine in the family to belong to the
burial society . . . and the pickings were lean. Each child had
to have a penny a week for Sunday School and grandma put
in two dimes a week for the church.

"Once in a while she squeezed out seven nickels so's the
children could go see lantern slides. Them kids wanted at
least one picnic during the summer. They ate up one can of
condensed milk a day . . . a tablespoon in a glass of water
. . . that's how they got their milk.

"Christmas and Easter was a terrible time of trouble and
worry to my grandma . . . with seven kids lookin' for somethin' new. . . . Toys? Grandma used to take a shoe box and
cut windows in the sides, then she'd cover the windows with
tissue paper, put a candle in the box, light it, cover it, cut a
hole in the top, tie a string on the box so it could be dragged
along and that was called a 'twilight trolley.'

"She'd pull up a clump of grass, tie it in the middle to make
a 'waist line' and then comb the dirt out of the roots so she
could braid them in two pigtails . . . and that would be a 'grass
doll' with 'root hair.' . . . She'd get seashells and they would
be 'play dishes' . . . and the boys got barrel wires for hoops
and pebbles and a ball for 'jacks.'

"Every minute of grandma's life was a struggle. She never
had a doctor except for 'sickness unto death' and neighbor
women helped bring her seven into this world. Sometimes
she'd get down to the 'nitty gritty' and have her back to the
wall . . . all the trouble lined up facing her. What to do! What
to do about . . . food . . . coats . . . shoes . . . sickness . . .

death . . . underwear . . . sheets . . . towels . . . toothaches
. . . childbirth . . . curtains . . . dishtowels . . . kerosene oil
. . . lamp chimneys . . . coal for the stove . . . diapers . . .
mittens . . . soap and hunger?

"Next thing, Grandma would get cross at the children and
she'd begin to grieve and cry if they'd make noise. . . . Then
she knew it was time to 'rally.' After the kids was off to bed
she'd sit in her rockin' chair in the dark kitchen . . . and that
old chair would weep sawdust tears as she rocked back and
forth.

"She'd start off singing real low-like. . . . 'I'm so glad
trouble don' las' always,' and switch off in the middle and
pick up with . . . 'Saviour, Saviour, hear my humble cry' . . .
and she'd keep jumpin' from tune to tune. . . . 'I'm gonna tell
God all of my troubles when I get home' . . . 'Come out the
wilderness leaning on the Lord' . . . 'When I've done the
best I can' . . . and her voice would grow stronger as she'd
go into 'It's not my mother but it's me oh Lord' . . . and
she'd pat her feet as she rocked and rassled with death, Jim
Crow and starvation.

"And all of a sudden the rockin' would stop and she'd jump
up, smack her hands together and say, 'Atcha dratcha!' . . .
and she'd come back revived and refreshed and ready to go
at them drat troubles. . . ."

That's what I told 'em, Marge. . . . *You know, it's amazing
that we're all here today!* . . . Well, the way they took it
you could tell that I was talkin' about their grandmas too.
. . . So I told 'em, "I bet Miss Tubman and Miss Truth
would like us to remember and give some time to the *many
others.* . . ."

I'm going upstairs and get some sleep now. . . . Stop that,
Marge. . . . If I'd known you would cry, I wouldn't of told it.

INTERESTIN' AND AMUSIN'

MARGE, TURN OFF the television so you can hear me talk because what I got to say is a lot more interestin' than hearin' that man singin' a song about a box of kitchen cleanser.

I served a buffet cocktail party this evenin' for Mrs. H., and of course her notion of a few friends is a lot different from mine, but be that as it may, we all got to work for a livin'. . . . Well, her crowd is what they call "smart," so after they ate up all the shrimp salad and chicken loaf, they lolled around chit-chattin' about poetry, paintin' and the problems of the world. . . . You know, Marge, it is easy to pass yourself off as one of the "smart" crowd because all you have to know is two words: "wonderful" and "amusin'." There's hardly anything they can think of that isn't "wonderful" or "amusin'," from the President to a pussy cat.

Well, yours truly was doin' her bit by emptyin' ashtrays and servin' martinis in between washin' dishes . . . and they was arguin' like sixty about first one thing and then another . . . then finally they started talkin' about war and peace. . . . Marge, for the first time "wonderful" and "amusin'" was squeezed out of the conversation.

Some of 'em was sayin' we couldn't have war and some was sayin' we couldn't have peace, and as I told you, I was mindin'

159

my cleanup business. . . . Well, one of 'em got the bright idea of tryin' to make a fool out of me by callin' me in and askin' my opinion. . . . Hold on, Marge! I did that. . . . "Excuse me," I said, "but I have to do my *work*."

"Oh, Mildred," Mrs. H. squeals, "don't be stuffy. I've told everyone how *wonderful* you are."

So I put down the silent butler and says short and quick, "I'm against war and if most of the people feel like that there'll be peace."

Well, honey, I could tell by the laughter in their eyes that they thought me "amusin'." Anyway, one arrogant young man speaks up. . . . "Why are you for peace . . . do you have a son?" "No," I says, "I do not have a son, but I got *me* and I have hope for better days and I'd like to be here to see 'em and I'm lookin' forward to someday bein' as much of a woman as I can be. . . . I also consider that all children belong to us whether we birthed them or not, be they girls or boys. . . ."

At this point, Marge, Mrs. H. starts wavin' her hands and smilin' as if to say that was enough, but I wasn't payin' her no mind whatsoever. . . . "Furthermore," I said, "I do not want to see people's blood and bones spattered about the streets and I do not want to see your eyes runnin' outta your head like water."

Mrs. H. says, "Oh, you'll turn my stomach, Mildred!" . . . "That is not me turnin' your stomach," I says, "that is war." . . . I looked at those young men in their fancy dinner jackets and the ladies in their strapless evening gowns and I went on, "I do not want to see you folks washed in oil and fire. . . . No, and I don't want to see your bodies stacked like kindlin' wood. . . . I don't want to see mothers and fathers screamin' in the streets. . . . I don't want to see blood flowin' like the Mississippi. . . . I don't want to see folks shakin' and tremblin' and runnin' and hidin' . . . but I *do* want to see the KINGDOM COME on *earth* as it is in Heaven and I do not think that bombs and blood and salty tears is a *Heavenly* condition."

Well, Marge, they were quiet and as I picked up the silent butler, I added one last remark. . . . "When there is true peace we'll have different notions about what is *amusin'* because *mankind* will be *wonderful*."

Marge, they were still quiet when I left.

A NEW KIND OF PRAYER

DEAR MARGE:

Hope this letter finds you well as it leaves me the same. My sister is much better now so I will be able to come home next week. Last night I went with her to prayer meeting at her church and I got so caught up with the spirit that I said a prayer. And afterwards somebody told my sister that it was a *dangerous* prayer to be making out loud.

Now Marge, whoever heard of a dangerous prayer? I listened to several prayers before mine and they were all good and sincere, but they were so *general-like*. I guess everyone asked help for the "poor and afflicted" but they'd leave it there and then jump to themselves and ask for special small favors—and it struck me that we were not praying right. We were praying general when we should be praying *specific*.

After all, Marge, there are so many people asking the Lord for things that it behooves us to pray clear and direct, with no fuzziness at all.

So I got up and said: "Dear Lord, will you please put a stop to the Klan, will you please? I ask this in the name of your son Jesus. In the first place they claim to follow his teachings, but they would not let Jesus join it if he were here (someone said Amen) and secondly they spend all their

162

time finding fault with your handiwork. They don't think much of you, Lord, and whenever they want to torment some of the folk you created they put up a cross like the one your son died on and set it on fire. And this means—'In the name of Jesus get going before you get killed' and on top of that, Lord, they got the nerve to say only white Christians can join it. (Right here the minister said 'Amen, Amen!')

"Dear Heavenly Father," I said, "I want you to notice what folk have been doing with the good things you put here on earth for *us*. They are grabbing everything up and putting a gate in front of it while some of your children are starving for what's inside! I am asking you, God, to stop men from killing in your name. Things have been destroyed in your name for a long time, but if you will notice, Lord, nothing is built in your name except churches and the main thing they are praying in them churches is: 'Oh Lord, help us overcome somebody!'" (There were some more Amens, Marge.) Then I went on to say, "Dear Lord, please, please stop people from saying God Is On Our Side because today if you say that, you can go out and do all manner of devilment and get away with it (I could feel the people praying with me Marge).

"Heavenly Father," I said, "we pray thee to go easy on Judas if he is still in torment, because men are still informing for the sake of silver only they haven't the shame to hang themselves afterward.

"Lord, there has been enough blood spilled, homes burned, enough arrogance in your name. Let it all change, Lord, and in thy name have Peace, Love and Plenty. (I walked to the front of the church and I opened my arms to everybody.) Dear Lord," I said, "I thank you for the gifts you gave me—a voice to speak, hands to work, eyes to see . . . that I might have the wherewithal to make a good and decent world . . . and I shall work, Lord, with all or any of these powers granted me, until the day I die. For I have faith when I look upon the innocence of the newborn who have but four needs: food, shelter, love and learning. . . .

"Dear Lord, we teach these little ones of hate and bloodshed. God, we are ashamed of the wickedness done in your name, Amen."

So you see, Marge, I only prayed what I thought, and it strikes me as an awful sign of the times, when it's even dangerous to tell God what is exactly on your mind.

Goodnight for now and don't forget to empty my ice pan for me.

Your friend,
MILDRED

HISTORY IN THE MAKIN'

HI MARGE! This is the time of year that we get to talkin' about Negro History. Well now! There you go startin' a argument before I even sit down. What do you mean you don't believe in no Negro History week or month? . . . Of course it should be all year round and of course everybody's history should be in the school books but I'm talkin' about what *is* and not about what *should be!* So now we are agreed on that!

But what gets me is the history that we are makin' right now. Doesn't it give you a funny feelin' when you notice that when one of our folks get a job it's headline news? Well, for an instance, Miss Marian Anderson made a long-overdue appearance at the Metropolitan Opera House lately and it broke the headlines everywhere. And here we are spang in the middle of the Twentieth Century and people are talkin' about rock-etin' to the *moon.* It strikes me that we oughta be working pretty near everywhere if folks have reached the point of workin' "out of this world," so to speak.

Oh, I so long to see the day when our doctors, lawyers, factory workers and politicians will be able to work as a matter of course. Every time I pick up the paper I see some-body gettin' a plaque for bein' the first Negro to work here or there. And all too often they are also the last. Another thing when one of our folk gets a job—be it playin' baseball or prizefightin' or what have you—we are always told that they are representin' the "race." To my way of thinkin', that's wrong. They look to me like real talented people making a living at something they are well suited for.

I never hear any stories about white actors and athletes representin' their race. It seems to me that the representatives should be in Congress and in the White House and in the Senate.

I think working for a livin' and enjoyin' freedom is a right guaranteed us by the law of the land, and some folk are breakin' the laws by holdin' back on our rights.

Yes, Marge, givin' full credit to all the good souls who fight the good fight to make a job openin' here and there. And I do hope they continue to do so. I long for the day when it will not be news for us to work anywhere, speak anywhere, ride anywhere, hold public office or do any of the things that all American citizens are by law entitled to do.

When that day comes, you will look in a newspaper and read announcements about *anybody* appearing *anywhere* and your only comment will be, "Oh my, isn't that nice, I sure want to see that." And all this huffin' and puffin' and blowin' will be past. And if you want to know anything about how things were in our time, you'll have to look in a book to find out. Because that's what history is—the things behind us that made the present.

Thank you, I will have some coffee.

DANCE WITH ME, HENRY

COME ON IN, MARGE, and shut the door behind you. If you want any coffee, tea, milk or whatever, just fix it for yourself because I don't feel like waitin' on you or anybody else! . . . No, I'm not mad at you in particular, but I'm mad at the world in general. . . . No, I have not been cryin'. . . . Well, looks are deceivin', that's all I can say. . . . And I wish you'd stop needlin' at me because I will tell you what it's all about as soon as I get ready. I'm not upset about what anybody said or did but I'm hoppin' mad about what they *didn't* say or *do* either! . . . Yes, I went to the Robinson's party this evenin' and I *know* I'm home early, and I know I sailed past your door without stoppin' by or anything, but I didn't feel like talkin'! . . . Don't bother to hang my dress up for me because I don't care if I never wear it again even if it did cost me twenty-six dollars and is the prettiest one I ever had! . . . If Eddie was here I bet I would of had a nice time! . . . Marge, I'm just about thinkin' I might soon get married to Eddie even though he is out on the road all the time sellin' records and books. . . . At least when he's here, it ain't so lonely-like all the time.

. . . I went out of here this evenin' as happy as a lark or at least as happy as a woman can try to be if she has to go to a party all by herself. . . . Yes, I could have gone with Dorothy and Rosalie, but you get sick and tired of walkin' in places with a whole bunch of women. So, I went alone. . . . But I didn't mind that part of it so much.

It was after I got there! . . . Oh yes, there was lots of folks there. Hardly anybody could be called a stranger, and they all talked friendly enough. . . .

Marge, I know I looked good in my new dress and shoes and everything, and you know I know how to laugh and talk and be sociable. . . . Well, at first everything was all right because I enjoyed listenin' to the music and watchin' everybody dressed up so nice, but after the record changer dropped six or seven tunes it suddenly came home to me that nobody had asked me to dance. The men were pickin' out women here and there, and most of those women had danced a lot already!

. . . Yes, I suppose you might say that they were kinda glamorous lookin', and I would be mighty small to get mad about a man preferrin' another woman to me. But I wasn't lookin' for someone to marry or be sweethearts with. I just wanted to dance some, too!

Timmy went flyin' by me several times with different girls. Oh yes, he waved and said, "Hey there!" And then Henry came up to me, and I was all ready to take off and do the mambo. But all he wanted was to ask me to please sell five tickets for his club dance. After I took the tickets, he just went on about his business. Milton introduced me to the girl he's gonna marry, and she asked me to hold her evenin' purse while they danced. John brought me a drink and left it on the end table for me and two minutes later I saw him whirlin' 'round the floor with somebody. Finally Mrs. Beecham called me over to sit with her and her husband when they were havin' refreshments. After a while she hunched him in the ribs with her elbow, and then he asked me to dance. But he looked so sorry-faced about it that I said, "No, thank you," and left them as soon as I could move without seemin' abrupt.

I felt so lost wanderin' around and smilin' at people that finally I went over in the corner with Dorothy and Rosalie, sat down and joined in with that everlastin' chit-chat. Who in the hell wants to go to a party and spend money for a new dress just to end up in a dark corner talkin' some made-up conversation just to cover your feelin's and brazen out the evenin'! It seems like people could be more sociable to each other. These men think that dancin' with you is such a big old deal and they don't want to be bothered with nobody unless they wish to follow up the whole business and try to make some time with you. Oh honey, if I was to ask one of 'em to dance with me, they'd run for cover and swear you was after gettin' them for your very own, to have and to hold from this day forward 'til death do part!

. . . People at parties owe it to each other to try and enjoy each other's company. . . . I know it, they're busy pickin' out the glama-rama chicks who got long curlin' hair and shaped like models or something. Or else they expect you to be a ice-skatin' champion or a movie star. Well, they don't know that if things was turned around and it was women who did the askin' and we picked *them* by their looks! Well, all I can say is that there would be a devilish lot of them sittin' around the sidelines twiddlin' their thumbs.

One time some fella came over to where we girls was sittin', and it was plain to see that he was gonna ask one of us to dance. But which one? He stood there lookin' each of us up and down like he was gonna *buy* somebody. He finally asked Rosalie although it seems he wasn't too delighted after he had picked her. And after him studyin' our legs and hair-do's and everything!

That's another thing! How come they can march around pickin' and choosin' who they think is best to dance with while we gotta sit there waitin' for whatever comes by? . . . Yes, I know that's supposed to be womanlike and modest, but it's also somethin' for the birds!

Well, I decided that I'd had enough, so I squared my shoulders back, put on a big old smile and told the host and hostess that I was sorry to leave, but I was sufferin' with the worst kind of headache. I was girl, I really was.

No, I'm not goin' to bed yet. I'm gonna first write a letter to Henry and tell him what he can do with these five tickets! 'Cause if Henry can't dance with me, why should I care whether his club's affair is a success or has a big crowd? And if it's the last thing I do, I'm gonna write Eddie a letter tonight and tell him I miss him!

AIN'T YOU MAD?

MARGE, I AM SICK to my soul and stomach. . . . Well, this morning I report on the job, and Mr. and Mrs. B. arc finishing their breakfast. Mr. B. is finishing on the last piece of buttered, jellied toast when he looks up from his paper and says to me, "Isn't it too bad about this girl tryin' to get into Alabama University?" And then Mrs. B. swashes down her bacon with a gulp of coffee and says, "Tch, tch, tch, I know *you people* are angry about this. What is going to be done?"

My hand started jumpin' and I was twitchin' my pocketbook, tryin' my best not to pop her in the mouth with that heavy plastic bag. All of a sudden, Marge, something hit me! I could feel a hotness creepin' over me from my feet on up and when it hit my head, bells started ringin' and I hollered at her, "What the hamfat is the matter with you? *Ain't you mad?* Now you either be *mad* or *shame*, but don't you sit there with your mouth full 'tut-tuttin' at me! Now if you mad, you'd of told me what *you done* and if you shame, you oughta be hangin' your head instead of smackin' your lips over them goodies!"

. . . Now wait a minute, Marge. Please let me finish. Mr. B. stops chewin' with the jam fairly skeetin' out of his mouth and says, "Don't upset Mrs. B. We were only tryin' to be sympathetic." Marge! I whammed my pocketbook down on the table, put my hands on my side and started pattin' my foot, and I yelled at him: "Don't you worry about Mrs. B. bein' upset 'cause if she gets too wrought up she can *scream* and the law, the klan and them men that ganged up on that young lady to keep her out of school, that's right, every one of 'em will come runnin' in here and move me off the premises piece by piece!"

At this point, Marge, he was gaspin' and sputterin' while she was puffin' and blowin' and I wheeled on him and said, "You tryin' to tell me about you bein' sympathetic . . . how do I know you wasn't in sympathy with them grown-up men that was throwin' eggs and stones at a defenseless colored woman? In the first place, you are white and you haven't opened your mouth to do a thing but put toast in it, and first thing I walk in you come askin' me what am *I* gonna do."

Then guess what, Marge! Mrs. B. jumps up wavin' her newspaper at me, talkin' about "Go home, go home *immediately*, you're in no condition to work here today!" Honey, never fear! I reached over and snatched that paper out of her hand and says, "Don't you be wavin' and fannin' nothin' in my face! My mama don't do that!" Then Mr. B. jumps up and hollers "Are you out of your mind, snatching things like that!" . . . "Well," I told him, "you can thank your lucky stars that paper is the only thing I'm snatchin' this morning!" He tried to cut me off, but I wouldn't let him, "If you ain't got the grace to stand up and fight for your own decency and good name, don't you dare ask me what *I'm* gonna do, because as long as *you* ain't *doin'* I ain't gonna tell you, 'cause then you'd know as much as I do, and that might be too much!"

Marge, I didn't want to cry because it do look so weak, but the tears were streamin' down and it seemed like their faces were floatin' in a sea of water. I could hear their voices but no words, just a rush of murmurin' in my ears. "Yes,"

I went on, "black folks want decent educations and the right to work at decent jobs and also every kind of right there is! And we bein' mobbed and killed and shot at. . . . That's right, they're shootin' at little children ridin' school buses! They're shootin' down their fathers for tryin' to get 'em into the schools, they won't sell us no food because we want our children educated, they turnin' us off of jobs and tryin' to drive us out of our homes, they draggin' people out of their beds in the middle of the night and burnin' them with oil and fire. And you ask me what *I'm* gonna do!"

Marge, the next thing you know he says real nasty-like, "When there's a Negro crime wave, I don't throw it in your face." . . . Sit down, Marge, keep still. Girl, I opened up on him and said, "You better not! 'Cause whenever a Negro does somethin' it's a *wave*, but your doggone newspapers is full of nothin' but white folks murderin' and robbin' *every day* that the Lord sends ever since there's been a newspaper and you folks done got so numb inside 'til you think that's how it *should be!*" Then I says, "Why, I can't turn on the television without seeing you all killin' each other up just for the sake of *entertainment*. So you just keep on eatin' your breakfast same as ever, you just keep 'tut-tuttin'. The world's just goin' to pass you by." He jumps up again and says, "Go home!" . . . "I'm goin'," I says, "but remember this: everybody that don't like the idea of white folks warrin' on my people, everybody that feels they don't want to be included in the mob crowd, all those kind of folks speak up and let the world know!" Yes indeed, I told him, "All those that keep quiet are with the mob whether they agree with 'em or not!"

And with that, Marge, I walked out and left them sittin' there big-eyed. . . . Yes, dear, I'll take a cup of coffee—strong. Yes, your friend Mildred is *upset!*

DISCONTENT

MARGE, I don't usually interfere with strangers on the street and neither do I butt my nose into people's business 'cause folks have been known to get killed on account of that sort of thing, and I want to be around here for a long time to come . . . but as the man says, it's the exception that proves the rule.

Girl, I'm not interested in how much you spent on your Christmas presents 'cause that money is as gone as yesterday's snow, I don't care how you figure it. Let's talk about *now*. . . . Of course, I liked my present, and by the way, how did you know I needed a sequin bed jacket? . . . Well, you sure are a good guesser because I know I never mentioned it!

Getting back to my story, when I was comin' home from work this evenin', I passed one of them step-ladder speakers, and I mean to tell you he had some lot of people standin' around listenin' to him. There he was just a-wavin' his arms and hollerin' real loud 'bout food prices bein' so high and the bus and subway fares goin' up, and honey that cold weather wind was whippin' his coattail to a frazzle, so I thought to myself, "If he got the gumption to stand on that cold corner and talk, I'll have the grace to stay with him a while."

Well, he did right well, although I figured he jumped around too much instead of stickin' to one subject. . . . You know what I mean. He'd talk about Jim Crow a bit and just when you got interested in hearin' all about that, he'd go talkin' about unemployment, and then on top of that he was talkin' too long, and I got to go to work in the mornin', so as much as I wanted to hear it all, I had to leave. . . .

No, Marge! I didn't tell him all that! I just left peaceable and quiet. . . . Well, another woman was leavin' at the same time and I heard her grumble, *"If he don't like it here, why don't he go somewhere else!"* I turned around to look at her and she looked a whole lot better than she sounded, so I said to her, "You better wish he stays right here, if you know what's good for you."

"Well," she says, "if he's discontented he oughta go where he'll be content. After all, everybody ain't dissatisfied!" Since she was travellin' in my direction, I walked right along beside her. "Listen here, lady," I says, "you work eight hours a day instead of twelve or fourteen because a gang of dissatisfied folks raised sand until they made it a law, and if they had all gone somewhere else you would still be on the job now instead of on your way home for supper.

"Discontented brothers and sisters made little children go to school instead of workin' in the factory. A whole lot of angry, discontented women fixed things so that we womenfolk could vote. All these different denominations of churches were set up because folks were discontented with one or another of them. Look at these housing projects—they were built because some folks were fightin' mad about livin' in slums. And you get paid a certain amount of money per hour 'cause folks were discontented with less, and if you belong to a union you know full well that it wasn't started by folks that loved their bosses.

"Another thing . . . public schools were not started by parents who were content with private ones. Why, whoever invented a washing machine must have figured that an awful lot of women were discontented with washin' boards . . . and when it comes to your remarkin' the fact that everybody ain't dissatisfied, all I can say is there was a whole gang of folks who didn't think Social Security or Unemployment Insurance was necessary, *but try to take it away from them now that they've got it, and you'll hear a different tone!*"

. . . No, Marge, she didn't get mad. All she said was, "My, I never looked at it that way, I guess you're right." We parted good friends and the last thing I told her was, "When we get peace in the world it will only go to prove my point: people are sure discontented and dissatisfied with war!"

. . . That's right, Marge! Why if man was content to walk there would be no airplanes or trains! Girl, some people spend a lot of time fightin' advancement, but after all the Good Book says, *"Whoso loveth instruction loveth knowledge; but he that hateth reproof is brutish."*

NORTHERNERS CAN BE SO SMUG

GIRL, I TRIED to hold my peace, I tried to let things go by the board, I did my best to remember all the things you told me, but before the night was over, I just had to speak my mind! . . . Yes, it was a nice meetin' as meetin's go. Of course you know I don't consider a meetin' to be the last word as far as a good time is concerned. I go to them 'cause sometimes folks got to meet in order to straighten out things, and I feel that it's my beholden duty to be right there meetin' along with everybody else.

Marge, the church was crowded, and it would have done your heart good if you could of been there to see that fine turnout! . . . It's a good thing that you had a toothache 'cause I wouldn't of taken nothin' else for a excuse! . . . No, I don't mean that I'm glad your tooth is achin', and you know it! . . . Why do you always twist and turn every word I say. . . . I don't mean *every* word, I only mean *some* words! . . . Are you feelin' better now? . . . Well, that's good. Do you want me to tell you 'bout the meetin'? . . . All right, I'll begin at the beginnin'.

Honey, they raised some money this evenin'! This civil rights business has got folks so tore up 'til they're really ready to dig down in their pocketbooks and put some money where their mouth is! The whole idea of givin' the money is simply this: they're gonna send it down South to help out people who are catchin' a hard time 'cause they want to vote and ride the buses and things like that. . . . Yes, they had several speakers there and they spoke right well.

The minister introduced one white man who got up and started his speech by sayin', "The South today is in a state . . ." and then he went on to tell us all about the state of things. After he finished a colored man got up and started his speech by sayin' "The South has *always* been in a state . . ." Then he went on to further tell us 'bout the state of things. Two or three more people spoke a little bit, and I'm here to tell you that they gave the South a *hard* way to go! Oh, it was the South this and the South that and by the time they got through, I don't think there was another bad word to say 'bout the South 'cause they had said 'em all!

When the question and answer time came, everybody started in on the South all over again and took it from slavery and traveled each day and year right back on up to nineteen hundred and fifty-six. I learned a lot, but it seemed to me that we was forgettin' that this land also has a North, East and West to it! Since I didn't think we should be so forgetful I got up to say my say.

When it came my turn, I said, "We have heard a great deal about the South tonight and rightly so, but I'm wonderin' if we got room to just low-rate the South in such a sweepin' manner. . . ." Marge, before I could go on with what I had to say, there was a little disturbance in the back of the auditorium, and one squeaky-voiced little man jumped up and said, "Yes, that's right, *before* we get on the South, let's take care of the North!"

. . . Now, he wasn't doin' a thing but tryin' to mislead the people, so I kept standin' and got him out of my way! "Never mind that *before* business," I says, "but let's take care of the North *while* we're gettin' on the South! To hear us talk, anybody would think the North was some kind of promiseland come true. All is not sweetness and light just 'cause we're on the North side of the Mason and Dixon line!

"But the main thing I want us to remember is that there's lots of *good* people down South!" Marge, they started to mumble then, and I could see that I wasn't gettin' too much agreement on the last thing that I had said. "Yes," I says, "*good* people. When we talk about slave days let's bear in mind that there was plenty of white folks who helped the slaves to escape, Southern folks. No, they didn't get the honor and the glory like the Abolitionists in the North 'cause they had to work quiet and secret and it was worth their lives if they got caught. I heard about them Southern ship captains who took slaves out of the South and hid them 'til they got to freeland, I heard about Southerners who bought slaves in order to bring them to the North and set them free, I heard of Southern homes where the poor 'run-away' found rest and food and hope. Believe me, when I say that it took nerve and courage to fight slavery right there in the teeth of it, so to speak! It wouldn't be right for us to forget those things 'cause even though there was more help comin' from the North, it was harder to get help in the South and for that reason it was worth its weight in gold!"

One woman sittin' behind me, whispered, "We don't want to make them Southerners sound like no angels now." And I said, "We got to give credit where credit is due at the same time that we're puttin' the blame to the South! Are we goin' to forget the judge in Carolina that spoke up for us, are we goin' to forget how he had to leave his home for sayin' what was on his mind? . . . Are we gonna forget the man in Kentucky who sold a colored family a home and got put in jail for it? Are we goin' to forget those youngsters in Alabama who signed a paper sayin' that they didn't want to have nothin' to do with mobs and that they were for the right of a colored student to go to their college? Are we gonna forget the folks who *refuse* to join up with klans and such? Are we gonna forget them Southerners who made trips to people's homes to warn them that bad white folks was comin' over to molest them? Oh, yes, there's been a lot of good Southerners who took a stand for the right even when the goin' was lonely-like and frightenin', when they got chased from their homes, when 'friends' wouldn't talk to them, when they got ugly telephone calls and letters. Oh, my, but it ain't easy to do right in the midst of all that killin', burnin' and mobbin' that's goin' on!"

One of the speakers interrupted me and said, "They ought to be doin' a whole lot more. After all, it's *their* laws that's makin' all the trouble!" "You are so right," I says, "and we oughta encourage 'em! We got to start showin' that we know how some of the folks are scared and pep-talk 'em a little bit! When we hear that there's a mob made up of hundreds of folks, we got to realize that the other thousands upon thousands was *not* out there with 'em and got to ask 'em how come they can't show some gumption and start doin' and speakin' against the mobs instead of sittin' home washin' their hands of it like Pontius Pilate. For too long they have been allowed to think that we don't expect any *good* to come from them, that we just fold our hands and say, 'Oh, well, they're Southerners, so what can you expect?' We got to start sayin' to 'em, 'Speak up so's we can hear you, if everybody ain't for oppressin', then let those that's against it stand up and be counted!

We got to include 'em in the *stand!* We got to write some of their churches and clubs and things and ask 'em, 'Where are you and what are you goin' to do?' When we get their answers, we'll have it down in black and white for the whole world to see! And I bet we'll rack up a few more friends down that way!"

The lady behind me says to me, "Honey, they should speak if they feel right! Looks like we'd be goin' out of our way to be askin' 'em about it."

"Yes," I says, "we would, but it's goin' to take some out-of-the-way things to change them Southern laws! After all, we sure hear plenty from the folks who don't want the law to change and from the Northerners who're willin' to go part-way with the civil rights but hang back some when it comes to *livin'* the thing right down the line!"

Marge, I got solid agreement on that 'cause folks know that even though our laws are much better than down home, we still got to put up such a to-do to get what the law promises. Didn't they try to keep the man out of the housin' project out in Chicago, didn't *they* have mobs gatherin'? How 'bout folks tarrin' the colored woman's home out in *Long Island?* Mobs and meanness can happen in any part of the land but them *laws* in the South just make it easier for it to go on!

Sure, I told them all those things and they had to listen to me, too, 'cause while we're settlin' the trouble down South, we got to remember that we want *all our rights, everywhere* and this is no time for Northerners to get so smug. . . . You're right, girl! All the colored folk that's standin' up and talkin' out in Mississippi, Alabama, Kentucky, Carolina and all over the South, ain't they *Southerners*, too! Yes, indeed, we got to send the message East, West, *North* and *South*. . . . It's high time that the land should be free, from one corner to the other!

LET'S FACE IT

TODAY I HAVE a good feelin'! Marge, life has its moments and every once in a while you hit up on one of them and you wouldn't take anything in the world for what it feels like! One good day like this one will last me a long time to come!

You know I worked hard today, but I really enjoyed every blessed minute of it because my mornin' got off to a rousin' good start! Well, Mrs. M . . . has house guests visitin' her. Guess where they are from! . . . Well, no point in you guessin' 'cause I'm glad to tell you. They are from *Alabama!* It seems they are some kind of far-removed cousins, and they are up here doin' the town for a couple of weeks. I don't get to see much of the woman because she is out shoppin' and seein' shows durin' the daytime, but her husband sticks close to the house and spends his time scribblin' things down on paper.

They have been hangin' around for nearly a week already and I was feelin' kinda sorry for Mr. and Mrs. M . . . 'cause the whole business is developin' into quite a strain. Mrs. M. . . . was followin' me from room to room in order to keep him out of my way and whenever I had to do any cleanin' in Mr. Alabama's, she would try to steer him to the other end of the house. Oh, I was wise to the drift of things and as I said, I felt sorry for Mrs. M . . . .

She was scared out of her wits that Mr. Alabama was gonna

say somethin' *wrong*. It seems like I was drawin' him like a magnet 'cause she really had her work cut out for her. Every time he'd come hoverin' around she'd think up some reason to call him into another room. "Come on in here, Billy, I'm goin' to fix us some coffee," or, "come here, Billy, there's a very interestin' program on T.V.," and things like that.

I guess it had her pure wore-out because after a while she calls me in her bedroom and whispers to me, "Mildred, Billy is from Alabama, and he has some strange ways and right now he is just catcn up with what's goin' on down there." "Is that so?" I says. "Yes," she answered, "you know how the colored people are insistin' on the school situation and things like that." "Indeed," says I. "Oh, yes," she says, "and while Mr. M . . . and I are very up-to-date in our ideas, Billy sees things a little differently." "You don't say!" I says.

You should have seen her runnin' her hands through her hair and glancin' back over her shoulder like she expected Billy Alabama to come in on us any moment. "Mildred," she mumbled, "I'm so afraid he'll say or do somethin' offensive, but I can't keep him out of your way all the time, so if he says anything to you I want you to feel perfectly free to speak right up and express yourself." I laughed a little then, "Put your mind at ease, Mrs. M. . . . because I will surely do just that!"

Marge, when I said that she began to look more worried than ever and adds, "I wish you would handle the matter without name-callin' or makin' a big scene. I'd consider that a favor because Billy is very stubborn about certain things, but on the other hand he is a good man in a great many ways. For example, when my mother died, he was real nice about helpin' out the family and he did see that my brother was able to finish school and . . ."

I held my hand up real calm and solemn-like, "Don't worry about it 'cause if *he* don't holler and beller at me, I don't see any reason why I should lose my head about anything." She sighed a big sigh of relief and went on, "No, he wouldn't do that and although he's a bit narrowminded, he is genteel." I nodded and smiled my agreement, and she and I parted company and went on about our business.

I was dustin' the books in the library when Mr. Billy Alabama of the genteel, narrowminded school of thought finally caught up with me. Marge, that man's eyes was as cold as a icecube at the North Pole! But his mouth was neatly tucked up at each corner so that he looked like he was wearin' some kinda false-face smile.

"Well, sister . . ." Yes, that's just the way he started off! My mind started runnin' like a sewin' machine, and before he got the next words out I had given myself two or three private words of instruction. "Mildred," I says to myself, "don't ask him if you look like one of his mother's children, don't call him 'brother' and don't tip your hand one way or the other until you get the full message that's on Billy Alabama's mind."

Just as these thoughts twittered through my mind, he was still talkin'. ". . . seems like you kinda busy there this afternoon! I was just tellin' my cousin how I couldn't help but admire your ways. Yes, indeed, I told her, 'That girl really impresses me as bein' right smart and you mighty luck to have her, what with times bein' what they are today with first one thing and then another.' "

Honey, I pinned a smile on, too, and sorta nodded in a general kinda way. Of course he took that as the high-sign to move on up a little higher. "I'm tellin' you these are some terrible times we livin' in and like I was sayin' to my wife this mornin', 'Darlin', between the atomic bomb and the races fightin' one another and the high cost of livin', it strikes me that it just ain't worth a man's time to get out of bed in the mornin'.' Yes, that's what I told her. But she's a *very* remarkable woman, and I'm glad to say that she always looks at things on the brighter side, so she says, 'Billy, there's no sense in bein' down at the mouth all the time because the world is gonna keep on turnin' and the sun's gonna keep on risin', and this race business is gonna straighten out, no matter how dark the picture might be at the present moment!' Yes, that's what she said! Her words started me to thinkin' and the more I thought the more convinced I was that she just *might* be dead right. Well, sister, I'm not losin' my faith in Nigras. . . ."

Marge, I wish you wouldn't be laughin' through every word I say. . . . Well, if you think my imitation is good, you shoulda dug *him!* Girl, there I was *tryin'* to control myself, and you know how a vein in your temple can start to throbbin' and beatin' when you're holdin' somethin' inside of you that ought to come out! . . . No, I didn't bust or cuss, but I held fast to the smile, determined to hear him through although I had to ease in a couple of words. "You can call me, Mildred." I says.

Billy Alabama looks a little shook up for a minute and then he says, "All right, *Millie*, now, as I was sayin', I am not goin' to lose *my* faith in the Nigras no matter what *anybody* says. I have known some really *fine* Nigras over the years and I say that they were some of the *greatest* people I ever met."

By this time Marge, he decided to settle down to business and really chat a while so he takes a seat in Mrs. M . . . 's leather chair. Well, you know there's two of those armchairs that sits facin' each other right in front of the fireplace. So I sat down in the other one. Girl, he got a look on his face like somebody had just slammed a automobile door on his finger.

Sure, he had to go on or else get *ungenteel!* Well, I could see him strugglin' for strength. He swallowed hard and started in again, "Some of the greatest people I've ever met. There was one old colored gentleman in particular that I recall, Rev'rend Higgensby! Never had a day's schoolin in his life, but I don't think a wiser man ever trod this earth. He was humble and sort of quiet-spoken, but he had a heart as big as all out-doors and when I was a lad there was many a day that we'd go down to the old fishin' pond and just *laaaaazy* away the afternoon together. Old Rev'rend Higgensby would say, 'Mr. Billy, you gonna be a *great* man one o' dese days an' I'se gonna be pow'ful proud o' you, but I wonts you to 'member po' old me and when you gits up dere in de high-place I wonts you to sen' for de ol' man to take kere of you an' see dat no harm don' come to plague Mr. Billy.'

". . . Yes, that's what he said. He also said, 'Dis po' ol' man ain' nothin' no-how, but when you's struttin' in de high-place, I'se gonna be so proud o' what you's doin' 'til I'se gonna fol' my han's and say, "Lawdy, call dis ol' man home to Glory 'cause I'se had my reward!" ' "

Marge, Billy Alabama's eyes misted up so 'til he had to take off his glasses and polish 'em up while he paused for a breath.

"He sounds like a real character, all right," I says. "Is he dead?" He put his glasses on and shook his head. "No, the old man's still hobblin' around on a cane, he's pretty crippled up now, but he still has a light in his eye and a smile on his face."

Billy Alabama waited for me to say somethin' so I said, "No, nothin's gonna kill old reverend but time."

"Well," Billy says, "I talked with the old gentleman a few weeks ago and his mind is just as spry as ever." "Do tell!" I says, and Billy rambles on with his story, " '. . . Rev'rend,' I asked

186

him, 'what do you think is gettin' into these Nigras to make them carry on all this devilment about the schools and busses, where do you think it will end?' And the old man shook his head sadly as he looked up at me . . ."

I interrupted him then, "Where was he, on the floor?" "Oh, no," Billy says, "he was sick in bed, just kind of ailin', but he looked up at me and said, 'Mr. Billy, fo'give 'em fo' dey knows not what dey do, dey's pow'ful change comin' ovah folk and dey's fo'gettin' de ol' ways and dey's fo'gettin' de days when all wuz peace and dey's fo'gettin' dey place.' Yes, that's what the old man said. Now, Millie, I'd like to be able to go and see him when I get back home and tell about the fine girl that's workin' for my cousin up North. I'd like to tell him what *you* think about the fuss that's goin' on. I suppose you've heard something about what's goin' on down our way."

"Oh, yes," I say, "there's been a few rumors flyin' around, and we've been able to hear a bit of it now and then even though we do live way up here in New York City. It's really surprisin' how news travels these days."

"Well," he says, "I'm preparin' a paper for one of our Southern newspapers and it would help me if I could hear your viewpoint."

No, Marge, I wasn't ready to jump in yet so I put up my guard. "I'd like to know what *you* think." He fell right in and went to tellin' me. "The Lord, in His great wisdom, wanted the races to be as separate as the fingers on the hand, if He had wanted them to be together He would have made them all look the same, He would have mixed them up in the first place if that is what He wanted. Why try to improve on the Lord's handiwork. Mixin' the schools will mix the races!"

I gave him a real inquirin' look, "Do you think that the white folks will have so little control of their personal feelin's that they will up and marry us from kindergarten all the way through college?"

He turned a wee bit red in the face. "It's a very grave problem because the Nigra man is overly fond of white womanhood."

"Well," I says, "can he marry her if she doesn't want to marry him?"

He held up his hand like a traffic cop, "I'm not talkin' about marryin', I'm talkin' about mixin'! It's against the laws of state and God to mix the races!"

"But they are mixed already," I said.

No, Marge he didn't retire at all but kept right on wadin' in. "I want the Nigras to have fine schools of their own! I want the races to go their separate ways in peace, I want an end to this three-ring-circus called desegregation, I want an end to the American people makin' a laughin' stock of themselves before the world!"

His eyes misted up again, Marge, and his voice trembled. "And I resent, yes, *deeply* resent *anybody* who dares to say that I don't have a warm spot in my heart for the Nigras!" Then he leaned forward in his chair, Marge, and looked at me real earnest-like, "Millie, I'm askin' you to do me a favor, I'm askin' you to send a heartenin' message back to old man Higgensby."

Marge, I looked around the room real cautious and then got up and shut the door, I put my finger to my lips and said, "Shhhhhhh, we don't wanna make any noise" . . . and then I tip-toed back to my chair. I guess he thought I lost my mind because I started whisperin' . . . "Don't talk loud 'cause I don't wanna disturb anybody, shhhhhhh!" And he kept starin' at me kinda spellbound.

Then I whispered at him, "When you see that old Uncle

Tom you tell him I said that if I ever lay eyes on him I'm gonna kick that walkin' cane out of his hand and beat his tail with it."

"What!" says Billy Alabama. And I kept on whisperin' soft and rustly-like, "I got a message for you. We gonna change *all* these laws 'til there ain't a piece or a smithereen of Jim Crow left. Yes, we're gonna go to the schools, ride the buses, eat in the restaurants, work on all kinds of jobs, sit in the railroad stations, and do all the things that free people are supposed to have the right to do. As far as this Jim Crow is concerned, I expect to hear about him bein' dead any day, and when he goes, we're gonna bury him in a gray suit, stick a yellow rose in his hand and bury him so deep and so tight that when Judgment sounds, he'll have to sandblast to see Glory."

Marge, when I tiptoed out of the room, he was still sittin' there like a stone image except that his lips would move a little as he kept sayin' shhhhh, shhhhh, shhhhh, shhhh . . .

IF HEAVEN IS WHAT WE WANT

I REALLY ENJOYED the church service this mornin'! The minister was talkin' about the people in the South demandin' their rights and how so many church pastors are goin' to jail because they're demandin' that their people be able to ride the buses and go to school and things like that. He said that we must give them our support and help by sendin' money and doin' whatever things they want us to do. It was upliftin'!

He also spoke about Heaven in his sermon, and he told how Heaven was always held out to us as the promise of our every wish comin' through. He said, "If Heaven is going to be a place where we get everything we want it will have to be divided up into little sections." . . . Well, he said that, Marge, because it is plain to see that people want different things. Sure, what would make us happy might make somebody else sad as all get-out!

The way he put it, we could work it all out very well by havin' everybody pick the section of Heaven in which they wish to dwell. For example, some folks will want to live in the section where everyone is *white*. . . . That's right, there'll be no Chinese or Japanese or Philippino or Hawaiian or African or . . . well, you get the general idea! This particular kind of

Heaven will also exclude Jews and a whole lot of other kind of white people!

Can't you just picture it? Hitler would be the official greeter, and everybody that wanted to go there could dwell in peace and contentment with all the old slavemasters and slavetraders. Every last one of them would have blonde hair and blue eyes *except* Hitler. And they could go through the rest of ever-lastin' eternity just chattin' with each other, and they'd never hear anybody's music but their own, they'd never see anybody's paintin' but their own, they'd never hear anybody's ideas but their own and they'd be chock full of nothin' but themselves for zillions and trillion killions of centuries for all time to come!

Now as the minister pointed out, there'd be some who wouldn't want this kind of Heaven but would rather go to one where nothin' but top-society folk was to be found. People who worked for a livin' with their hands would be excluded from this place 'cause you would have to be terrible rich and trace your family tree with important names in order to get in. There would dwell princes and kings and billionaires and such. These people would never see a waiter or a shoemaker, a singer or a musician, a writer or a maid, a bartender or a lawyer. . . . That's right, they would see nobody but themselves!

. . . No, girl! They could not talk about fashions or boat races or horse races or diamonds! They couldn't do it because the people who built the boats, made the fashions, dug and cut the diamonds and took care of the horses would all be in some other section. . . . So there they would be just talkin' about by-gones and lookin' at each other from one corner of eternity to the other!

. . . No, I wouldn't want to be there either because it would bore me silly, but we couldn't be there because that wouldn't be *our* kinda Heaven! The minister really started me to thinkin' though, and I'll bet we could sit here and think of a thousand different kinds of Heaven that would just delight a thousand different kinds of people. Why, you could have hundreds of 'one-nationality' Heavens and all such as that!

. . . What kind would I want? Well, girl, if I ever get there I will shake hands with the official greeter and say, "The first thing I want to do is congratulate the plannin' committee on how well they fixed up everything back down on earth and I would appreciate it no end if you could send me to a Heaven almost like that."

Then, Marge, when he asked me *exactly* how I'd like it to be, I'd tell him, "I want to go to the section of Heaven that's all mixed with different kinds of folks. I want them to have all different kinds of ways of cookin' and dancin' and singin' and buildin' houses and things like that. I want to have a nice little house on a block that's peopled by all the kinds of people there are. And I want all of us to get to know each other real well and learn to speak at least one common language so that we can talk to each other about everything there is! And I want the kind of Heaven where all of us can go on a picnic and be together without me havin' saved up a lot of money to sail on a ship and just stare at them when I got to their homes!"

Oh, I'd speak my mind! "I want to meet ship-buildin' people, dancin' people, lawyers and doctors and vacuum cleaner salesmen, and subway motormen and poets and newspaper people and folks who pick fruit and plant fields and some of all the kind of folks that peopled the place where I came from —at least all of them that don't hate me or mine 'cause I can't think of anything better than meetin' and gettin' along with the whole world!"

Then, Marge, the official greeter would say, "Oh, you want it to be just like the earth." And I'd say, "No, I don't! I'd like you to leave out the bombs and wars. You can keep all the dispossess and charity agencies, also the miseries and diseases, the hatreds, the floods and tornadoes, Jim Crow houses and schools, and all manner of ugly things like that. And I don't want to spend all eternity restin' and takin' my ease 'cause I'm afraid I'd get weary of sittin' down! I want lots of work, lots of rest and lots of play!"

. . . Oh, go on, Marge! You so silly! . . . Okay, have your way, I will also ask for a T.V. set that gets nothin' but good shows!

WHERE IS THE SPEAKIN' PLACE?

WHAT IS POLITICS? . . . I know it's about elections and the government and things, but I mean what is it besides all of that?

Well, what I mean is just this, I have here a magazine piece that says that *famous* people like actors and writers and such *should not* be gettin' into politics! . . . You are right and I do agree with you! Anybody *oughta* be able to do what they want! But I'm not talkin' about folks runnin' to be governors or congressmen or anything like that! Oh, no, this piece is all about famous folks keepin' their mouth shut about *anything* that goes on that calls for folks speakin' out!

It sure taught me a whole lot 'cause I have always wondered why these big, famous, grand, important people never have a word to say about the most important things that's splashed all over the newspaper. You know, we have so many celebrities in this country that it would take you a lifetime to count 'em up! Just think of how many bigshot actors and musicians and writers and singers and things we see in the movies and on the television and stage and things like that!

Well, if you think about it some, you will find that whenever you read something they got to say or hear them speak on a T.V. interview they all pretty much speak about the same two or three little things all the time. Well, they will say what film they are gonna do next and maybe tell how nice it was to work with somebody or the other and they will also let you in on what they are gonna do next and also tell about how they might visit Italy or some country. And that is all. Have you ever noticed that Marge?

. . . No, it seems that famous doctors and folks like that can dilly-around with a few other subjects, so I guess it means that celebrities like famous show-folks are not supposed to have much *sense!* . . . No, I don't believe that, either! 'Cause I know it takes a lot of sense to act and write and sing good enough to be real famous.

I guess that the general idea is that big folks are too important to concern themselves with what happens to other people. And I think it's kinda sad 'cause most of the celebrities seem so warm-hearted and friendly-like and sunny.

I wonder if I could stand bein' famous if it had to mean that I couldn't ever talk about *nothin'!* It would torment my very soul if I had to shut up and pretend like they never murdered a little boy in Mississippi 'cause he was colored. I couldn't sleep at night thinkin' about all those ministers that was arrested 'cause they wanted the same kinda rights that I had! I couldn't sleep 'cause I'd be sick and 'shamed-to-my-heart that I dared not mention a word about it. I'm afraid I'd get weary just talkin' about Europe and all the other famous people I knew. I guess I would also feel kinda stupid and foolish too, especially if I was playin' parts and singin' things about great deeds and brave folks and big happenin's!

When I see some of these actors hangin' off of cliffs and fightin' a dozen people singlehanded or trackin' down dangerous, armed, crazy murderers, it strikes me that it wouldn't take a hair-breadth of that much nerve to speak out against murderin' real live people! . . . I know it is make-believe, but I am always readin' 'bout how one of them has hurt himself or almost froze to death 'cause he was tryin' to play the thing real-like.

. . . No, Marge, I don't think I'd like bein' a celebrity at all if it meant givin' up my speakin' place. Nobody could give me enough swimmin' pools or champagne cocktails or motorcars to make up for that.

. . . Yes, I guess you got a point there! Of course, some people might not like them speakin' up. But the people who wouldn't like it would be the ones who either wanted to murder folks or else wanted to see *somebody else* keep on doin' it. And I wouldn't care whether folks like that liked it or not! . . . You think they would lose their jobs! . . . Well, why should you think that? Do you believe that the folks they work for want to see the murderin' go on? . . . Well, then, what is it all about? Unless, unless . . . Marge, do you think them celebrities don't *care* even one little bit?

. . . No, honey, I could never be famous, it would cost too much! As short as life is, I sure wouldn't want to go to my grave havin' missed my chance to put in a little comment about this old world!

. . . That's a hard question, Marge, and I don't see how I can answer it but I'll try. If I was a celebrity and *had* to keep still 'cause I was told to, what would I do? Well, I can't see nobody tellin' me what I *have* to do. But if I was simple enough or scared enough to let 'em get away with it, I guess there'd be nothin' for me to do except go out and get *drunk!*

MISSIONARIES

MARGE, THE OTHER DAY I heard a very interesting radio program. It was all about missionaries and how hard they have to work to save "the heathen" in far-off places, and also how much hard cash they have to spend in order to keep up the soul savin' work and how we ought to chip in some dollars to keep the ball rollin'. . . . Who do I mean by "we"? I mean the two of us right here or rather I should say anybody that was listenin' to the program. . . . Well now, not so fast. I think missionary work is a good idea. What is more important than savin' people?

The man was all upset about savin' folks in India. He told all about how they worshipped false gods and shouted and hollered over sacrificing a goat as an offering. He was some distressed and told how his heart bled for the poor ignorant folks. The way he carried on it was enough to draw tears from a turnip. He got to warmin' up to his subject and tellin' of the many far-off places the missionaries have to go, and it struck me all of a sudden that he wasn't the least bit disturbed about raisin' funds for missionaries here at home, because there's a whole heap of savin' to be done right here under our very noses.

The kind of dim-minded, cruel human beings who will shoot a man down for voting certainly needs to be saved, those who go 'round preachin' they're superior because their skins have a certain tint need to be saved, adults who threaten to spill the blood of little children because they seek to find an education in the public schools, don't they need enlightenment? Oh, there are plenty of missions right here that need to be carried out. Everybody is busy these days talking about "equal" education, but I honestly question whether "equal" education is good enough as it now stands. The important thing is *what* we are teaching! All eyes are turned toward the "poor little Negro child" doing without the things the white children have, and nobody seems to question what is happening to the white child in the way of education, and their parents seem to smugly assume that they are getting the very best of everything. Doesn't it strike you as wrong that these children should be taught arrogance, scorn for others, darkness of ignorance instead of the light of knowledge, the nasty art of ridicule, slander, and yes, even violence? Some of these poor miseducated folks even *believe* they are being "patriotic" and "American" when they bomb homes, scare little children and murder men and women. A parent who willingly goes along with the idea of a poisonous education for his child has had a poisonous education himself.

. . . Oh Marge, of course I know that! Anybody that speaks up about these things kind of loud is going to get some of the same treatment from those who hold M.I.V. degrees. That means Master of Ignorance and Violence. But as the man said, "Missions aren't easy, but we must carry on."

Well, the mission is right here in front of our eyes and we need millions of missionaries right this minute to spread the light and bring joy to the hearts of the people, and anybody that undertakes the job should bear in mind that we got to move another step beyond "equal" education and start preachin' the doctrine of *enlightened education* for each and every child throughout this land. Anyhow that's what I think about that.

SO MUCH FOR NOTHING

HEY MARGE! Turn on your T.V. set. . . . No girl, I'm not off my trolley. Mrs. Tanner told me that the Twilight Movie has got a grand set of dishes for sale, so I rushed right over so I can take a look. There, that's it! Well, you don't have to watch the movie. My Lord! I don't think I want to watch it, either. Wouldn't that kill you? Everytime you turn on the set, there's some fool picture about a African leadin' the white man through the jungle. . . . No, there's nothin' wrong with leadin' him, but them guides are always takin' them some-where to take the gold from some tribe or somethin'. . . . Sure, they make it look all right by makin' their chief a wicked man that is scarin' his people to death. . . . Oh honey, you don't have to look at this because I can tell you how it will end. . . . Well, the white men will kill the chief and his medi-cine man, take all the gold and head back for civilization with the pretty white woman who has been queen of the jungle ever since she was dropped from a aeroplane when she was three years old. . . . Yes, sure, they all like that!

Hold on, Marge. Here, you take the pencil and paper, and I'll tell you what to write. Here comes the man with the dishes! My goodness, but that table is really set up, ain't it? . . . He sure can talk fast. . . . Put that down! A set of "Wild Moosehead Dinnerware." Sure is plenty of it, although I must say I'm not too fond of having a moose grinnin' up at me out of my dinner plate. Oh well, I guess you could cover him up with the mashed potatoes. I've seen the set enough now. I wish he'd get around to sayin' how much it costs. Here we go! . . . Not forty-nine dollars and fifty cents, not thirty-nine dollars and ninety-nine cents, not thirty-five dollars and thirty-three cents, but . . . here it is . . . he's holdin' up a sign now . . . it's, it's . . . thirty-three dollars and ninety-nine cents. Write that quick! Ain't that somethin', look at the stuff they're gonna give to the first hundred people that call: a free table-cloth, napkins, glasses, complete set of silverware, ashtrays and one week's supply of frozen food. Hold on, Marge, there's somethin' else: a extra bonus—one bowl of wax fruit to enhance the table. Oh my, and mercy do! . . . You gettin' the telephone number? . . . All right, be calm, he's repeatin' it for you. . . . Okay, we can turn off the set now.

He sounds like a regular Santa Claus! Marge, I just can't believe my ears! . . . No, wait a minute. Don't call the number yet. I smell a rat on that Moosehead offer. . . . Honey, I've lived long enough to find out that nobody is givin' anybody somethin' for nothin'! . . . That's a natural fact! Now it would be somethin' else if he was my nephew or brother or some kind of relative. It would even be different if I had saved his life one time or loaned his mother a thousand dollars or somethin'. But nobody's gonna tell me that some business firm is gonna hand me five or six hundred dollars worth of stuff for thirty-three dollars and ninety-nine cents! . . . Yes indeed, you got to work for each and every thing you get, and anybody that think different, well, they still believe in fairy tales.

THE BENEVOLENT CLUB

MARGE, SOMETIMES I can get so mad at my own folks that I could just scream. . . . Honey, I went over to Ruth's last night to talk about startin' up a benevolent social club for the church. Well, Clarice was there and you know that she don't allow *nobody* to call her a *Negro*. That is a fact. She is an *Afro-American!* And also Betty was present, and she says she is *colored*, and not no *Negro* or *Afro-American*.

Anyway, we made plans to give lectures and social teas and such. Next thing we went on to discuss what folks we would benefit through this benevolent society. You know, like people who have lost their homes because of tryin' to get their children into school and families of men that have been killed or run out of town. Well, during the talkin' Ruth made a crack, "If all those bombings had taken place in the *West Indies*, the people wouldn't have taken it." You know how airish she can be!

Since she is *from* the West Indies everybody else got quiet for a minute and then the conversation loped along kind of casual sort of. In a few minutes Betty says, "It's a strange thing, everything is so fine in the West Indies, but they keep comin' over here."

At that I chimed in to play peacemaker, "I guess Ruth came

from the West Indies for the same reason that I came here from South Carolina."

With that, Clarice gives us all a sharp look and comes up with, "All I can say is that if they had bombed them folks on the Gold Coast in Africa, them African leaders would have seen to it that somethin' more was done besides not eatin' oranges or doin' without soda pop."

Marge! By this time I could see this club fallin' apart before we could get it named hardly. Well, there we were about to bust up this club, so I took the floor. "Ladies," I said, "why is it that every time our folks get bombed or mobbed we got to get to arguin' amongst ourselves? Yes, we do. I noticed lately that some of our papers have been havin' a merry old time cloudin' up the issue. Why do we waste time like that, meanwhile callin' the Klan nothin' but 'dastardly and shameful'? I even read where somebody said, 'This bombin' has got to stop because it plays into the hands of the *Russians* and makes bad *propaganda* which they can use.'

"Now there must be many a brave man turnin' in his grave when he hears that. Imagine! We can't work up no more passion about our murdered dead than to call it 'bad propaganda'! I suppose that if we was real chummy with all the countries in the world then it would be all right to kill our people! Yes, indeed," I went on, "here we sit makin' a big fuss about who we are and who is better than the next one while that is the very kind of thinkin' that was turned on the people we're tryin' to help. So I propose, ladies, that we use our funds to help all these brave folk that are in distress, and that we ask every Afro-American, colored, black and Negro organization (in other words anybody that may get lynched) to help us do it." I had the floor and I held it: "We must also ask any *white* folks who are ashamed and fightin' mad about what's happenin' to also put their time and money in it, too."

Honey, one little lady that I hadn't seen before jumped up and told me, "I don't want any white people to have anything to do with it! After all, white people are the ones who are mistreatin' us!" I do hate anybody to take me for a fool so I answered her, "You don't think that I'm plannin' to invite no lynch mob to help us, do you? . . ." "No," she says, "but I've been around them, and I don't like their ways and some of them are rude and uppity and think they know everything and . . ."

"Wait a minute," I said. "When have you been around white people?" Then she sashayed out to the middle of the room and began to really wind up: "I have been around them when we was raisin' funds for the nursery school, when we was tryin' to get some colored elected at votin' time, at the parent-teachers, when we held Brotherhood Week, at the children's recital, also where I work. . . ."

Clarice hollered out, "Well, I guess she's really been around 'em, Mildred!" At that I took the floor back again while I could still get it: "Yes, and I want you all to remember that every one of us is better off when white folks (never mind the faults) would rather *be with us* in these things than stayin' at home never givin' a care or joinin' with mobs and murderers! We need all the white *friends* we can get and the fewer the enemies the better!" "Well," she adds, "I'm not gonna be givin' into them on everything and lettin' them run everything their way!"

"Well, I guess not," I said, "but we deal with that when we come to it, but for the time bein' I'm still gonna ask you ladies that we vote to include Afro-Americans, colored, Negro, white, Chinese, Japanese and every kind of American there is to join hands with us and help make everything peaceful and friendly."

No, Marge, they didn't settle down real quiet, and I'm sorry to say that a few more cracks were passed about "some people always do more talkin' than workin'," and "I swore I'd never join another club," and things of that nature. However, I'm pleased to report that they voted the way I asked them. Yes, I feel real good about that.

ALL ABOUT MISS TUBMAN

MARGE, this is Saturday afternoon and you must not be short with these children. They deserve to have a party. . . . Well, there are only nine of them. I didn't think you'd feel imposed on, and I would've naturally invited them to my apartment, but since I just waxed my floors I thought yours would be better. . . . After all, I did bring the refreshments, and it isn't like you don't know these kids. . . . Well, they belong to Mrs. Gordon on the top floor, the super in the basement, Mrs. Mack on the ground floor rear, and those two over there are little visitors from Virginia—Jimmy and Janey. They're twins, ain't they cute?

Now, Marge, if you will dish up the popcorn, peanuts, ice cream and cake, I'll tell them a story. Now, children, let us all say together: "Thank you, Miss Marge!"

Bobby, don't throw your grape skins on the floor, it's not nice. Gertrude, don't squeeze that glass ornament on the table or it will bust. Everybody sit down quiet 'cause we can all sing together, but we cannot talk together. Billy and Mabel! You will kindly stop smackin' each other on the knee before it turns into a bloody-nose fight! Quiet! . . . The first one that hollers or screams will get sent out of here fast as greased lightnin'! Place all feet on the floor and fold hands neatly in your laps. Now I'm goin' to tell you a story about Miss Harriet Tubman. . . . Put your hands down, children. . . . I know that you don't know anything about her, and that's why I'm tellin' you the story! Your school books say precious-little about Negro history, and I'm not goin' to have you kids goin' through life thinkin' that colored people don't have a history! . . . Another thing, pay attention to what I say because I did not go all the way to the one-hundred-and-thirty-fifth-street library and get the story in order to have you all whisperin' through every blessed word I say!

Once upon a long, long time ago and to be exact it was durin' the days of slavery . . . Jimmy, I'm surprised that you don't know what *slavery* is, I'm glad at the same time. . . . Slavery is buyin' people and puttin' them to work for you free. . . . No, there was no law against it. . . . That's right, Sylvia, the person who owned slaves could beat them or sell their children or kill them and it would be all right with the law. So, you can see what a terrible, monstrous thing it was. . . . Now, I have lost track of the story! Oh, yes! Once upon a time, way back in slavery days there was a little girl, she was born in Bucktown, Maryland.

Her childhood was not like yours, there was no school . . . and I'll thank you children not to grin when I say that because when you're not allowed to go to school, you soon know what a good thing it is to have one to go to. Well, anyway, she was not allowed to go simply because slave children had no rights, and furthermore it was against the law for them to learn how to read or write, much less count. . . . Yes, Bobby, some folks managed to learn anyhow, but they had to keep it a secret or else they would get a beatin'! . . . Who would beat them? . . . The slavemaster. Don't you kids understand nothin'?

. . . Look, Sylvia, I don't care if your schoolbook does say that the master took care of slaves and would be *kind* to them. I'm tellin' you different, I'm tellin' you what's true. . . . No, everything that is in your book is *not* true. . . . Well, you tell that teacher that your Aunt Mildred says it ain't so! . . . Are you goin' to let me tell this story?

Harriet spent her little-girl years workin' out in the fields plantin' and ploughin' and doin' all manner of hard work. . . . No, she could not go up to a cop and tell him about it! . . . Billy, I have explained already how slaves had no rights, and I'm not goin' to keep goin' over the same thing all the time!

Now, the overseer was very cruel. . . . Janey! Don't be interruptin'! . . . Oh, well, if you don't know what a overseer is, I guess I'll have to tell you. A overseer was a man hired by the slavemaster to see that the slaves did a lot of work and to also beat them if they didn't do everything the master wanted them to do.

One day the overseer hit Harriet in the head with a piece of iron because she tried to stop him from beatin' another slave. He hurt her real bad and for a time it looked like she wouldn't live. All winter long she was sick-unto-death, and she didn't have no hospital bed or doctors or trained nurses, but she lay on a heap of rags while her mother tried to nurse her back to health as best she could.

. . . Barbara, are you out of your mind? . . . No, Superman and Batman did not go after the overseer! I am tryin' to tell you kids a real story 'bout real, live people, if you will let me! There was no men flyin' through the air and swoopin' down on no overseers. . . . No, she did not have a ray-gun! Listen to what I'm sayin', please!

She did get back her health, except for one thing. Her poor head was so hurt that she was left with sleepin' sickness. . . . By that I mean, several times a day she would drop off to sleep for a minute or two without even knowin' it, and this sickness stayed with her for the rest of her life and she had a large scar on her head.

. . . Yes, indeed, she hated slavemasters, and her heart was troubled not only for herself but for all the rest of her people who were in bondage. . . . That's slavery! Some years later she told a friend, "I had seen their tears and sighs, and I had heard their groans, and I would give every drop of blood in my veins to free them." It became her burnin' desire to set them free.

Now, there was a thing talked about in those days that was called the "underground railroad," and it was her dream to ride it to freedom. . . . No, children, it was not a subway or any other kind of train that you could see and neither was it no fairytale. It was a string of human bein's, black and white folks who met the slaves and secretly took them from house to house, over field and hill and meadow, through the forests and streams, across rivers, always followin' the North star in the sky, on toward freedom in the Northland.

. . . Kenny, what do you mean by sayin', "Miss Mildred sure makes up good stories!" Didn't I tell you that every bit of this is true! . . . I cannot help it if it is not in your school book! Didn't I explain that to you! That's why I'm *tellin'* the doggone story! The reason you won't find it in your dag-nabbit book is because . . . You're right, Marge, I must not lose my temper and get to usin' bad language in front of these little ones. Children, forget that I said dag-nabbit and dog-gone and don't any of you *ever* let Aunt Mildred hear you sayin' words like that 'cause it's ugliness and also rude.

. . . Janey, you can ask enough questions to keep a soul tongue-tied! . . . If you children will be patient, I will be able to tell you all about Miss Tubman because you are *guessin'*, but I *know!* One night Harriet ran away and kept goin' until she got out of slaveland and arrived in Pennsylvania. She found many friends in the new land, but she was not completely happy because it made her sad to think of her brothers and sisters and friends still sufferin', and she made up her mind that she would free them also, so she looked around to find a way to go back down South and bring her friends up to free-land.

No, there was no airplanes at that time or motorcars either. The first thing she had to do was make some money, so she did domestic work the same as me and Miss Marge, only she worked a lot harder in laundry rooms and such.

Harriet decided that she'd be a conductor on the Eastern line of the underground railroad. Oh my, that underground railroad was somethin'! Folks who went down to lead the slaves over the right paths was called "conductors"; folks who took them into their homes to rest and receive shelter from the law was called "stationmasters" and their homes was called "stations."

Harriet met a lot of these good people and she was so delighted to find out that there were so many good white folks called "Abolitionists." . . . Bobby, before you ask me what that means, I will tell you. Abolitionists were people who thought slavery was wicked and thus made up their minds to do away with it as fast as they could. . . . Yes, Jimmy, there were plenty of colored ones, and they all worked together nicely so Harriet decided to join up with them. She became a "conductor" on the underground railroad.

. . . No, children, I do not think that she knew Davy Crockett. Now let me go on with the story! Harriet was a conductor for ten years and never lost *one* of her passengers. Her name became so famous that everybody who loved her called her "Moses." I won't tell you what the other folks called her because you are little children and the less you hear of such, the better.

Sometimes as she neared a slave plantation, she would sing spirituals to call the slaves to her and I like to think that she sang "Steal away home to Jesus" or "Swing low sweet chariot."

Now, Mabel, you are bein' rude and a little bit sassy. I would expect that you'd behave better. . . . What do you mean by sayin' "I don't believe you?" I told you that it is not in the schoolbooks because bad folks don't want us to know about all the great things our people did. . . . They don't want us to know 'cause if we think that we did nothin' at all, we will feel *inferior* and if we feel like we're lower than other folk, then we will expect to be treated like we're lower!

No, Marshall, there's no movin' pictures been made about Miss Tubman. Mabel, if you tune up to cry just 'cause I scolded you, I'm gonna send you home. . . . Marge, you see how these children are bein' kept in the dark? It's a wonder they know anything at all. It makes me mad through and through. It ain't right!

Yes, Kenny, I'm goin' to tell the rest of the story, but I'll thank you children not to be almost callin' me a outright liar! . . . You can ask questions, but don't be holdin' me up for scorn! Do you really believe that I would sit down and tell you a pack of lies? Do you think that I'm so sneaky and mean as to make fun of you and try to fool you?

All right then! Harriet took so many slaves out of the South 'til they tacked up signs on the trees, offerin' a big reward for her capture. Forty thousand dollars! . . . No, they never did catch her, although once she had a sleepin' spell overtake her, and she fell asleep smack-dab underneath one of them signs. . . . No, nobody noticed her 'cause they was as uppity as you children and couldn't believe that a woman sleepin' under a tree could be the great "Moses."

Of course, you have all heard of the great John Brown. . . . Well, I'm glad to see that Janey is raisin' her hand and is able to tell us something about him. . . . Janey, you can sit right down 'cause I can see that you don't know very much about him. . . . Who told you that John Brown was crazy? . . . No, he wasn't, he was a good man who wanted to do away with slavery! . . . All right, Jimmy, if you know a song about him, you may sing it. . . . Marge, do you hear that?—"John Brown's baby had a cold upon its chest, so they rubbed it with camphorated oil!" . . . Children, John Brown was hanged, they took his life 'cause he helped to take us out of slavery! We oughta know all about him and love him dearly for what he did.

Yes, Lincoln was a great man and signed those papers, but he didn't just up and set slaves free! There was all kinds of great fightin' goin' on about slavery before that happened. Did any of you ever hear about Nat Turner? . . . Lord, Marge, do you see what I see? . . . Not a one of these children has heard a word about him, can't a one of them raise their hand!

. . . Yes, bless your little hearts, I will tell you a few more things about Miss Tubman, and I'm sorry to lose patience so easy. It sure ain't your fault that you know nothin' at all 'bout these things.

One time when Harriet was in Troy, New York, she heard that the law was holdin' a man who was an escaped slave in the courthouse and plannin' to return him to his former master. Harriet called on all her friends in Troy, and they went down to the courthouse. Harriet got past the door guards by stoopin' over and walkin' like she was a decrepit old lady. When the officers started to lead the prisoner from the court,

Harriet seized hold of him and called out to the crowd to help her and they did.

. . . Marshall! Get down off Miss Marge's couch, and stop pullin' on Janey's hair! . . . Stop playin' like she's the man I'm talkin' about, or I'll stop the story and you'll *never* know what happened! That's better!

Well, that crowd got into the biggest fight and Harriet kept hold of that man while her friends beat off the people who were tryin' to take him away. . . . Children, if you scream one more time! . . . Yes, they got him and put him in a wagon and drove him straight into Canada, where he was as free as a bird! . . . Oh, excuse me, was I hollerin', too? . . .

Yes, Janey, I guess you could say that she was like Joan of Arc. She did serve in the Civil War. . . . Sure, she was a soldier. She always worked in the Union Blue and was never without her rifle.

. . . Jimmy, please do not pinch the other children because I'm now near the end of the story, and you will only have to sit still for a short spell longer.

When Harriet was old and her work was almost over a lot of people showed respect and paid honor to her. Queen Victoria sent her a medal, a silk shawl and a letter invitin' her to come to Great Britain because everybody there had such admiration for her. But she was too tired and old to go anywhere by the time she got it. Sad to relate, she spent her last, remainin' years in poverty and want. One day she told somebody, "I liked apples when I was young and I said to myself: 'Someday I'll plant apples myself for other young folks to eat'; and I guess I did."

Now do you children know what she meant by that? . . . You are right, Jimmy. . . . She did mean that she had done things to make our lives better. . . .

What? . . . Why, of course, Mabel, you speak right up and say whatever is on your mind. . . . Well, thank you, I'm glad to know that you *believe* me. . . . How many of you would like to hear some more true stories some other time? . . . No, no, I can't tell any more today, but it's nice to know that you're all so earnest about it. . . . No, Barbara, I don't think you should change your name to Harriet, but you could read and study some about her when you go to the library 'cause you will find her name in some of those books even though she's left out of the schoolbook. . . .

Marge, ain't this enough to break your heart! . . . Of course, Marshall, there were great *men*, too, a lot of them, and next time I'll tell you about Frederick Douglas who was braver than brave. . . . That's right, Sylvia, he was true to life also. . . . Well, you just go right ahead and *ask* your teacher why he isn't in your book, and if she tells you that he never happened, you come to me and I promise you this: I'll go to school with this book and prove it to her and the whole class and also the principal, if need be! . . . Sure, we got a grand history!

Now, children, you will kindly pick up all the popcorn off the rug, wipe all sticky hands and then thank Miss Marge for havin' us in her house. Now, all together with Mildred, say, "Thank you, Miss Marge!" . . . You're welcome, Jimmy, the ice cream and cake wasn't so much. Aunt Mildred wishes she could give you a whole lot more 'cause you youngsters are starved in more ways than one. . . .

THE A B C'S OF LIFE AND LEARNING

OH WELL, it's all very fine for us grown-ups to worry and fret all kinds of ways about this desegregation business, but I wonder what it feels like to be a little child goin' to school and gettin' right into the thick of things as it were.

Marge, can you imagine a little seven-year-old colored child goin' off to his first day at a school that's just turnin' democratic? It's so hard to explain everything to the little ones so's they will really understand what's goin' on. They must feel all the uneasiness that's in the air and what with the parents bein' worried and cautionin' them about bein' careful and not walkin' down certain streets and comin' directly home and things like that, their little hearts must be awful burdened and put upon.

Is there any grown person that can put themselves in that child's place without feelin' angry and ashamed that this can be done to children? What does it do to a child when he sees adults throwin' things at him and jeerin' at him? How does it feel to walk in a classroom and have no one say a kind word? What does it feel like to sit in the back of the room all by yourself and try to study your lessons? What does it feel like to eat your lunch all alone and off to one side?

What does it feel like to have to run part of the way home

in order not to be beat up or even maybe killed? What does it feel like to have to wait for your mama or papa to call for you and take you home by the long, round-about way? Don't you think these children are wonderin' and thinkin' some big, solemn thoughts?

. . . Sure, I know there's people who try to give this as the excuse not to have the schools mixed, but I don't go along with that at all, and it seems that you can say the same thing for the children. These brave little people take their lives in hand and walk the pathways leadin' to the schools all over the country. They want to learn, and they don't want to keep goin' to school buildin's that get a second place break on the money deal!

Oh, Marge, we got a lot to feel proud about! I wouldn't take anything for livin' right now in this day and time! I'm glad to my heart to see these brave children marchin' to the schools throughout the land, claimin' their rights and plowin' ahead in the face of mobs and threats and all manner of ugliness. These colored boys and girls got their hands stretched out in friendship to the white boys and girls in this land. And you know one thing? They're gonna clasp hands and walk together and get along and learn from each other and be peaceful and enjoy life in spite of these grown-ups tryin' to spread malice and hate. And one of these days this land is gonna be truly beautiful. Yes mam, every square inch of it!

SOMEHOW I'D LIKE TO THANK THEM

EVERY ONCE IN A WHILE you read about something that really stays with you, something that makes you keep faith in people in spite of how the world is always at sixes and sevens in the midst of so much hatred and greediness and pure downright meanness. Sometimes what you read is just a few lines tucked away in some far corner of a magazine. . . . Yes, isn't it strange that all the ugliness is spread across the front pages of the newspaper where you couldn't miss it if you wanted to! When it comes to findin' the good you have to look sharp between the ads and things in order to find it.

This piece that I read was in a magazine and it told all about how some white women down in Capetown, South Africa had done a truly fine and beautiful thing. Just readin' about it gave me a glowy feelin' and although they are in a way-far-off place, I felt real close to them!

Well, it happened like this. It seems that the lawmakers down in that part of the world are terrible hard and mean on the African people and any other colored people that might be around. . . . Yes, I know that Capetown is in Africa, but all the say-so is done by white folks. You know how they have been doin' about keepin' the Africans down and makin' it against the law for them to do anything that any citizen should have a perfect right to do!

Well, accordin' to this piece I was readin', it seems that they had kept most of the African people from votin', but that they allowed a few colored folks to vote a little bit. Well, after them lawmakers studied over it for a while, they decided that even this was too much and they passed a law declarin' that *no colored* could vote at all!

The day they were passin' the law in their courts, a lot of white women got together and marched before the courthouse with black mournin' bands stretched across their dresses. They were doin' this to show that they were mournin' the death of justice!

Some of the women went into the courtroom and sat down. And those black bands they were wearin' upset the court so much that the lawmakers made them take them off. . . . Oh yes, they took them off, but then they went in their pocketbooks and each one of them took a black artificial flower out of her purse and pinned it on her dress. That upset them, too, but they didn't try to make them take it off because it seems like a flower is supposed to be a decoration for ladies' dresses.

. . . Yes, I'd say it was just a small, orderly little way for them to show that all white people did not uphold those people in carryin' out their meanness and cruelty! But what got me was how those women were treated in the streets! Do you know what they did to them?

. . . Oh, yes, they did somethin'! A bunch of mean, devilish, ignorant white folks gathered in the streets and threw garbage and stones at those women! . . . You heard me! So, you see, it wasn't safe for them to even *quietly* and peaceably show what was on their minds!

Marge, that's why a lot of white people don't speak up when they see how ugly the darker peoples are treated. . . . Sure, they're afraid *they'll* be stoned to death or run out of town! That's why I feel so respectful about what those women have done.

It takes a lot of strength for a white person who has privileges to take a just stand for everybody's right. He knows that the bad folks will not spare him just 'cause he is *white!* . . . No, indeed, he will treat them like dirt, take their jobs, threaten his life and even take it sometimes!

But I think what is even more hurtful than that is the treatment they get from folks who are near to them like relatives and friends! They will give them a hard way to go, too, and shut them out of their homes and things like that! I imagine that a whole lot of white people do not go along with all this hatred and meanness that's goin' on, but they are scared stiff to speak out and maybe get garbage and stones thrown at them and perhaps lose their jobs and everything.

. . . Well, you're perfectly right! It does mean that they are not free either, or else they would be able to speak up as free citizens and say whatever happens to be on their minds without losin' their lives about it!

. . . Yes, I'm sorry that so many of them are frightened and hidin' their heads in the sand. . . . No, I don't think those white women that I mentioned were braver than anybody else. Who knows? Maybe they were kinda frightened when they did that. But I do believe that they were the kind of folks that would have felt more miserable if they hadn't done something to let everybody know where they stood and what was in their hearts. It would have cost them too much to be quiet and still and not listen to the voice of truth that was whisperin' to them. You know, Marge, some people *have* to do right even if it kills them!

Yes, readin' about that gave me a good feelin'. And wherever those women are tonight I wish them pleasant dreams and happy goin' in all that they might ever do because I know that it will always be something that is fine and helpful to everybody.

Marge, can't you just see them standin' up straight and proud, wearin' those black flowers! . . . No, I would not call them ladies although I know exactly what you mean. I call them *women*. And I feel as proud of them as I do of my folks who are fightin' to go to school and get all of *their* rights. There are a lot of good folks on this earth!

MEN IN YOUR LIFE

No, MARGE, I don't think you have any more hard luck with men than anybody else. Neither do I go in for this downin' of men all the time like they are so many strange bein's or enemies. I think men are people the same as women and you will run into some bad characters in this life be they men or women!

. . . Well, I'm in perfect agreement with that! A lot of men *do* think that they are just the cock o' the walk and oughta have the last word about everything! There are also a lot of them that look down on women and make fun of everything we say and do. I'm tellin' you they really can rile me when they end up sayin' something like, "Women! can't live with 'em or without, bless their souls!" Of course, rilin' is what they usually got in mind when they say those things.

But, Marge, we women are also the first ones that get a crack at these men. . . . Well, I mean, ain't we the ones that get to raise them from the time they are babies? While it's true that a heap of women have drawn some sad pick of husbands, it is also true that they raise their sons to make somebody else a mighty poor kinda spouse!

It is not a easy thing to raise a boy so's that he'll be as

close to right as you can make him! It takes more than a bit of commonsense and a whole lot of tryin'. If I had a son, I would want him to be fair and square and good and worthwhile and at the same time not let anybody walk over him. Well, you know how Marie can hang-dog her husband around! . . . No, that is not at all necessary, and he shouldn't allow it! I would raise a son of mine to think for himself and get a good feelin' for the right and wrong of things! And I think a little application of the golden rule toward everybody oughta get him off to a good start! . . . Sure, everybody *says* they live by the golden rule, but how many people really and truly treat other folks like they'd like to be treated themselves? Not too many, you can be sure, 'cause everybody wants the tip-top best for themselves and then a *little bit more!*

I stopped off to see Tessie the other day in order to go over her club minutes. You know, I would never have gone if I thought Clarence was gonna be home from work that day! He can make me so mad 'til it ain't funny!

That man can say and do some of the worst kinda things! In the first place, he is *grumpy.* Yes, always frownin' up and mumblin' under his breath about nothin' in particular! . . . That alone would get me in a fistfight or a strait-jacket or both! I couldn't stand somebody goin', "mumble-mumble-make me sick-mumble-mumble-my dinner-mumble mumble-tired of this. . . ." Yes, that's the way he goes on all the time! And don't let her have a visitor 'cause that's when he'll do it most!

It gets real embarrassin' to sit around pretendin' that you don't notice it. Lots of times when I've been there he would come walkin' in and say, "Where's my dinner?" before he would say good evenin' to anybody! And no matter how I try to recollect I can never remember a time when I could say I saw him laughin'!

The other day she went in the kitchen when he called her, and I could hear him sayin' "Where's that ten dollars I gave you last week?" And Tessie was whisperin' soft-like so's I couldn't hear what she was sayin', but it was plain to see that he was mad 'cause she wanted to pay out two dollars for club dues. When I left, I said, "Good night folks!" and he says, "mumble-mumble-night." Like it was killin' him to even do that much. He acts that way with everybody but mostly with Tessie!

I'll never forget the time when I went out with his brother Wallace! He was supposed to be takin' me out on this bang-up dinner date! Honey, as soon as we got in the restaurant he says, "The hash is real good in this place, they make it better than any other restaurant."

. . . . No, dear, I wasn't payin' him no mind! I hadn't asked him to take me out to dinner! Neither had I told him to pick out a expensive restaurant, so I went ahead and ordered me some spring lamb chops with a salad on the side! I can stand a *broke* man but I dearly detest a *cheap* man! And he was just pure *cheap!*

Next thing he started lookin' in his newspaper for a good movie and the way he told it everything that was playin' at the high-priced picture houses was *no good*, but there was a couple of fine things showin' in the neighborhood places! So, since he'd asked me what *I* wanted to see, I picked out the exact one I had in mind. However, I didn't pick it out 'til I had ordered me a cocktail!

Then you should have heard him twistin' and turnin'! Started talkin' 'bout how long he'd been alone since his wife died and how he really *needed* somebody and things like that. I just sat there sippin' and noddin' in a understandin' way, but every once in a while I'd take a peek at my watch 'cause it was gettin' mighty close to bein' too late to catch a movie.

Next thing you know, he starts talkin' about *wastin'* our time. He says, "We're both grown and there ain't no need of us wastin' each other's time if we're not gonna get anywhere!" . . . Honey, I caught on real fast! He was lettin' me know that he didn't *want* to go to the movies unless I would come on out and declare how obligin' I was gonna be in the love-makin' department! . . . So I says, "It's gettin' late Wallace, I have a splittin' headache and I think I'd better get on back home before we waste any more time *or* money!" And that was that! . . . Yes, he took me home and when we got to my door he says, "Do you want to give me a little kiss?" I just looked at him real calm-like and says, "Get off of that act, Wallace. You can tell whether somebody wants to kiss you or not, you don't have to ask! Now look at me and tell me whether I want to kiss you or not!" He didn't say another word, all he did was turn around and go on home!

I hate any man to be creepin' and pinchin' along tryin' all kinds of tricks and foolishness with me. . . . Of course, he had money, Marge! He has been workin' on a good steady job for the last fifteen years and ain't never missed a day's work in all that time. . . . Tessie was the one who really talked me into goin' out with him 'cause she told me I ought to go out with a "good steady fellow who has a reliable job."

I guess she was takin' a dig at Eddie 'cause he is a salesman and don't seem to be doin' so hot at sellin' them race-records and books. But I'll take Eddie any day and you can *have* Wallace! Eddie is the kind of man I like. He doesn't play any games or try no four-flushin'!

Whenever Eddie's in town I have a grand time and even a

letter from him is worth more than a whole evenin' with somebody else. Sometimes he will say, "Well, honey, there ain't but five dollars in the cash register so let's try and stretch it into a good time!" And he can figure out a lot of swell things to do. We will go dancin' and then have a few beers and take the subway home or sometimes walk even! But the whole time we're laughin' and talkin' and enjoyin' ourselves so much 'til you couldn't believe how happy I feel!

Some Sunday afternoons Eddie is *broke* and then we go walkin' and he will take me up to a pawnshop window and turn it into a regular movin' picture show. . . . Well, I mean he will make up stories about the things that he sees in the window and try to figure out who they belonged to in the first place and how they happen to be in the pawnshop window now. . . . Oh, foolishness stories like, "I see where some cat had to pawn his saxophone, now why do you think he did that?" And I'll say, "To pay his room-rent!" And he'll say, "No, he got a letter tellin' him that if he came to East Jalappi, there would be a fine old steady job waitin' for him, so he hocked his horn in order to buy a ticket, only when he got off the boat he didn't have no horn to play so the poor old guy is hangin' 'round Jalappi tryin' to save up enough money to buy him a second-hand horn, and this horn is hangin' here in the window tryin' to tempt some youngster into takin' up music so that he can get to Jalappi some day himself!"

I like him to tell me them pawnshop stories. He can tell electric-iron stories, radio stories, ring stories, suitcase stories, silverware stories, and all manner of tales about cocktail shakers, toasters, suits and overcoats, cameras and all such things as that!

Eddie will do me favors, too. Like goin' downtown to buy

things that I don't have time to pick up, washin' dishes for me, mindin' my cousin's kids so's she can go to church and a whole lot of other things like that. But what I really like about him is that sometimes when I ask him to do a lot of things, one comin' right after the other, he will say, "You runnin' a good thing in the ground, and furthermore I don't feel like it, what do you take me for?" I'm glad when he does that, too, 'cause just like I don't want nobody walkin' all over me, I sure wouldn't have any use for a man that's gonna let people trample him!

Marge, you know Eddie has loaned me money, too. But the first time he tried to borrow some from me, I got real scared 'cause you do hear so many stories 'bout how men try to take advantage of women sometimes by gettin' their money away from them. . . . Yes, I loaned it to him, but I worried him to death until I got it back. When he returned it, he said, "Whew! I don't *never* want to borrow *nothin'* from you no more 'cause it's too much of a strain!"

I felt a little bit shamed about that, but now we don't never have that kind of trouble no more 'cause all the time we know we can depend on each other no matter what happens! . . . Yes, we have been talkin' 'bout gettin' married, but neither one of us got enough change to start up family life in the way we'd want it to be, and you know how you can start puttin' things off 'til everything is shaped up just right.

But I get to thinkin' awful deep sometimes. And when Eddie is away, I start picturin' his easy-goin', happy ways, how he likes children, how he looks at me so that I don't have to wonder how he feels, how he never had to ask for a "little kiss" but knew when was the right time to kiss me, how he loves people, how he hates meanness and ugliness— how he wants me to get out of other folks' kitchens, when

I think on all of that and stand him up side of those steady, reliable guys like Clarence and Wallace, it seems like Wallace and Clarence don't look so hot!

Yes, I think I will marry Eddie 'cause the only, single thing we will have to worry about is bein' poor. . . . Yes, that is a pretty big thing to have to worry about all the time, but if a man gives you all of the very best that he has to offer, all the time, what more could a woman want? . . .